THE SUITE

THE SUITE

A NOVEL

Susanne Perry

This is a work of fiction. All of the characters, names, incidents, organizations, and dialogue in this novel are either the products of the author's imagination or are used fictitiously.

Archway Publishing books may be ordered through booksellers or by contacting:

Archway Publishing
1663 Liberty Drive
Bloomington, IN 47403
www.archwaypublishing.com
1 (888) 242-5904

ISBN: 978-1-4808-5506-9 (sc)
ISBN: 978-1-4808-5508-3 (hc)
ISBN: 978-1-4808-5507-6 (e)

Library of Congress Control Number: 2017916793

Print information available on the last page.

Archway Publishing rev. date: 1/10/2018

For David
…who keeps me laughing.

"The Philosophers have only interpreted the world, in various ways. The point, however, is to change it."
Karl Marx

"Be ashamed to die before you have won some victory for humanity."
Horace Mann

SUNDAY

Chapter 1

The girl was dead, that was a sure bet. By the time the shelter residents returned from looking for housing, work, help, whatever, they knew she was dead. When asked by the investigators, no one seemed to have noticed whether she had been at breakfast, nor could they remember if the girl had been around the night before. No one noticed. It was the story of her life, really. No one noticed whether she was around unless it was some degenerate Fagin-like creep who saw her as a commodity. They noticed her now, now that she was dead. The shelter is called the Avalon Street Center, a shelter for the homeless.

Being that it was mid-November, wet from the incessant rain and cold at night, Avalon was a busy place. Homeless families with children or single women can stay at Avalon for thirty days. Then they have to move on. Move on to permanent housing, to in-patient treatment, to transitional housing, to another shelter, back with relations or friends, or back on the street. Avalon has a dorm, one large room really, called The Suite. The Suite is made available to up to four single women at a time. Our unnoticed girl had a bed in the Suite and had been there three days before she was found dead in the alley. Mark Twain was quoted to say that the rumors of his death were greatly exaggerated. Not so with the girl. Her death was a sure bet.

Avalon is in Columbia City, Washington, on the north bank

of the mighty Columbia River for which the town is named. On the south side of the river is Oregon. Indigenous peoples, the Cascade Chinook, inhabited the area for centuries. Names of nearby landmarks and areas still bear Native American names. A town and a river are both called Washougal which means "rushing water" or "land of plenty" depending on whom you ask. The nearby city of Yacolt got its name from a Klickitat word meaning "haunted place."

The area is near the destination of the Lewis and Clark Expedition and, because of its proximity to the Columbia River, was ideal for some of the first non-native settlements in the Pacific Northwest. Logging, trapping, and military interests continued into the mid-twentieth century. Columbia City existed before either Seattle or Portland. It began as a garrison to protect the interests of the Hudson Bay Company, which today would be a trading conglomerate. A few years later, Ulysses S. Grant lived here with his family before returning east and assuming command of the Union army. Rumor was that the Grants hated the rainy, wet weather. The Grant home still stands, carefully preserved, on a street named East Reserve, but locally known as Officers Row. The Oliver O. Howard home on the Row is named for the Civil War general for whom Howard University is named. Half a century later George C. Marshall had a residence on the Row, now a popular venue for social events. And decades later, in an alley only a few miles north of the stately old Row of historic houses, lay a dead girl.

The first one to see her body lying in the alley was Ty. A decent sort, Ty returned from Iraq a very different guy from the one sent there. Ty never blamed anyone else for his plight. He had been in the infantry and had simply heard, seen, and smelled more than anyone should ever have to in this lifetime and he was haunted by an inability to forget. He tried to work, tried to relate to people, tried to quell the nightmares, but they defeated him and he toppled down like one of Saddam's statues. Ty was a regular at the men's shelter down the street. Actually, Ty was a fixture there. And because he was a decent guy and he didn't have a temper, the staff liked him.

Ty walked from the bus stop to Avalon every Sunday at five p.m. because Mike worked the Sunday evening shift. Ty looked forward to seeing Mike on Sundays. Mike treated him like a man instead of some wasted shell person. Mike didn't divert his eyes when Ty looked him in the face and he even greeted him when he saw Ty approach. Days could go by on the street without that happening. Ty and Mike would have a cup of awful coffee and visit like old friends.

But on this Sunday, as soon as Ty walked past the alley, he smelled it. He knew what it was. For a few seconds he was there in the smoke and the stink and the fire. He made himself approach the lump at the side of the alley entrance and saw that it was the girl. What was her name? Had he ever heard her name? He must have. Ty took in the ugly gash at the side of her head. It was just above her right ear but more to the front. Something heavy had slammed into the side of her head, cleaving skin, tissue, and part of the skull. There was a lot of blood producing the sour smell that had brought Ty to her. The blow or blows had missed her open right eye. The girl stared into hell without seeing or caring that she had arrived.

Two others came along just a few minutes after Ty. It was Marco and Genevieve, the seniors. Marco spoke with a heavy accent although he had been in the States forty years. Having never learned to read and write and with no driver's license or Social Security number, Marco was a ghost really. He had worked as an itinerant laborer until the pain in his back became too intense to handle. The volunteer doctors at the free clinic were nice and tried to help, but the only relief for an indigent with a ruptured lumbar disc was oxycodone. No way would the state pay for surgery for the likes of Marco. So after years of dependence on the stuff, guess what? Marco would have sold his Mama for a hit of whatever he could get every four to six hours if that's what it took to take the edge off. Thank God for the doctors at the free clinic.

Marco's sidekick, Genevieve, was a small, stooped woman with hair that had long ago lost its color. The gray was not just gray; it was as if some blight had infested her hair and robbed it of all life. As a young woman living in Texas, Genevieve had been married with a family. She had four children with her husband and "functioned well" until the voices started to dictate how to raise those children. "Functioned well" is social service talk for didn't scare the shit out of anyone by doing some off-the-wall crap such as holding Davey's head under running water because the voices said it would heal his ear infection. The last straw was the incident when Maureen, her youngest, was in kindergarten. Gen was asked to send snacks for the class of five-year-olds.

Miss Holcomb, the kindergarten teacher, opened the box expecting snacks but instead was greeted with a box of dead cockroaches. The problem was that Genevieve had been working to clear the critters out of the kitchen for weeks and got the containers confused. She never realized that she burned a box of perfectly good saltine crackers.

The school called social services and Genevieve was put into a day program so she could be observed and evaluated. Observed and evaluated led to a diagnosis of schizophrenia and more attempts at treatment than can be imagined by the average person. Genevieve ended up more or less escorted out of central Texas, away from her children. They were told she was nuts. Husband filed for divorce and took up with a less crazy mate. At some point, Genevieve ended up in New Mexico and her path crossed with Marco's. Marco didn't mind that Genevieve heard voices. His concern was that her check came through each month and she helped him keep a stash of pain meds handy. The arrangement worked for Genevieve, as well, because Marco kept the street predators at bay and reminded Genevieve to eat.

Soon after Ty saw the girl, along came Marco and Genevieve. They were following Ty from the bus stop and when they saw him enter the alley, they followed like lemmings. Ty stopped short and called to Marco, "Hey man, go get Mike. Now, man, get Mike."

Ty didn't stop to consider whether Marco knew who Mike was or if he'd know where to go to find him. Ty knew that Marco and Gen had been around the streets awhile and most folks on the street knew Mike was the guy at Avalon.

Marco and Gen stopped short of approaching the girl. *Too intense; too much,* they thought. Marco's back hurt since he hadn't had a pill since mid-day. Marco ambled slowly toward the alley entrance and yelled for someone to get Mike. Gen was looking but not really looking. *Too much,* she thought. They both took cues from Ty's demeanor. Marco and Gen could tell a hard rain had fallen. The Fates told them in their souls to be reverent because a fellow traveler had met with a bad end due to no fault of her own. A death, even of a disenfranchised soul, is sacrosanct.

Marco yelled again, for Mike, while heading down the alley toward Avalon. Several other residents appeared and wandered into the alley, stopping short when they realized that Ty had discovered tragedy. Ty is a leader of sorts, a role he neither wants nor feels qualified to hold. But Ty can appear to take charge and that's all it takes. Ty has a connection to reality that the others only aspire to and that's why he stands out as capable and relatively reliable.

Soon, the buzz filtered to the shelter, and Mike came running around the corner into the alley with cell phone in hand. "Who is it, Ty? Is it bad?" he asked.

"Yeah, man. It's the girl," Ty answered, then paused before adding, "and she's dead. What's her name, Mike?"

Mike dialed 911 and waited for dispatch to pick up. "Hell, Ty, I don't remember. I'll have to check her intake card." By then an emergency dispatcher was on the line. "Yeah, this is Mike Dwyer at the Avalon Street shelter. We just found one of our female residents in the back alley." Mike paused to listen to the emergency dispatcher. "No, there's no doubt." Mike listened again, said, "Yeah...I know."

Chapter 2

The first officer to respond was Connors. Kyle Connors, a rookie cop, was known on the street to be fair. He didn't add insult to injury when there was a problem with folks on the street. Tall and fast, Connors played basketball in high school in Portland and snagged an athletic scholarship to Oregon State, down Interstate 5, in Corvallis. He minored in Spanish at OSU and was fluent enough to converse. His brown hair, blue eyes and fair-with-freckles complexion worked to his advantage. His graduating class his senior year in high school had voted him Best All Around. He was never quite sure why law enforcement appealed to him, but he had decided to be a cop at a fairly young age.

Most street folks knew and liked Connors and if they were in need of help, they knew he would be square with them. They knew this, as long as they didn't steal or harass anyone, didn't lie to him, and most of all, didn't break a law. Connors was fair but he wasn't a marshmallow. So after arriving, Connors immediately took over and was securing the crime scene by the time the investigator showed up.

Detective Sergeant Liz Jordan had been an investigator with the Metro Police Bureau for twelve years. Elizabeth Marie Jordan was a third generation graduate of Washington State University, and she grew up in a home where college football was a religion.

At five nine, she was on the tall side for a woman. She wore her hair straight and mid-length so she could pin it up or put it in a ponytail when on the job to keep it out of the way. The simple style meant low maintenance in the morning and few salon appointments. She liked keeping fit and it was a requisite of the job, but the workout routine that she had enjoyed in her twenties had become more of a necessary evil in her thirties.

The daughter of a high school history teacher and an eighth grade science teacher, Liz never wanted to become a teacher herself. She loved teachers, she knew how hard the job was, but she didn't want to spend her days in a classroom. Besides, she asked herself, what subject did she know enough about that she would want to share? She preferred asking questions to answering them. Liz, as she was known, made eye contact with Connors as she approached the body. "Tell me," was all she said.

Connors was looking around the alley taking in details. "Female victim, late teens or early twenties, white, average build. Homeless guy found her and alerted Mike Dwyer from the shelter. Mike called 911 about twenty-five minutes ago. I checked for vitals but she's dead. Not been here for more than a few hours is my guess, but dead all the same. M.E.'s on the way." Liz looked at the girl, soaking in what details she could from observation. Her hair was long, straight and light brown with a bit of blonde. Her skin had been fair even before the deathly pallor had taken over.

She wore jeans and a leather belt, the simple buckle constructed of two small iron rings. A long-sleeved, faded-out black thermal shirt was worn under a plaid flannel. There may have been another layer under that, hard to tell. Basic street-kids uniform with a decent pair of hiking boots and thick socks. The girl had two earrings in the right earlobe, the earlobe that was visible just inches below what appeared to be the fatal wound on the side of her head. One earring resembled a small silver dragonfly. The other was a tiny silver sphere on a post. No backpack. No purse.

No wallet. An amount of some liquid appeared to have been spilled near the body, close to where she landed on her left side as she fell. It looked to have been spilled or dumped from a cup or bottle. But there was no cup or bottle in the alley. The lab may be able to identify it. It was a liquid other than blood, that is. But there was a lot of that, too. At least the weather had been on their side. It hadn't rained since early morning.

Connors' voice broke into her thoughts as he gestured and said, "Mike's over there with the guy who found her. You know Mike, right?"

Liz nodded yes. She did, indeed, know Mike. Mike Dwyer and Liz had been best friends for years. They met as students at WSU. Bright eyed, overly self-righteous students of social change, Liz and Mike had found themselves on the same side of many classroom debates. The culminating argument their senior year was a study of a legislative proposition that would have brought devastating consequences to immigrants and anyone else who didn't speak English as their first language.

Mike and Liz had been friends, occasionally intimate friends, ever since. Like all relationships, theirs had its ebbs and flows. The last time they talked it was over a late Sunday afternoon lunch of burgers and onion rings. Liz recalled the look of disgust on Mike's face as she ordered another beer. A non-drinker, or more precisely, a former drinker, Mike could keep his patience with imbibing a beverage along with a meal, but not as a continuing pastime for its sake only.

"Okay, Connors. I'll talk with Mike and the man who found her. Let me know when someone arrives from the M.E." Liz waited a beat, and then asked Connors, "You wouldn't happen to know who's in the rotation?"

Connors shook his head. "Should be Myers but maybe you'll get lucky."

The Myers to whom Connors referred was a pathologist

with the medical examiner's office. To be perfectly blunt, Liz detested Myers and actually had come to blows with him once in the corridor of the morgue. Although neither of them had divulged the details, the altercation had become legend around the department. Anyone who knew Liz would have had the sense to back down and the incident earned Myers the distinction of having had his clock cleaned by a girl -- a really tough cop of a girl, but a girl nonetheless.

The episode had resulted in reprimands and some continuing chagrin. With any luck, thought Liz, it would be Stein, the Chief himself, who would show up for the girl. Liz Jordan had a lot of respect for Dr. David Stein but how he kept idiots like Myers on his staff was beyond her comprehension.

Liz resolved to purge thoughts of the idiot Myers and focus on what deserved her attention -- the girl in the alley. Liz canvassed the immediate area with her eyes trained for detail but well aware that crime scene forensics would provide more information than her visual assessment. Other than the girl and the mystery fluid, there was nothing to see.

Liz walked over to where Mike, her old friend, was waiting. Mike Dwyer, late thirties, was sporting a bit of grey on the temples. A dedicated runner, even during his drinking years, Mike was in good shape. The excessive physical activity had kept the ravages of a stressful career in social service at bay. Running had been a source of focus and power for him when he gave up drinking.

Next to Mike was a man who looked to be a few years older, although with homeless men, age was relative to how long they had been invisible. Both men were in a full crouch position leaning a bit forward, a defensive posture Liz had seen before. Mike patted the man's shoulder and they both stood as they looked in Liz's direction.

Mike took a deep breath, keeping his hand on the other man's shoulder. "I know you need to talk to us, Liz, but can we walk back to the shelter? I left Kelly kind of in charge when I ran out here. She's probably trying to keep everyone from freaking out." He looked from the fellow to Liz, from Liz to the fellow. "Ty, this is Liz. I've mentioned her to you once or twice."

Liz studied the man as he responded with an almost imperceptible nod, the rest of his body uncannily still. "Ty, I'm Liz Jordan with Metro Police. You found the girl?" she asked. He nodded. Liz looked at Mike who also was nodding his head. "If we walk over to Mike's place and sit down, can you tell me about it?" Ty nodded again. Liz turned around and called to Connors that the three of them were heading up the alley to the shelter and reminded him to call her cell as soon as the M.E. showed up.

There were residents standing in groups of two and three along the street near the entrance to the alley. Several adults held young children and the protective posturing was palpable. "Ty, what's going on? What is it?" several of them asked. The residents were looking at Mike and Liz warily but they only spoke directly to Ty as if that was as far as their trust could extend for the moment.

"Just stay away from the alley, you'll be okay," Ty told them. "It'll be okay. I'm going inside with Mike for a while. I'll be back. Remember to stay out of the alley."

"Who's this Kelly?" Liz asked Mike as they walked toward the shelter.

"Kelly works for the city," Mike replied, "kind of a liaison between the street and the shelter. She most likely had some interaction with the girl. Glad she's here today. This will be rough on the residents." He looked at Ty, who seemed to agree.

Liz turned to Ty and said, "The folks out here trust you." He looked her in the eye for the briefest of moments and for the first time, Ty spoke directly to Liz.

In a quiet, calm and somewhat deep voice, Ty said, "Kel's okay." Ty turned to Mike and said, "Shit. I just wish I knew the girl's name. I mean jeez, man, we know it's her but I don't know her name."

Chapter 3

The building they approached was neat and clean outside with minimal landscaping. A large sign indicated that this was the Avalon Street Center and listed the building's street address. Below the address were the names of the cooperating agencies responsible for operations: Community of Episcopal Fellowships, Sinai Ministries, and the Department of Public Housing. Liz was familiar with two of the agencies but had not heard of Sinai. They went through two sets of double doors leading inside the shelter. The double entry created a vestibule and gave the impression of entering a church although security or heat conservation was the more likely concern. The doors each had a bar release that when pressed, enabled the door to open.

The lobby area was small and resembled the waiting area in a bus depot with six to eight metal and vinyl chairs. There were two baskets of assorted toys and a few children's books and a small table with a surface that doubled as a chalkboard. Bulletin boards heralded a slew of options for free programs, the community health clinic hours, where to apply for food stamps, and the nearest businesses seeking day laborers. The lobby was neat as a pin and smelled faintly of a lemon disinfectant. Opposite the entry doors was a counter area backed by sliding windows similar to those in a doctor's office, and a single locked door leading to staff offices. Currently the office area was empty. To the left, double swinging doors with small windows were labeled Dining Room.

Liz asked Mike if there was a room she could use to speak with Ty, and then with Mike himself. "There's a small meeting room we use for conferences with case managers. You and Ty head into the dining room and grab coffees while I get the girl's intake info from the office."

As Ty and Liz entered the dining room, she realized it could have been the fellowship hall in any number of small houses of worship in any town, although there were no discernible clues as to faith or denomination. Liz had been here a few times to meet up with Mike but this was her first official visit and she noticed it always looked the same. Long, cafeteria style tables covered with vinyl tablecloths with the edges wrapped underneath and pinned down tight. A few chairs were available at one table but the rest were stacked and lined up against a wall. Four highchairs stood neatly in a row against another wall. A side table near the pass-through kitchen window held the ever-present, all-important five gallon coffee urn, assorted ceramic mugs, powdered creamer and sugar. The coffee urn produced gallon after gallon of coffee, day and night. There was a large, plastic water container with a push spout. Other than water and coffee, there were no other beverages or edibles in sight.

Liz recalled Mike explaining to her that the shelter adhered to strict hours for meals, with the exception of infant formula, baby food, and snacks for children. Residents went through staff to obtain items for their children outside of regular meals, and although it was nearly always available for the kids, every distributed food item was documented. In the world of the homeless, food is money.

There were few residents present in the dining room. At the table sat a young Latina woman and a child of maybe three years. She had a coffee cup in front of her and was encouraging the child to eat bits of something that looked like a mixture of raisins, nuts and crackers. Near them sat two young women side by side, quietly talking. One of the women held an infant in the crook of one arm with her opposite arm around the shoulder of the other woman, who sat with her face in her hands.

As Ty and Liz found a place to sit, coffee mugs in hand, Mike joined them with a clip board in one hand and a sheet of yellow paper in the other. All eyes were on him for a moment. He walked over to the woman and the child having the snack. He smiled and spoke to the child, rubbed the top of his head. He asked the woman a question or two and she nodded yes. Mike told her thank you and touched her lightly on the shoulder.

As he turned to join them, Liz saw him glance at the young woman holding the baby and as their eyes met she nodded an acknowledgment, and looked in Liz's direction. Everyone seemed stunned by the events of the afternoon, just slightly short of full blown shock.

Mike led them to a small room furnished with a table and two chairs. The attempt to create a homelike feel extended here, as well. There was a lamp on a low table and a couple of generic pictures on the wall.

"Leah. She told me her name was Leah, but it's possible that's the name she used on the street." He was talking to the two of them but looking at Ty as he spoke.

"Leah…," repeated Ty, deep in thought. "I was thinking it was an unusual name like that."

Mike continued. "The Washington ID she produced at intake is for a Leah Bishop, nineteen, but I'd say she was closer to seventeen." Mike handed the paperwork to Liz and said, "Take the time you need with Ty. I'll ask Kelly to stick around. You may want to talk with her." The statement struck Liz as peculiar because she had not seen anyone who looked like shelter staff or anyone who appeared to be in charge in Mike's absence.

Mike closed the door as he left. Liz explained to Ty that as a formality she needed to show him her shield and ID and asked if he understood that this was an official interview into a death. It took about ten minutes to hear from Ty about how he happened upon Leah on his way to the shelter for his weekly chat with Mike. Yes, he'd seen the girl once before at the Avalon shelter, on Friday afternoon when he'd helped one of the staff from the men's shelter pick up supplies. Ty said he'd seen her a couple times in the park too. He hadn't had a real conversation with her but got the feeling Leah was sharp.

"Describe sharp for me," said Liz.

Ty looked a bit puzzled and with a frown, he answered, "She didn't seem to have given up."

Liz's cell phone rang. It was Connors informing her that crime scene techs and the M.E. had arrived and that the death had been pronounced. Liz informed Connors that they had a somewhat positive ID as one Leah Bishop. Connors said crime techs were coming up with very little but it appeared she had died there in the alley. Nothing that indicated a weapon had been found. The M.E., in the form of Chief Stein himself, guesses time of death at about twelve p.m. today but would know more after autopsy. Stein would like to transport the body to the morgue after techs were finished with scene photos, etc. Liz told Connors she was taking statements and asked if Stein wanted her on scene before transport. She heard him ask Stein, who said no need but that he'd be at the morgue most of the evening and to please find him there.

As Liz hung up with Connors she looked at Ty. He appeared to be sitting in repose with eyes closed, his shoulders relaxed. Both feet were on the floor, his fingers interlaced, and hands in his lap. His eyes opened. After a moment Liz said, "Rough afternoon."

Ty nodded and said, "Yes, indeed, it has been." Liz thanked him for the information and asked where he could be reached if there were more questions. "You can let Mike know you need me; or Gary at the men's shelter. That's where I get mail. I'll be around." He looked her straight in the eye while he put both hands on the table and stood up. "It'll be a damned ugly nightmare out there as if it isn't ugly enough."

Mike's face appeared at the window insert in the door and she waved him in. Behind him, Liz saw the young woman who had been holding the infant in the dining room. She looked to be in her late twenties but again, hard to gauge. She wore her dark hair in a long, thick braid and wore older, heavy, military-style olive drab pants with button flap pockets and a tee shirt. On her feet were running shoes, worn but with a lot of miles left in them. Liz trusted that Mike had his reasons for wanting her to talk to another resident. Maybe she knew Leah better than the others and could shed some light.

As Liz started to introduce herself, Mike interrupted. "Kelly Blevins, this is Sgt. Liz Jordan with Metro Police. Liz, this is Kelly. I can't remember if you two have met before but I'm a bit off kilter right now. I need to get back to the dining room. Maria's getting the casseroles out of the oven and I'm helping with little Javier while she's busy. Folks are coming back in. Maybe not with a lot of appetite but some comfort food is in order. I'm glad you had asked Maria to handle dinner, Kelly. Thanks."

Chapter 4

When Kelly Blevins had looked in the mirror that Sunday morning, she gave herself a pep talk. It will be easy, she thought. I've stated my case before and this will be a repeat performance. I'll begin by stating for the City Council the positives that have been accomplished by having someone in my position out on the street. I'll go over the impact on the social services budget and how much money has been saved by addressing concerns proactively. I'll have the stats to back me up: that fewer indigents have had need to visit the city's ERs, that higher numbers of homeless families are securing housing.

Mike told Kelly the hardest part would be to make it sound like her motivation wasn't just to keep her job without sounding like a bleeding heart do-gooder. People who make decisions with other people's money hate listening to do-gooders. So Kelly will hit them with numbers. They will need to see in black and white that they cannot possibly eliminate her position without costing the city more of the taxpayers' money. At least she had more than a week to prepare for the City Council meeting that would decide the fate of her position.

Kelly went into the tiny kitchen in the tiny fourth floor apartment. The place cost them too much rent but this part of town was quiet and she was reasonably close to the areas of the city in which she worked. Besides, once she and Peter had seen the view of the river they were hooked. She rinsed her coffee mug and placed it in the dish drainer, braided her hair and left a note for Peter, her boyfriend of seven years, that she would only be working for a couple of hours today. She wanted that to be a promise but knew from experience it wasn't smart.

Working on Sunday wasn't the plan when she accepted the position of Outreach Manager working with the homeless, but more and more Sundays found her with appointments that the folks on the street just couldn't make any other time or day. Other than scheduled meetings with clients, there were often incidents that popped up and required her presence or her help. Sometimes it was a matter of helping them with their meds, finding a meal or a place to shower. Sometimes it was a message about a job interview (Kel, can you just go over the questions with me, please?) or locating a family that had made it to the top of the list for a spot in transitional housing. Those important events made the job worthwhile.

Kelly planned to head over to the park to find Nyla and Skip and see how they were doing. Skip worked as a temp doing a variety of manual labor jobs. He had hurt his shoulder working for a landscaper. His girlfriend, Nyla worked in housekeeping at a hotel and she was recovering from a bout of pneumonia. Skip and Nyla weren't old, mid-thirties. But fighting addiction and living on the margins had taken a toll on them. Both were expected at the community clinic on Beaumont tomorrow for follow up. Kelly hoped they were managing to hang in there. A couple without children had no option for extended shelter stays, so that meant night-to-night arrangements around town or sleeping on the street. Nyla had spent a few nights in The Suite at Avalon after a brief hospital stay for the pneumonia but she worried about Skip and she gave up her bed. It's difficult to stay healthy on the street and they needed to work. A few more weeks and they'd have enough for a place. It'd be a dump but it'd be a place. Kelly hoped they remembered about the clinic tomorrow.

Checking the time, Kelly realized she had better get moving. She wanted to take a walk under the bridge and see if anyone spending their nights there was in need of a hand but that may have to wait until tomorrow.

Kelly was due at Avalon Street around two p.m. She would follow up with Candy, a new mother whose baby girl was just nine weeks old. Candy was a challenge but Kelly was unsure as to why. She would talk with Candy, yet again, about mom and baby's health and applying for temporary assistance. Kelly would take along a postpartum depression questionnaire that they most likely would not complete. It was too soon. Another chat or two together and Candy might trust Kelly enough to answer the sensitive questions. But, hell, thought Kelly, she's young and on her own with an infant and staying in a shelter. Wouldn't anyone be depressed?

In contrast, Kelly hoped to connect with Darlene, a woman who had a bed in The Suite. Darlene had just started a job cleaning offices. She worked nights, so it could be tough to meet up with her but they had seemed to manage it and met together often. Darlene had left Kelly a note on Friday that she would be around Sunday afternoon after church. Darlene's dream was to keep her job, get an apartment, move her mother out of the rest home in Tacoma, bringing her here to live with her.

The run down, low rent area of Columbia City is known as the Beaumont District or the Beau for short. Bordered by the river on the south and the downtown business district to the north, the Beau runs from Interstate 5 on the east to Beaumont Street as its western boundary. The only thing farther west was marshland that led to a lake fed by the river. Kelly walked the few blocks to the park, a routine with which she often started her work day.

Kelly found Nyla sitting alone in the rare autumn sun at a

picnic table. Nyla waved her over and Kelly took a seat on the opposite bench. Nyla kept her red hair very short and the absence of any intended style seemed to produce that very thing. A small, thin woman, Nyla looked alert, her color was good, and she was clean. She once had confided in Kelly that she was able to shower occasionally after her shifts at the hotel. They chatted for a few minutes. Nyla assured her that Skip was doing okay. He had walked over to the convenience store for coffee. Yes, she was feeling decent. Less chest pain when she took a breath. Yes, still taking medicine for the pneumonia and was adamant about being at the clinic in the morning to see the volunteer physician's assistant who had treated them both. Gary at the men's shelter had been letting Skip ice his shoulder three times a day. He had only been using Advil, but Kelly knew that pain management was dicey for Skip and that Nyla was staying with him on the street as a support for him to stay clean.

Nyla and Kelly heard a voice call out a greeting from the corner and turned to see Skip walking toward them. He was carrying two large paper coffee cups. In contrast to Nyla's short, red hair, Skip wore his salt-and-pepper hair long, preferring to tie it back. He wore jeans and a flannel shirt over a tee shirt and a hooded sweatshirt was tied at his waist. Handing Nyla a coffee, he took the backpack off and placed it on the picnic table. He rotated his right shoulder slowly and took an Advil bottle out of the backpack, opened it and shook out four of them, all the while telling Kelly he was sorry to have not brought coffee for her, as well. Kelly told him thanks, that she'd had some earlier but that it smelled great. Before he popped the pills into his mouth, she noticed that the small round, brown tablets in Skip's hand did, indeed, look like Advil. Funny the things she noticed.

Kelly asked about the shoulder and how his supply of Advil was holding out. Skip said he was okay. Ice and Advil were helping but the volunteer PA suggested alternating ice and heat and they were trying to figure that one out. Kelly asked if he had been attending meetings. Skip said that he was and Nyla nodded yes, as well. Skip made little eye contact with Kelly but that was normal for him when he was the subject of conversation. When Skip asked Kelly if she could talk Nyla into returning to The Suite, however, he was more direct.

As Nyla took a bottle of pills from her own pack, she said that she was doing better and didn't want to discuss it. Her decision was firm. She and Skip were going to stay together even if it meant that she would stay on the street. End of discussion. Nyla was due to work her regular four hour shifts at the hotel today and tomorrow. Skip would hope to get a few hours temp work after the clinic tomorrow. Kelly asked if she could check in with them over the next couple of days. Nyla and Skip both urged her to please feel free. They always appreciated talking with her, they said.

When Kelly walked into the lobby of the Avalon Street shelter she was surprised at how empty and quiet it was until she remembered it was nearly two p.m. on Sunday. She knocked on the sliding window separating the lobby from the offices.

Mike peered from around the corner, said "Oh hey, Kelly," and buzzed her in.

"You're here early, aren't you?" asked Kelly. Mike usually worked Sunday evenings, rarely taking over for the day shift before four or five p.m. Mike agreed that yes, indeed, he was on site early but that paperwork called. Few confidants knew that the main reason Mike made a late afternoon appearance was due to his history with the group of volunteers known as the Episcopal Fellowship.

For several years, a group of ten to twelve helpful Episcopalians from assorted congregations arrived every Sunday morning at ten o'clock. For a long time, the Episcopalians attempted to hold a worship service for the shelter residents but it was not well received and only a few folks attended. Mike held many spirited "discussions" with the group's organizer about how to better serve the shelter. At one point, Mike was asked why it wasn't required of the residents that they attend the service, after all the Fellowship was one of the agencies supporting the shelter's very existence.

After first explaining that perhaps not all homeless families ascribe to the Episcopal faith, Mike went on to say that the group was welcome to continue to visit on Sundays because (1) the Fellowship was one of their supporting agencies and (2) because they made a great breakfast, giving the resident currently responsible for that meal a break once a week. The discussions ended and Mike decided it was best to turn the place over to the Episcopal group on Sunday mornings and to stay away.

At some point, lo and behold, Mike was contacted by the newly-ordained organizer of the ministry who seriously wanted to make the Sunday visits worthwhile for both the Episcopal volunteers and the residents. Mike suggested that they might best engage homeless families by engaging their children. Since then, every Sunday visit began with the big breakfast, as always, but was followed by children's activities centered on fun. They enlisted help from Episcopal teenagers with the energy to handle a group of unruly children powered by pancakes and applesauce. The traditional worship service was replaced by an opportunity for the families to enjoy themselves together. Shelter parents felt more inclined to talk with the adult volunteers than they had previously.

Soon the Sunday morning event was full to capacity. Families who had left the shelter wanted to come back for Sunday morning "Kids Church" and within a few months the doors opened to other families in the community, homeless and thriving. Residents began to make more frequent use of other support resources at Avalon like the AA and NA groups, parenting help, and housing and work connections. Mike was sure that this increase in interest was due to the new approach. Sundays became the shift of choice for staff, but Mike had been accustomed to the Sunday evenings by then and kept the routine going.

Kelly and Mike talked about her plans for the visit, and who she hoped to connect with but shared few details out of respect for confidentiality. Kelly looked at the board, a large dry-erase surface with a grid resembling patient stats posted behind the nurse's station on a hospital wing. As with patients in a hospital, the board listed intake dates, due dates of progress reviews, and expected exit dates.

Capacity at the shelter was 78 and there were currently 72 residents: 13 men, 24 women, and 35 children. Of the 23 family rooms, only one was empty and available and there were two beds available in The Suite. If the intake line called with a family of three to four or with one to two single women requesting a bed in The Suite, they could help, otherwise folks would be turned away. The staff at Avalon played a daily numbers game. Staying close to capacity kept more families from sleeping in the street. Kelly told Mike she planned to be on site only a couple of hours today but would seek him out later in the week. She wished him a quiet night and went to find Candy and the baby.

By quarter to five, Kelly had spent significant time with Candy, which created some additional concerns and raised other questions. Candy had not yet arranged for the baby to be seen for her two-month well child exam and Candy hadn't been seen by a doctor since leaving the hospital after delivery. Candy's own health care could merely be encouraged but the baby's welfare was a different matter. If neglected, the baby could be removed from Candy's care. Kelly had to make a decision; not about what to say but in how to say it. Ultimately, she told Candy – firmly, that she must have her baby seen by a pediatrician or at the community clinic within one week because not doing so was neglectful.

Kelly explained it wasn't anyone's opinion, it was a fact. Her baby needed and deserved a doctor's care.

Kelly also had met with Darlene, always a bright spot. Darlene had been hired by a couple who owned a janitorial service, primarily cleaning offices. It was hard work and although she was on a crew with another woman and a man, she was able to work somewhat independently, which she liked. Darlene learned recently that her employers also owned rental properties and were looking for an assistant manager to live on site at a small, older apartment complex. They had urged the woman on Darlene's crew to apply but she wasn't interested in more work and had suggested Darlene.

As Darlene explained to Kelly, she could be earning her rent by being available to the renters after hours and on weekends. This was the break Darlene had been waiting for and working toward since a bitter divorce four years ago had left her with virtually nothing. Darlene was thrilled that she could have a two-bedroom apartment on the ground floor; just what she and her mother needed.

They talked about Darlene's stay at Avalon, too. Darlene's adult children in Seattle didn't know she was living in the shelter. She felt they had lives of their own and didn't need another responsibility. Kelly thought for a moment of how Darlene was so intent on helping her mother but wouldn't consider the parallel of help from her own children. Kelly knew that times had been tough for Darlene and that she had made positive strides, but wondered at what point Darlene might be reconciled with going to her children for help.

Kelly looked around the room and saw a pack and duffle under the desk near the bed. She assumed these items belonged to Leah whom Kelly had met on Friday. Kelly asked if Darlene had met Leah. Darlene replied that yes, she had seen her briefly a couple of times. Darlene said Leah struck her as a loner, read a lot, and kept her area of the room picked up. She and Leah had talked about what Darlene knew of the area of town around Avalon. She seemed aware for her safety. Resourceful girl, thought Kelly. Darlene mentioned that Leah was nice enough to sit outside and read so Darlene could get some sleep during the day -- a concern for Darlene with other roommates in the Suite.

Before they ended their meeting, Kelly and Darlene discussed a lease agreement with her potential landlords for the apartment. The agreement should include parameters for exchanging work hours at a defined wage, for rent at a defined market value. She added that Darlene needed to protect herself, her means of employment, and her future living situation, which would be cast into one big pot controlled by her boss/landlord. Kelly reminded Darlene that she owed her mother that protection, as well, if she moved her in. Kelly suggested the local Legal Assistance Office. When Darlene asked, Kelly agreed to visit Legal Assistance with her. What a strange assortment of things I find myself doing, Kelly thought to herself.

Kelly had stopped for a few minutes to talk with another resident, Maria, playing with her son, a toddler named Javier, when she heard shouting from the back of the building. Through the commotion they heard people screaming for Mike. Kelly saw a couple of folks she knew from the street. She thought his name was Marco but wasn't sure of the name of the woman with him. He was standing at the back door yelling in broken English for Mike to come with them to the alley. "Please Miguel, come, you come now!" Marco, obviously upset, was waving his arms, gesturing for Mike to follow him. "Ty, he found a girl from here. She hurt. Maybe died. Ty, he need you."

Mike looked at Kelly. "Ah, shit! Kel, stay with them while I check this out!" His cell in his hand, he threw the building keys to Kelly and followed Marco back to the alley. A group of younger people Kelly hadn't met were outside in the smoking area. She asked Maria if she knew them. Maria said they were here with their families. Kelly asked one of the guys if he knew what was going on.

After a deep draw on his cigarette, he said, "We just heard the dude yelling for the old guy to get Mike. We didn't see anything but they were pretty freaked out. The old gal started to wander away so my girlfriend brought her back here."

Within a few minutes several residents had come from the alley in back of the building. Sirens were common in this part of town, but when folks realized they were headed to the alley behind Avalon, it got scary fast and stayed that way. Darlene heard the sirens and came running from the hallway in a panic. The fellow with the smokes said there were two police vehicles and an emergency vehicle in the alley and repeated what Marco had said about the girl.

Darlene absorbed it all quickly, put her hand to her chest and said, "Jesus God, no!" then went straight outside. Candy had come out from her room by this time having heard sirens, visibly shaken and with baby in arms. Her baby must have sensed the tension and was crying. Candy sat down at a table and Kelly brought her a cup of water.

"This is bad, I just know it," Candy said and she started to cry. Kelly grabbed a few paper napkins for Candy to wipe her face, and took the baby from her arms, hoping she could settle her. She couldn't think of a thing to say that didn't sound like a lie, such as, *Don't worry Candy, it'll be fine.* It certainly wasn't going to be fine.

Kelly and Maria made eye contact several times. Kelly checked the time. She wasn't sure how much longer Mike would be or what terrible news he would bring. Kelly asked Maria about the evening meal for the residents. She handed the sleeping infant back to Candy, and then she and Maria took three large tuna casseroles from the freezer and placed them in the ovens. Maria asked Javier if he wanted a snack. He nodded yes, and Kelly smiled and told him that sounded like a good idea. As Kelly sat back down with Candy and offered to hold the baby again, she was surprised to realize she felt selfish for feeling glad that Maria was there.

Chapter 5

It was almost six o'clock when Mike appeared at the door to the dining room. With him was Ty, the Gulf War vet whom Kelly knew fairly well. Apparently, it had been Ty who had raised the alarm and had kept folks away from the sad scene. A woman was with them. Kelly was sure she had to be a cop. Tall and fit, with blonde hair and dressed for business in a rugged sort of way, Kelly wondered if she was Mike's cop friend from college.

Mike turned around and headed in the direction of the offices while Ty and the cop each got a cup of coffee. Mike returned with paperwork, went over to talk with Maria. Mike looked in Kelly's direction, saw that she was comforting Candy, nodded an acknowledgement and led Ty and the cop to the little conference room. He returned to the dining room within just a minute or two, alone.

Mike approached Candy, Maria and Kelly and, crouching down, delivered the terrible news. "It's Leah. She's gone." Candy continued to sob and tremble. Kelly heard Maria's breath catch in her throat and saw her eyes tear up as she looked at Javier.

Kelly's thoughts returned to two nights ago at Avalon when she met Leah. She happened to be there to introduce herself to new residents and the girl had just settled in. She claimed to be nineteen and gave Kelly a look that dared her to prove otherwise. Leah seemed more interested in having a conversation than most of the women on the street or at a shelter. Often they are suspicious that you're going to accuse them of using drugs or find cause to remove their children. But Leah gravitated toward Kelly and made eye contact. Kelly seldom experienced this at the onset of working with the women in The Suite so it was a significant detail.

Kelly asked if she was comfortable, how she liked the place. She said it was okay, better than others. Smaller than some she'd been in, she said. Kelly asked Leah how long she planned to stay. "Until they kick my ass out or some jerk steals something." Kelly had wanted Leah to understand that if she needed to see a doctor or a dentist, she would try to help her work that out. Or if there was anyone Leah wanted to contact, Kelly would assist her. Leah looked off into space, said, "Yeah, well...." then turned and walked away. That was Friday and by Sunday she was dead.

Kelly's cell phone rang, bringing her back to the present and the shock of Leah's death. The screen said it was Peter, probably wondering where the hell she was. He would be surprised, but knowing Pete, forgiving when he heard her excuse this time.

Mike approached Kelly as she finished her brief call with Peter. He said he knew she hadn't planned to be around so long but that Liz wanted to ask about Leah. "Was that the cop you've told me about?" asked Kelly.

"Yes," he said, "she doesn't visit here much so I forget whom she's met and whom she hasn't. You'll like her. You two have a lot in common." Mike saw Maria checking the food in the oven and told her he would return to help. Kelly followed him to the conference room, wondering what she possibly had in common with the hyper-alert, in-control authority figure she had just seen come through the dining room. Ty and Liz, the cop, were standing and she waved Mike in. Ty turned to leave and when he saw Kelly, he stopped and touched her arm for a moment. Ty said he was going to check in with Marco and Genevieve. *That's right. Marco's friend is named Genevieve.* Mike introduced Kelly to Liz Jordan, said he'd be helping Maria serve dinner. He thanked Kelly for all her help and returned to the dining room.

Looking a bit stunned, Liz offered her hand and asked Kelly to please sit. Kelly told Liz she was glad to meet her but regretted the circumstances. Liz apologized, but said she was surprised. "To be honest, I thought you were a resident," Liz said. She looked so embarrassed, Kelly had to laugh.

"Don't feel too bad," Kelly told her. "It's actually a compliment of sorts. I'm probably more effective if I blend in."

Liz looked more confused by that. "Let's begin on that note," she said. "Can you tell me in a nutshell what it is you do?"

Kelly began to describe her work. "My official title is Outreach Manager but, trust me, I don't manage anything. What my title should be is Street to English Interpreter or Buffer Zone Coordinator. My job description would have you think that I make wonderful, daily strides into helping the poor, unfortunate homeless get that foot up to self-sufficiency that the fortunate all think they want. The reality is that three months into this job as a professional do-gooder I discovered that most of the people on the street and in the parks and alleys still didn't trust me enough to tell me where they spend their time. It took another three months to gain a reputation as someone who wasn't going to have them picked up for vagrancy and thrown in the tank."

"So, when I came to the conclusion that help is best offered on their terms, I began to earn their acceptance, at least, if not their trust. The level of education I began to receive from my clients on the street wasn't even approached in the university setting. I sometimes wonder if the true masters of the universe are the ones who can get from one side of town to the other, on three buses, within thirty minutes to make it to dinner at the shelter before the kitchen closes down. Now, that's a feat in schedule coordination."

Liz listened with interest as Kelly explained things as she

saw them. When Kelly realized that she had been talking for several minutes, she stopped herself. "Sorry about the diatribe. I guess it's too late to get it back into that nutshell you mentioned but I'll try. Basically, my job is to communicate with homeless individuals and families in such a way as to connect them with available services."

"Right," said Liz, "Mike used the term liaison. It didn't make sense to me then, but I see it now."

Liz was impressed not just by what Kelly had to say but in the passionate way she conveyed it. Kelly went on to describe her brief interactions with the girl they knew as Leah. Liz mentioned the intake paperwork Mike had supplied and asked for any additional information Kelly could offer. Kelly related her conversation with Darlene about having met Leah and that Leah's things were in The Suite.

"The Suite?" asked Liz.

"Oh, uh...yes, that's what we call it. Makes it sound like a lovely room in some big hotel, doesn't it?" replied Kelly. "Mike started calling it The Suite when the large room on the end was set aside for single women. You see, the men's shelter provides short term beds and day services for homeless men, and anyone can get a meal there. There isn't anything comparable for women unless they have children or are victims of domestic violence. Mike didn't like calling it The Dorm or The Ward because he didn't like the connotations, like it was part of a college or a hospital. He thought calling it The Suite was a good alternative. And I agree."

Chapter 6

Mike Dwyer was distracted. He was beside himself with sadness, anger, and concern. In fourteen years of case management he had never before had a client die. At least he'd never had a client die under these circumstances: a current resident, discovered by another homeless person. He had spent the last couple of hours with the residents attempting to calm them down. Shelter life can turn stormy rather easily. Constant crises and regular states of emergency keep you on the edge of your seat.

There was usually a buzz in the air at Avalon but the current atmosphere was different. It was as if the oxygen had been sucked out of the place and everyone had to gasp for every breath. Mike had known less about Leah than Kelly. He had met with her briefly as was the rule before she was allowed to move into The Suite. He had assessed her level of function (capable) and her basic ability to reside within the shelter community (strong). Leah had agreed to urinalysis to determine if she had drugs in her system. This didn't surprise Mike because he saw no evidence of recent drug use. The intake had taken about thirty minutes. She claimed to be from the Tri Cities and had been in the city on and off for a few months.

Leah struck Mike as younger than the nineteen years of age she claimed. She said she had quit school after tenth grade and had worked as a waitress until the boss kept hitting on her and she walked out. She answered no to every question regarding whether she had family or anyone to contact in case there was a need. "What kind of need?" she had asked Mike, with a sarcastic, but amused smirk. "Like if I end up homeless and in a shelter? No, man, there's no one to contact."

According to the info Leah provided, she had never served in the military so referring her to the VA wouldn't be an option. They always asked this question, even when it was doubtful. Leah was assigned to a bed in The Suite and was given a tour by Ada, one of the shelter staff. She was assigned the daily task of cleaning the community room, kind of a living room/work area for residents, and was offered access to basic necessities, toiletry items, etc. As a condition of residence at the shelter, Leah would be expected to meet with a case manager within her first week at Avalon and to check in with shelter staff each evening before lock down at ten p.m. She could choose to meet with Kelly and take advantage of Homeless Outreach Services, but that was optional for shelter residents.

For many potential residents, the cost of following rules was just too high. Many preferred the street and the freedom of nothing left to lose over having to check in with someone they deemed an authority figure. Mike had been told by more than one homeless person that trying to exist in a shelter was like sacrificing their dignity and that was often the only thing they had left. Mike wondered even at Leah's tender age if she wasn't one of those folks. But he had told himself it was too early to judge.

Mike had talked with Liz, had given his statement about the events surrounding the discovery of Leah's body, and had provided all he knew of the girl. Liz had looked through Leah's few possessions for additional clues and had headed downtown to meet up with the M.E. Under the watchful eye of Officer Connors, Mike had removed all of Leah's possessions from The Suite. As a rule, Mike and the other male staff members did not enter The Suite. Any need to do so, like for room checks, was conducted by female staff. If the women in The Suite chose to, they could meet with female staff or with Kelly in The Suite but this was up to them. Avalon was, after all, their temporary home and The Suite was meant to be a place of safety and privacy. Mike felt like an intruder. He convinced Connors to have Darlene present in the room with them by telling him that Darlene could verify that things had actually belonged to the dead girl.

Leah had brought with her a total of two bags, one a backpack and the other, a small duffle. Inside a small inner pocket of the backpack was the ID she had shown Mike at intake. It was current, issued in Washington, with an address in Spokane. Her few items of apparel were clean although worn. There was a small, wool fleece blanket, a hair brush and two elastics for securing a ponytail. In an inside pocket that was easy to miss was a small metal container that held mints. Under the mints and paper, was a small envelope containing $74.00 cash. A small piece of paper contained the printed notation "10/08 @ 1423" circled by a handwritten heart. Bus schedule, maybe? Plans to meet a loved one? Was it an appointment? The paper resembled a receipt but held no other information as to its origin.

Mike knew that Liz had noted the details of the items and Connors did the same. There were no pictures, no letters, nothing to provide any clue as to who might want to know she was dead. Maybe she'd given a name of a contact when she got the ID. There was a takeout menu from a rib restaurant in Kennewick called Barbecue Betty's. Leah had used it as a bookmark about half way through a paperback copy of Wuthering Heights. The menu was old and ragged and didn't look significant. The paperback book was tattered, the spine and back cover had been reinforced with packing tape. The police, namely Liz, probably would try to make a connection to Leah through the restaurant, if it even still existed. There were no indications where or when she may have picked up the Bronte novel.

While Liz and Connors consulted with Mike, Kelly finally had a chance to return Pete's call. He was sorry to hear about the girl's death because the death of anyone, especially one so young, is sad. Peter also felt sorry because he knew how it would take a toll on Kelly and her work with the homeless community. "Let's take a rain check on our plans for dinner out. I can whip up food here. How does that sound?" he asked.

Kelly was relieved. She wanted to go home, to the tiny fourth floor apartment and spend a quiet evening with Peter. She would resist the urge to make the rounds and check in with her clients on the street. She knew that word of Leah's death, and that it was a violent one, would get around fast. "I would like staying in," Kelly told him. "It's just what I need. And I owe you one. I'll be heading out in just a few minutes. Love you."

Kelly walked through the dining room, out to the courtyard area where the adult residents could smoke. Ty was sitting with several of the residents. But Kelly knew that Mike was talking with Liz, giving a statement. Mike would know that the residents may need a calming hand so he may have asked Ty to hang around until he was free. There wasn't much conversation happening between residents. A few looked stressed almost to panic. Kelly knew that a crisis or situation of extreme stress was hard on those who may be in recovery. Ty looked up, saw Kelly. He stood and walked over to the door leading to the alley. Kelly followed him, then turned to look at the residents in the courtyard and told him in a low voice, "I'm heading out, Ty. Mike should be free shortly. How are you doing?"

He let out a long, deep sigh and said, "It was pretty bad, Kel. Marco and Gen were right behind me but they didn't get too close." Bless his heart. Ty's voice sounded steady and his manner was composed but on closer study, the cigarette in his fingers was shaking.

"I'm sorry you had to be the one to find her, Ty, but you got Mike out there and kept the folks away. What time was it when you found her?" Kelly asked.

Ty took a long drag off his smoke and blew it out with his face pointing straight up at the sky. He closed his eyes and said, "Five o'clock. I was on my way to see Mike. It's Sunday." Kelly told herself they could bank on that. Ty's Sunday routine visiting Mike was well known. She patted his shoulder and as Kelly turned to walk away, Ty's hand came up and covered hers ever so lightly and only for a second. Kelly made it to the front door and out to the street without meeting anyone's eyes. She was suddenly very tired and relieved to be heading home.

Chapter 7

Dr. David Stein, the Chief Medical Examiner, was in an autopsy suite doing a preliminary examination of the dead girl, when Calvin in the front office buzzed him. Dr. Stein straightened his posture from bending over the body. He looked up over his half glasses, took the latex glove from his right hand, pressed the intercom button, and asked, "Yes?"

"Dr. Stein, Detective Sgt. Jordan is here and said you'd be expecting her. Should I send her back?" Having left word for Liz to find him at the morgue, Stein told Cal to please send her to autopsy suite three. As Liz walked in through the swinging doors, Stein realized that he hadn't seen her in the morgue in a few weeks.

"Hello Detective Sgt. Jordan. Seems you and I need to do some catching up. Not exactly my choice of the best way to connect with people, but nonetheless, here we are." Liz noticed that Stein's slender six-foot frame was dressed casually under the protective gown in what appeared to be khakis and a polo shirt. His partially bald, mid-sixties forehead was tan and his graying hair was definitely a shade whiter.

"What a way to come back from vacation," Liz said, looking at the girl. Chief Medical Examiner Stein and his wife, Beverly, celebrated their fortieth wedding anniversary a couple of months before and it had been a point of contention between them that the good doctor had not taken a vacation since their thirtieth. Taking the bull by the horns, Beverly made arrangements with everyone from the Police Chief to the head of the city's Human Resources department to extract her husband physically from his responsibilities for two entire weeks. Now, that's love, Liz told herself. "How was the Caribbean?" Liz asked.

"Good. We had a wonderful time," he told her, "but let's save that conversation for another time. I happened to be in my office reviewing the cases that came in during the two weeks I was out of the country. I heard the call come in for our girl here and decided to take it myself." Stein, seeing the sheepish expression on Liz's face, added, "…and no, I wasn't sparing you an interaction with my colleague, Dr. Myers. I refuse to treat the two of you like children who can't play on the same monkey bars. I was more concerned for the girl. Everyone was stretched thin in my absence and I figured it was time to jump in rather than wait until tomorrow morning."

Liz averted her gaze, glad to move from the subject of Myers, and asked, "What can you tell me?"

"At this stage, only a few things," said Stein. "The information from Officer Connors at the scene identifies her as Leah Bishop, nineteen years, but you already know that. She appears to be between sixteen and twenty years old, about five foot six and one twenty. With the amount of blood loss at the scene, I'd say she probably died there and that cause of death was blunt force trauma to the head. I'm not ready to rule it a homicide but I doubt she did this to herself, even accidentally. I'd place time of death at about noon today but we'll narrow that down. She wasn't in bad health when she died, which is surprising if she had been on the street very long. Maybe she was a recent arrival, Liz. I'm intrigued by some of what I'm finding, for example, the condition of her skin, her hair. There's no sign on the outside of the body indicating drug use. No needle marks, nose and sinuses look healthy, finger tips are clean. My guess is she was able to take fairly good care of herself."

As Liz listened to the details, she thought back to the search through Leah's few possessions. There was nothing to indicate she hadn't been homeless and on the street for a while other than that her clothes were relatively clean. That didn't mean much really, as Leah had struck people as resourceful. "We'll be working on verifying her ID. That may take some time," said Liz. "If she was a runaway street kid with fake ID, she could be anyone from anywhere." Dr. Stein put one hand on the table near the girl's shoulder and studied her, almost tenderly.

"Let's see what she tells us. I'll be using any information I discover to confirm ID, as well, from labs to dental records. You know I'll be in touch as soon as I know more."

The clock on the wall in the corridor said it was nine thirty p.m. It had been four and one half hours since Ty found Leah in the alley. And according to Stein, it had been about nine and a half hours since someone, in anger or with a plan, hit the girl in the head with enough force to end her life.

Liz walked out of the building, grateful for the fresh air. The city tried hard to keep the morgue habitable for the staff and for the family members of the deceased. But it was still the morgue, and visiting there meant only one of two things: either someone you loved was dead or you'd been asked to confirm that someone you loved was dead. It wasn't that Liz needed the fresh air because it was a foul environment as much as the place made her feel physically stifled. At least she was walking out of the place. Feeling stifled was nothing compared to the state of those souls who weren't walking out.

Liz put a call in to Mike. "How are you holding up?" she asked when he answered his cell phone.

"It's tough, Liz. It's hard to think clearly. The residents are either in shock or at a high state of alert, which is status quo for many of them anyway. I keep thinking about the girl, Leah, and what may have brought her here. We all have questions and not enough time or clarity to deal with any of them." Mike sounded calm, in control. Liz knew that his crisis management skills had kicked in. Always sound in control even if your words betray you. She had seen a similar, almost autonomic response earlier, from Ty. "Is there anything you know? How long she might have been lying there before Ty found her?" he asked.

Liz measured her response carefully. "I can't tell you a lot and I can't get into specifics, but she was dead a few hours. You were right that she may have been younger than nineteen. In reasonably good shape, health-wise before she died. The M.E. and I are thinking she may not have been on the street long." Liz gave her friend a chance to absorb the information before she went on. "Mike, I'm going to need to come back and talk to anyone who knew Leah as well as anyone who may have seen or heard something, whether they think it significant or not. Kelly mentioned someone named Darlene, who had been rooming with Leah. But I'm going to wait until tomorrow." Liz hesitated before she continued. "I think the folks there need some time although I can't give them much."

Mike thanked her for the consideration, processing the details Liz had shared. Liz went on, "I'm sure you've already thought of it, Mike, but it's not looking like an accident." Mike knew that much already but hearing Liz say it out loud made it real and even more of a tragedy.

"Liz, is there anything else I need to know right now?" Mike still sounded in control but it was slipping. "Should we consider the residents to be in danger? We need to know. These people are homeless, Liz. They're in a damn shelter, remember? They may have been on the street for months before they landed here and into relative safety. It's no picnic here but most think it's better than the street. But they deserve to know if they'd be safer somewhere else."

Liz felt for him but she respected him enough to be honest. "I understand what you're asking, Mike, and yes, safety is important. We're going to provide a greater police presence near Avalon and the park until this case is solved, but we don't exactly have fans down there."

Mike replied, "It would go a long way with folks if they felt the cops were around for their protection, Liz. They are rarely made to feel like part of the bigger community, you know? It would help them feel more willing to help, I can almost guarantee."

Liz considered Mike's words but felt compelled to add, "There are also other possibilities to consider. I hope for your sake whoever is responsible is not from within the homeless community. At this point, we don't even know if it was random or not. My view is that life is hard enough for folks on the street, and for those of you who work with them, the job is already tough."

Liz waited a beat while Mike absorbed her words, then she continued. "If someone outside the homeless community did this, it may be easier to catch them because they can't hide as well. They're not off the grid. But random or not, it may have been someone inside, someone who may still be around and it's nearly impossible to find someone who has left virtually no paper trial. I'm going to need you to help us keep tabs on people. At this point, everyone in the homeless community is suspect, including staff. But unfortunately, depending on what we learn and which way this goes, you all may be in danger, as well. We just don't know enough yet."

Liz's words made Mike feel suddenly cold. As much as he was concerned for the safety of the residents, he knew that the staff was not immune to being victimized. If he were truly honest with himself, he had to admit that neither was he.

Chapter 8

Traffic had eased and Liz made it home within an hour of leaving the morgue. "Home" was the third floor apartment in what had once been a large single-family dwelling. Instead of overlooking the river, the lake, or the rolling hills above the east side of town, Liz's view was of the football stadium and track at Columbia City High School.

"How can you stand it?" Mike had asked her more than once. "It's so freaking loud when there's a Friday night game, not to mention marching band practice."

But Liz liked living there. She liked using the track on the weekends. A football fan, she enjoyed the sights and sounds of the game. Although he complained about the noise, Mike had joined her on her little balcony more than a few times to watch the local kids compete on the gridiron.

As Liz unlocked her door, she was met by Eddie and Little Kurt, her cats. Eddie, a calico, was rescued as a kitten years ago from the parking lot of a run-down building where Liz had served papers. Little Kurt, a tabby, was a more recent addition. Having taken up residence near the dumpster at Avalon, Mike had found him and begged Liz to take him home. The cats were named for two of Liz's favorite musicians, Eddie Vedder and the late Kurt Cobain. A native of rainy western Washington, she'd been partial to the grunge music of Pearl Jam and Nirvana since high school.

Liz and Mike had spent evenings together arguing about a variety of things. But they always agreed on their choice of tunes.

"Hey, guys. You're hungry, huh?" Liz knelt as she petted her cats and then fed Eddie and Little Kurt. Liz had planned to return a call to her folks about Thanksgiving, but she decided to wait until tomorrow. She sliced an apple and grabbed a few cheddar chunks and a beer. She turned on the music and sat down just as Cobain started singing, "All Apologies."

As she noshed, sipped, and listened, Liz's thoughts returned to the case of the dead girl. What had happened in this girl's life that led it to end in that alley? Liz considered the line in the song about being easily amused. She had wished that for herself on occasion, to be easily amused. But Liz knew herself well enough to know that she was not. That's probably what made her a good cop. Had the girl ever felt that way? Had she wished to be easily amused? Liz shook her head with dismay. There were many things about the girl she would never know and Liz was saddened by her death. Apologies to you, Leah Bishop.

When Kelly opened the door to the apartment she shared with Peter, she was overcome with the delicious aroma of homemade marinara sauce. It smelled good enough to make her swoon.

"Great timing!" she heard Peter call from their small galley kitchen. He came around the corner just as Kelly hung her small backpack on a hook and squeezed her feet out of her shoes. He handed her a glass of Merlot and wrapped an arm around her tightly and kissed the top of her head. Peter told her he was glad she was home and that he thought rigatoni was in order. "I remembered the leftover sauce in the freezer. My mother would be so proud."

Peter Denuccio was a fourth-generation Italian-American with a huge extended family and they had adopted Kelly as their own. One of the things she loved about Peter's family was their belief that every problem, situation, or decision was made easier by lots of good food. Peter was over six feet tall and kept a trim physique by playing basketball at least twice each week. He was at his Sunday game that morning when she had headed out for the park and written him a quick note. That seemed like ages ago now.

"Smells wonderful," Kelly told him. "I'm exhausted and numb. When I left home this morning I had hoped to be back before your game with the guys ended but the day spiraled out of control. How was b-ball anyway?"

Peter steered Kelly to a chair, urging her sit while he put the pasta on. He went around into the kitchen, sipped a bit of his wine, measured sea salt into his hand and added it to the pasta pot. While he moved, he talked. "Game was good, mildly brutal. Gillman took an elbow to the side of his head. Not my elbow," he shared proudly, "and I came out of it unscathed, for once."

Kelly admired how Peter could carry on a conversation while completing any number of tasks. Classroom practice, she thought. Peter was currently one of the two male teachers at the elementary school where he taught second graders. Peter surprised everyone when in his junior year of college he announced that he was changing his major from physical education to elementary education. The decision followed a summer job as counselor at a camp for foster kids. He loved teaching and although he had been approached a few times about positions in administration, Peter was happy in the classroom.

Kelly had visited him at work for school assemblies and holiday programs and loved to watch him as he interacted with his young students. He would fold his tall frame into a human pretzel and sit on the floor, seeming to shrink before her eyes, reading a chapter of Lewis's *The Lion, the Witch, and the Wardrobe* aloud to the children. "Thanks for asking, but I'm fine, Kel. I'd like to know how you're doing."

Kelly sometimes related a few details about her work but both she and Peter knew that healthy boundaries were important. The events of today with Leah's death, however, were beyond that reality. Kelly talked with Peter about how the day unfolded and as she talked she realized how it was good for her, almost cathartic, to review it all out loud.

As they ate Peter's rigatoni with marinara, Kelly thought of the huge pans of tuna casserole she had helped Maria place in the oven to warm and she wondered how Mike and the residents were coping.

After dinner, Peter insisted that Kelly sit down and sip a bit more Merlot while he handled clean up. "Ugh," said Kelly with a frown as she rested her head in her hands. "I just realized I need to give Don a heads up about today. I better call him now."

Councilman Don Collier was Kelly's boss. He was an okay sort who had worked as an accountant most of his adult life. Don was assigned responsibility for administering the Homeless Outreach grant, in part, because many of his fellow councilmen wanted a close eye on how the funds were distributed. The other reason was that no one else would touch it. The grant was up for review and Kelly knew she needed to win their continued support with solid numbers. She could just imagine how the city council would interpret the impact of poor Leah's death. Kelly felt sick to even think in those terms. She abhorred bureaucracy, but it was a necessary ally, linked hand in hand with social programs for funding. Kelly felt both sadness and anger as she thought of the dead girl. Maybe she could use her connections to help find some justice for Leah.

When Kelly returned to the living room after her phone call to Don, Peter was sitting on the couch, wine glass in his hand, thoughtful look on his face. "How did the phone call go?" he asked.

"Okay. Don was grateful that I called him myself. He even thought to ask how I was doing with it all." She had sat down next to Peter and snuggled under his arm when the weight of the day hit her. Peter pulled her close. A few seconds passed before Kelly was aware that she was sobbing.

MONDAY

Chapter 9

At seven a.m. Monday morning, Liz walked into the precinct, making a mental list of how to proceed. She had given a lot of thought to her conversation with Mike the evening before. Liz was convinced that as with any investigation, the best clues would come from people closest to the victim and the circles they moved in. The help she received from Mike, Kelly and others would mean solving this case or not.

As Liz made her way to her office, she spotted Connors. In addition to being young and having a reputation for fairness and genuine concern, Connors was a good resource in the department regarding the folks on the street and in the shelters. Liz asked if he had a few minutes before starting his patrol shift.

After they settled at her desk, Liz began by sharing what she had learned from Stein at the morgue and from her talk with Mike the evening before. "I want your thoughts on this case, Connors. Anything you've picked up on that you can share? Do you think the residents at Avalon are in danger?"

Connors looked at Liz as if she'd grown horns. "Aside from this girl's death, they were in danger already." The young officer stopped for a moment, placed his hands out, palms up. "Yeah, I know what you're asking, but it's a dangerous way to have to live. They're homeless. They often resort to selling plasma for bus fare or just to make it to the end of the month when they get a re-up for the meager assistance they receive. Those that are able function at a high state of alert."

Liz had a distinct feeling of deja vu of last night's conversation with Mike. She put her hands up as if to say, *whoa, slow down*, but instead said, "Of course, you're right about that and I get it." Liz tried to rephrase her query. "Let me start over...what I'm asking about is danger outside the norm...danger of this happening again? If it is the homicide it looks like, what's your theory at this point? What's that Dunkin' Donuts-eating cop gut of yours telling you?"

Connors smiled at the jibe, sat back in his chair, and looked around the office. "I'm probably seeing the situation the same way you are," Connors began. "The girl was hit with something heavy, hard enough to kill her. If she died in that alley, which is how it looks, she may have had something someone wanted and it turned bad. Value is relative; we can't think in terms of whom the aggressor was unless we know what it was they wanted. There's a chance that it was someone on the street or another shelter resident."

Connors paused to consider how to proceed. "But, Sergeant, I hesitate to assume that this was a homeless on homeless crime. It may have been, sure. It might have been response to a threat, real or imagined, or extreme anger out of control from someone too ill to be on their own out there. But we should keep in mind that the homeless, especially women, can be victimized same as any other. And it's harder for them to defend themselves."

Liz nodded, considered what Connors was telling her and she realized he had as good a grasp on street peril as did Mike or Kelly; and listening to Connors made Liz realize how much she needed to learn. "I agree. I'm thinking that if Leah was killed by another street person, it was random or at least some momentary rage or impulse. She claimed to be around the area on and off and wasn't too well known on the street around here. If her assailant was not from within our homeless community, it's not looking random, unless her assailant was a predator who happened upon a defenseless homeless girl. If that's not the case, then whoever killed her sought her out."

Connors agreed, nodded his head firmly, and added, "Sergeant, if that's what happened to her, we need to know as much as possible about who she was and where she was before she came here. And why she ended up at Avalon. How difficult that task will be depends on how long she was on the street."

"Connors, I'm going to be straight with you. You have expertise about being on the street and you aren't a stranger down there. That would give us a huge advantage. I'd like to request pulling you from patrol and placing you on special detail under my supervision as part of the investigative team. Do you have any objection?"

Connors stood and answered, "No, Sergeant Jordan, no objection whatsoever."

Liz nodded. She told him to expect a call from Command with a change in assignment. "When we get the okay on this, change into street clothes and call my cell. I'll let you know where I am." As Connors left her office, Liz logged in and put in a special personnel request.

Chapter 10

As Kelly rounded the corner onto Beaumont Street, she realized that traffic was still heavy for mid-morning on Monday. The community clinic was a block further up and it opened at nine a.m. There was a line of patients forming already. As Kelly walked nearer she saw Nyla and Skip in the line. Kelly recognized several people with young children waiting to be seen by the doctors and nurses at the clinic. Some looked as if they hadn't slept, others coughed or sniffed, babies cried or slept on shoulders. Several of them recognized Kelly and as they acknowledged her, she realized they were visibly concerned. Kelly knew they'd probably heard about the girl's death on top of whatever health problem brought them to Beaumont Street that morning.

As Kelly approached Nyla and Skip, they turned toward her and immediately started to ask questions. "Jeez, Kelly, we heard about the girl. Everyone has. Did you know her? Who was she?" Kelly felt for them; so much to deal with and then to hear sad news.

"Yes, it's sad," said Kelly. "Her name was Leah. She was a resident at Avalon for a few days and I had spoken with her briefly. I don't know how long she had been in the area."

Skip looked sad and his eyes rested on Nyla, who appeared pretty shaken. If Kelly was reading Nyla's thoughts correctly, she was thinking about how hard it was on the street for young women. Nyla shook herself and tightened her grip on Skip's arm. Nyla looked over at the door into the clinic and sighed. She turned back to Kelly and said, "We should be able to sit down inside soon. It's almost nine." Kelly nodded and mentioned that she was glad to see that she and Skip were recovering well.

"I'm not going to ask where you've been sleeping. It's not my business but I hope it's dry and warm, at least." Skip and Nyla shared a glance at each other. They both nodded yes but didn't say a word.

Kelly wanted to keep the conversation going. Her hope was to stay here and visit with Skip and Nyla until they were seen by the practitioners at the clinic but if they shut her down Kelly wasn't going to intrude; that was the fastest way to break the tenuous connection she worked so hard to establish with folks on the street. This was unlikely to happen with Skip and Nyla. They had been easy to connect with but if they weren't interested in talking she'd just have to move on.

"Did you work yesterday, Nyla?" Kelly asked her although she knew the answer but it kept the conversation going.

"Yes, I worked my usual four hours after we talked with you in the park. That's all I can handle right now anyway," she said.

Skip pointed over to the corner, took a cigarette pack from his pocket and said he'd be right back. As they turned back to the building's entrance, Nyla half whispered to Kelly. "Skip met me at the hotel when my shift ended. He's been doing that most days since I've been sick. I snuck him into the shower so he could clean up and run some hot water on that sore shoulder. I was worried we'd get caught. I mean, Keith, the manager, is pretty cool and he treats me okay. But Skip and I don't need hassles. I knew his shoulder was sore," she continued, "and I thought Skip would want to clean up before seeing the Doc this morning."

Kelly smiled at Nyla and put her arm around her small shoulders. Nyla was slight enough that she was one of the few women Kelly knew who was smaller than she was. "That was thoughtful of you, Nyla. I'm sure Skip was glad to get some heat on that shoulder."

Nyla glanced toward Skip, who was walking back to their place in line. "Yeah, he's worth the risk of getting in trouble. I should have asked Keith beforehand but it was kind of spur of the moment." Kelly smiled at Nyla, happy to share her secret and thought maybe she was talking about more than just a shower. If it had been Peter, she thought, she might have taken the same risk to do something nice for the guy.

Kelly added, "It's great to see you're doing better, Nyla. A few weeks ago it was harder for you to talk this much without coughing and your breathing seems easier. The Doc will be pleased."

Nyla took a breath and exhaled slowly. "So this girl that died, we heard she was pretty young. You said she had been at Avalon but I don't remember a chick like that." Nyla looked up at Skip who had joined her in line, then returned her gaze to Kelly and frowned as if thinking deeply. "I was just out of the hospital though. I slept all the time. Poor gal; what did you say her name was?"

"Leah," answered Kelly. "Her name was Leah. She wasn't at Avalon more than a couple days. You were back out here with Skip by then. I don't know where she was before that. I'm sure the police will try to figure all that out."

Just then the door to the clinic opened and the receptionist stepped out, keys in hand. As she unlocked the door and held it open, she said in a loud voice to no one in particular, "Good morning! If you have an appointment, step to the window and check in. If you're a walk-in, take a number and have a seat."

Chapter 11

The line moved slowly through the door and into the waiting area of the community health clinic. The place resembled the lobby at Avalon but was more run down and grimly antiseptic. Operating on a bare-bones budget, the clinic was staffed by a rotating crew of volunteer doctors and nurses. There was one paid RN named Fran who had retired after twenty-five years working in county hospital emergency rooms. With her pension, Fran was able to work at half salary and was fond of saying her job at the clinic was better than bingo with her sister or golf with her also-retired husband.

The only other full time staff was the receptionist named Adele who had opened up that morning as she did every day. Adele also was the unofficial bouncer of sorts, because as a large, loud woman with obvious street smarts, no one messed with Adele. With volunteer practitioners, the clinic directed every possible dollar to patient supplies: medications, bandages, analgesics, compresses, oral and topical antibiotics. The chairs were old, the linoleum was worn. There were few amusements for the children. The stark, empty room was simple to keep reasonably clean. Besides, the patients who came through didn't care what it looked like or how comfortable it was. Most were happy to have a chance to see a doctor. That was comfort enough.

Kelly walked in with Skip and Nyla but there were a few

others she hoped to connect with this morning and she wouldn't take up a chair. Judging by the line it looked to be a packed house. Kelly wondered to herself if Leah had known about the Beaumont Street clinic or if she possibly had been seen there by one of the medical staff. Kelly knew better than to ask. The medical staff, and especially Fran and Adele, knew Kelly and were familiar with the work she did. She'd had a cooperative relationship with them in as much as directing the homeless to their care and occasionally helping find people who needed follow up. However, the staff would be tight-lipped about patients and Kelly had no authority to expect otherwise.

Kelly turned around just as Liz Jordan walked in the door. Kelly watched as Liz made her way toward the appointment window. She was obviously out of place, dressed as she was in a striped oxford shirt with slacks, overcoat and boots, even though she hadn't yet shown her badge. Just before Liz started to interrupt Adele as she checked in a young woman with a toddler, Kelly approached the window. "Liz, welcome to Monday morning at the clinic. Have you been here before?"

"Oh ... Kelly... hello," said Liz. After glancing around the room, Liz looked at Kelly and answered, "Uh, no, first time."

Before Liz had a chance to continue, Kelly motioned her over to the corner away from the check-in window. "You're here to ask about Leah."

"I am," Liz replied. "It seems a good place to start. At least we have the picture from the ID she used at Avalon; smart of Mike to make a photocopy." Liz handed her a grainy copy of a copy and Kelly saw that it was, without question, the young woman she knew as Leah. Kelly noticed the people in the waiting room had started watching them curiously.

"Let me see if we can grab Fran, the nurse here. She'll be able to offer you more help than Adele who's covering the window." Liz was thankful to avoid getting between the formidable looking receptionist and the stressed-out looking woman with the very gooey-faced kid. Kelly and Liz both looked up as the locked door leading to the examination rooms opened. A petite woman looking to be in her sixties with a kind face and short, silver hair stepped out.

She studied the file in her hand and called, "Carlisle, Anthony." The woman smiled as she looked up over her half glasses expecting someone to claim the name she had called, but she saw Kelly first. "Well, hey, Miss Kel. Who's with you today?" She looked at Liz and said, "I doubt that you're a patient, my dear."

An older man with a stoop was slowly ambling over, waving one hand and clutching what may have been a handkerchief at one time, in the other. "Carlisle, that's me." The man named Carlisle stepped past Kelly and Liz like they weren't there.

"How are you today, Mr. Carlisle?" asked Fran. "Come on back and sit in that chair so I can take your blood pressure."

Kelly hurried to say, "Hey Fran, this is Sgt. Liz Jordan with Metro. Can she ask you a few questions?"

Fran halfway turned to Kelly, saying, "You and your friend can follow me back too. Find a chair in my office and I'll be with you in a minute."

Liz and Kelly walked down a short hallway and entered an open doorway on the right. Fran's office was shared with assorted volunteer nurses. It was furnished with three huge ancient desks, several four-drawer filing cabinets, and two large locked metal cabinets. Liz saw three phone lines and a couple of outdated PCs. Two of the three desks were neatly organized but had a vacant efficiency about them. The third one of the three appeared even more organized than the other two. On the desk was a framed photo of a grinning Fran and a smiling gentlemen with three small children dressed as pumpkins.

Kelly gestured to a couple of chairs and they each sat down. "Nicely done out there, paving the way for me, Kelly," said Liz.

"And I didn't even need to show my badge. If I didn't know better, I'd guess that was by design."

Kelly replied with caution. "Well...it is a medical office... and you're interested in talking with the staff, not the patients. I guess I saw the logic in not upsetting sick people any further. Did I overstep my bounds?"

"No worries. I can be as discreet as my position legally allows," said Liz, and then added with an eye roll, "...no matter what you've heard from Mike about me." Kelly chuckled and Liz asked her, "Are you working around here today? I'd hate to think running into me derailed your morning."

"No, this is fine for now. I saw two people I had hoped to catch here this morning. A lot of what I do is kind of impromptu." As Kelly was talking Liz's cellphone rang. It was Connors.

"Yeah, Connors," she answered. After listening for a few seconds she said, "Great…how soon? I'm at the Health Clinic on Beaumont. Kelly Blevins was here when I arrived. She's handling my introductions, so to speak." Kelly could hear one side of the conversation. "Not sure, but here's the plan for now: head to Avalon and start interviewing anyone who knew Leah or saw her on Sunday morning. We need to establish a timeline for her whereabouts yesterday. I'll meet you there. I will inform the M.E.'s office that you're working with me on this case. I'm hoping to hear from Stein this afternoon and get the report from the crime scene crew. By the end of the day we'll sit down and assess our information and where to go from there. I'd give Mike at the shelter a heads up that you're coming to conduct interviews but ask him not to tell residents beforehand."

At this point, Liz glanced at Kelly while she listened to Connors on the other end. "Sure, I'll tell her." Liz ended the call and explained to Kelly that she'd requested Officer Connors to assist with the investigation into Leah's death. Kelly nodded and said she thought that would prove helpful.

Liz then offered Kelly a half smile and said, "Connors seemed relieved that I had run into you, like he thinks I need an escort or something. Oh, and he asked me to say hello. Is there anyone down here that you don't know?"

Kelly smiled as she thought of Connors and said, "Kyle is a great guy. Our professional paths cross on a fairly regular basis. He looks out for everyone on the street, including those of us that work down here, and," shared Kelly, "he shoots hoops occasionally with my boyfriend." Liz instantly felt stupid. Until now she hadn't even known Connors' first name.

Just then, Fran walked into the office with the cordial but brisk efficiency of someone used to juggling interactions with a number of people. As she greeted them again she separated the stack of files in her arms into two smaller bundles and placed one on her desk, the other on top of a filing cabinet. "I've got about three minutes, friends." She offered Liz her hand and said, "Francine Michaels, but please call me Fran. How can I help you, Detective?"

Liz shook the nurse's hand then retrieved another copy of Leah's ID picture from her case. "We're looking into the death of this young woman. The name we know her as was Leah Bishop. If you recognize her or if she was a patient here I'd appreciate anything you can tell me." Fran's demeanor slowed abruptly. She sighed and looked at the picture of Leah. She continued to study it, then walked around and sat down at her desk.

"This is the girl I heard about on the news." Shaking her head, she added, "She doesn't look familiar to me." She hesitated, then asked, "But you knew her, didn't you, Kelly?" As Kelly nodded yes, Fran turned to her PC, fingers on the keyboard, repeating the name, "Leah Bishop...doesn't ring a bell ...let's see. Not many patients here I don't run into but it's possible." Fran scanned the screen of patient names. "No, we've not seen anyone by that name. I'm sorry."

Fran closed the file she had accessed. She placed both palms on the top of her desk and slowly stood. She turned to Liz. "I'd like to keep this picture, if I may. There are others working here that come and go. They should see it too, if your time frame fits. Tell me though, the news said it looked violent but that her death may have been an accident?"

Liz and Kelly rose from their seats and Liz addressed Fran's question. "We are expecting an official cause of death soon. We haven't ruled out an accident at this point and her injuries didn't appear to be self-inflicted. If that's true, accident or not, someone knows what happened. Yes, please keep the picture and if anything comes to mind for you or from your colleagues that could assist us, please be in touch." Liz handed Fran her card and said, "Thanks for your time, Fran." Fran walked around her desk and the three women stepped toward the door to the hallway leading to the exam rooms and the lobby.

"There's an unofficial network of sorts between clinics," Fran explained. "We don't violate medical confidentiality, you understand. We follow the law because we believe it protects our patients. However, patients get creative if they need pain medications or are fighting addictions. Practitioners rely on a heads-up from each other. The volunteers who work here work in other clinics, as well. Maybe one of them will know of her from somewhere else. Anyway, right now I need to take care of the patients here. I'm sure Adele has a full room out front."

Kelly and Liz followed Fran to the lobby waiting area. As they opened the door, they heard raised voices, quickly identified as Adele arguing with a man who was clearly agitated. "I've asked you to lower your voice and take a seat. Or you can wait outside, but I'm not going to ask you again," they heard Adele tell him firmly.

Liz could now see that the man was really just a kid, slight of build and near Liz's height. Dark eyes revealed panic in a face that may have had an olive complexion but looked bruised and battered, and dark, unkempt hair that may have been curly. He was jumpy and belligerent, clearly dealing with the desperation of withdrawal from some chemical he had in his system.

"Why you treatin' me like shit? I'm sick, lady! I thought this was a place for sick people." He continued to rant although difficult to understand because he spoke so fast.

Adele continued, "Do you need me to come over there and help you sit? If you don't listen to what I'm telling you, we can't help you."

For a moment or two it looked as though the young man had calmed down as he stared at Adele. Suddenly, he grabbed a chair, hefting it up with both arms, ready to hurl it at Adele's check-in window. Everyone's instinct kicked in. Kelly and Fran stepped closer to the frightened patients who had the bad luck to be sitting closest to the action. Every patient waiting in the lobby became still and silent, protective postures shielding the children. Liz quickly placed herself between the man and the window, put the case she carried on the floor, and moved her jacket out of the way to show both her badge and her sidearm.

"Easy there, dude," she told the kid. "I know you're sick but I need you to put the chair down. We don't want any of these little kids to get hurt."

The man didn't appear to look at Liz but he growled at her words. "Shut up! I'm already hurtin'! That's what I been saying to her!" Adele had come out to the lobby and was looking back and forth between Liz and the man holding the chair, wondering how the hell this would end but appeared ready for anything.

"Hey, man. Let's go outside for a smoke." All eyes turned. It was Skip, who had been waiting for his follow-up with the doctor for his shoulder. Ty, the homeless man who knew Mike so well, the man who found Leah, stood behind Skip. Skip held out an unlit cigarette in one hand like a dog biscuit to a pet spaniel. His other hand was extended toward the chair but low and non- threatening.

The man looked at the cigarette in Skip's hand but didn't move. Skip made eye contact with Liz, who very slightly nodded her head. The man put the chair down and wiped the sweat from his face with his sleeve. Skip stepped between the man and the chair and motioned toward the door. Ty opened it and the man walked outside taking the proffered cigarette as he went out. Skip followed him and the door closed behind the three of them as they stepped outside.

"Whew! Nice job, everyone," said Liz as she turned to Kelly and Fran. "Is everybody okay?"

"Yes, everybody's okay," said Adele, waving her hands in dismissal of Liz's concern. "This wasn't the first time a junkie came in trying to get some relief. Just the first time we had a cop in plainclothes here to see it. And you can haul his scrawny ass in but it won't help him." Adele turned and went back into the office, resuming her place at the check-in window.

Liz headed out the door. Skip, Ty, and the kid were standing together a few yards down the street, smoking. The three men were of similar size but the two older men had assumed control of the kid and he seemed fine with it. Liz walked up slowly and asked Skip, "So how are we doing?"

Skip looked her way and said, "I think we're alright. My man here is Malachi. I'm Skip." The young man had calmed considerably, sucking on a second smoke for dear life, the nicotine kicking in. Skip and Ty seemed to know each other.

Liz looked at Ty as he surreptitiously surveyed the street. The military bearing was unmistakable. She noticed that Skip and Ty had positioned themselves to assume both safety for themselves and control of the poor kid should he attempt to bolt. Their stance and bearing would have come natural to either police officers or peace keepers. Liz lowered her voice and spoke to the kid, keeping a distance of a couple steps. "My name is Liz. I'm a cop. Ty here knows me, right, Ty?" Ty glanced from the street to the kid briefly and nodded yes.

"Okay, look Malachi, I know you feel like crap but you can't scare people like that. Threatening to throw a chair? I can take you to jail for that," said Liz. "Threatening a clinic full of sick people? It's called menacing. There were kids in there, man." Malachi looked like he might get agitated again, but he seemed to be listening. "If you check yourself into treatment, I won't arrest you. Yet. I'll get you a ride to in-patient or detox, whatever it takes. It'll be a black and white but it'll be a ride, okay?" Malachi said okay, puffing away. "I have to pat you down and have you empty your pockets before I can put you in a car. Do you understand that?" Again, Malachi agreed. "I'm going to check, too, Malachi," Liz told him emphatically, "and you better be there or you'll end up in lock-up and you'll be sick as a dog until they figure out what you need, you know?" He nodded yes again.

Skip spoke up at this point, saying, "Man, that's a deal, you know?" Ty looked at Liz and she sensed not only approval from him, but trust.

Liz gloved up from the kit she kept in her pocket. She patted the kid down and emptied his pockets while Ty and Skip served to form a visual barrier of sorts from the folks on the street. In his possession the kid had a meth pipe, half a book of matches, two one dollar bills and a few coins, two tiny, empty plastic bags, no ID but a card from the Grayson Avenue Hotel with the name Gary and a number handwritten on the back. Liz used her cell to call dispatch and explained she needed uniforms and a patrol car but no lights or siren. Skip saw the card and asked the kid, "You've been staying at the Grayson?"

"No, man, I got no money for that," he replied. "Keith just gimme a cup o'coffee. He said to go see Gary."

Ty looked at Liz and said, "That's Gary at the men's shelter." He then looked back at Malachi and said, "Gary's cool but that pipe will lose you your bed, you know?" Malachi didn't appear to hear him.

A few minutes later Liz put Malachi into the custody of the patrol officers and explained to them what had transpired. She turned to Skip and Ty, who had waited with Malachi, and thanked them for helping.

As they walked back toward the clinic, Skip said to Liz, "That card Malachi had, for the Grayson? That's the place my girlfriend works. The manager Keith is okay; must have tried to get him to the shelter. He frowns on tweakers hanging around the place."

Kelly was outside. "Hey. Nyla's finished," Kelly said to Skip, "and Fran's looking for you, Skip. That was quick thinking in there. You okay?"

"Yeah," he said, "just a sick meathead kid. I cringe thinking I was like that once." Skip offered Liz his hand. As they shook hands, Skip said to Kelly, "Your friend here was pretty cool. She sent the kid to treatment instead of jail. The kid will most likely stay on the shit but you never can tell."

Ty and Skip bumped fists. Ty nodded toward Liz and said, "I'm outta here then. I'll be at the men's shelter helping Gary most of today. Busy there. Been cold at night." He turned to Skip and said, "I'll catch up with you later, Bro. Take care of that shoulder." And off he went.

Skip went inside the clinic. Kelly and Liz heard applause and saw him get a hug from Nyla before he went through the door to the examination rooms with Fran.

Kelly smiled at Liz, shaking her head. "Welcome to our world, Sergeant. Connors would be impressed."

Liz looked back at Kelly and said, "I don't know how you do this every day. It's like working in a war zone."

Kelly just kept smiling and reminded Liz that at least she goes home at night. "I've got some news for you. I showed Leah's picture to Nyla. She recognized her from the hotel where she works. She doesn't want to talk to you here. Nyla's hoping you can come by her work later today. She'll be there after two. She works at the Grayson Avenue Hotel."

Chapter 12

When Liz returned to Avalon, she had wanted a chance to debrief with Connors about the incident at the clinic, but Mike met her at the locked front entrance. "We're in lock down. An irate ex showed up looking for his ex-girlfriend and their kids. She's okay, just shaken. He was pretty nasty but controlled himself. He didn't threaten her but I know their history, so I'm locking up for everyone's safety. Connors escorted him off the premises. She's getting on a bus to Sacramento tomorrow. Her mother is expecting them."

Liz asked where Connors was interviewing residents. Mike directed her to the small room where she had talked with Ty and Mike the evening before. He told her to help herself to coffee if she wanted. Liz started to decline, but reconsidered. Mike and Liz headed to the coffee urn. Liz sipped and said, "Not bad. I guess morning brew is fresher, huh?"

Mike shrugged. "You'll need me to let you out when you're ready. And I'd appreciate any updates you can share before you leave; if you don't mind."

Liz bristled. "Mike, what's with the attitude? We're on it. These investigations are slow to start." The dining room was empty of residents at the moment. She put her cup down and took off her coat. "I'm getting with Connors as soon as interviews are done here. I should hear from the M.E. and crime scene techs any time. That should tell us a lot. At least I'm hoping. Am I missing something, in your estimation?"

Mike glared at Liz. "Look," he said, "we're all on edge here. That ex-boyfriend probably heard about the girl's death. That's probably what prompted his visit; his own twisted way of showing concern. I'd like to avoid many more scenes like that. We've had two families leave this morning. They like their chances on the street better than in here. These are folks with small kids, Liz." Mike took a breath and eased his stance a bit. "I know you're doing your job. Sorry."

Liz exhaled and said, "Yeah, I got it. Connors and I will finish talking to residents and get out of here."

"Actually, it was handy having a cop here this morning," Mike told her. "Connors is okay."

Jeez, thought Liz, as she rolled her eyes. She took a bow and said, "That's what I hear. All us cops are just in the right place at the right time today." Mike shook his head and went back to his office, puzzled.

Liz found Connors between interviews, documenting his efforts into the case file. "A bit of an incident here earlier, huh, Connors?" she asked.

Connors shrugged. "No big deal, really, Sergeant. The guy was worried about his kids. Once he realized there was a cop on the premises, he left without incident. I'd be surprised if we see him again before the ex and the kids leave tomorrow."

"So, tell me what you've learned," said Liz. Connors began by sharing that he had seen Marco and Genevieve on the street on his way in. Marco knew Connors. They had talked a few times in Spanish. Connors took the opportunity to ask him if he had been familiar with a girl named Leah or had seen her on the street. He wasn't sure but said he may have. Connors knew that Gen wouldn't talk to him. Gen never talked to anyone except Marco. She would occasionally acknowledge Ty, maybe Skip or Nyla. But that was it. He asked Marco if Gen may have seen her around. Marco shook his head and told Connors he didn't think she had.

Connors had talked with six residents at Avalon, only three of whom had even spoken to Leah. They knew nothing of her personally nor did they recall anything very specific from speaking with her. The comment Connors heard more than once was that she hadn't been around long, but then neither had many of them. There were a few others to talk with so he and Liz split it up.

After nearly an hour of interviews, only one person was able to offer something useful. Liz remembered the young woman named Maria. She'd been in the dining room at Avalon after Leah had been found in the alley. She'd been sitting with a small child. It was Maria that Mike had thanked for getting dinner started for the residents.

Connors spoke with Maria because she felt more comfortable using Spanish. As Connors explained to Liz, Maria was able to converse in English but preferred Spanish, maybe for the privacy it afforded. Whatever the reason, Liz believed that when asking for information it was best to use the subject's first language out of respect. Liz appreciated Connors all the more.

Maria told Connors that she and her son, Javier, were eating dinner on Friday evening when Leah sat down near them with a plate of food. Maria said that Leah acknowledged her by briefly meeting her eye and asking if anyone was sitting at the table near them. Maria thought this was odd as few of the residents ever thought to ask. Maria had told Leah that she was welcome to sit. They ate in silence, but Maria noticed that Leah and Javier had engaged in a back and forth exchange of funny faces. Maria was touched that Leah took a moment to enjoy her child.

Later that evening, after Jav was asleep in their room, Maria went down to the women's bathroom to shower, as she did most evenings. As Maria finished her shower and walked out of the bathroom, she saw Leah in the corridor talking with another resident whom she identified as Candy. The dialogue she had overheard had not sounded friendly.

Connors pressed Maria for any detail of what she heard. Maria heard Candy say something like, "... but they were straight with you" to which Leah said, "How can this be straight?" Leah had turned away from Candy and walking away, replied, "This isn't over." Candy then said "It is over. Jeez, just go back to Richmond." Connors had asked if she might have heard Richland, being the name of one of the Tri Cities. Maria said, maybe, but she thought she heard Richmond.

Liz remembered the menu Leah had used as a bookmark from the BBQ restaurant in Kennewick. Would Candy and Leah have known each other from the Tri Cities in the eastern part of the state -- Pasco, Kennewick and Richland? Was Candy telling her to just go home? Connors hadn't yet interviewed Candy. Mike thought she'd headed to an appointment with her baby that morning and would alert them when she returned to the shelter. She was due back in time to handle afternoon snack for the residents.

Liz shared with Connors about Nyla recognizing Leah's picture and being asked to come by the hotel later. "That was smart of Kelly. I don't think I would have placed Nyla and Leah together or thought to ask her. Sounds like a stroke of luck."

Liz nodded and answered, "Yeah, and it was lucky that Nyla's boyfriend and Ty stepped up and helped this morning at the clinic." Connors, somewhat bemused, listened as Liz recalled for him the Malachi incident at the clinic.

"His name's Malachi, huh? Don't recall anyone by that name. The incident doesn't surprise me though. There are a lot of sad cases out there. Folks resort to desperate measures trying to get some help. And we both know the stats, Sergeant. Chances are this Malachi kid will slip back into it, even if he makes it through de-tox. But you never know. When they're motivated, for whatever reason, to try and clean up, their chances are better. I know where to find Ty and he'll know where to find Skip. Maybe they can help us check up on the kid. Sounds like Skip might have connected with him. I can see that happening." Connors grinned and added, "And we can hold the benevolence of the good Sergeant Jordan over his head; 'stay in treatment or go to lock up.' That's incentive, all right."

Liz updated her notes, as Connors had done earlier. As she finished, she saw notations that indicated that the report from the crime scene technicians was available for her review as well as the official M.E.'s report from Stein.

Chapter 13

Liz asked Connors to call the crime scene unit for a quick rundown while she checked in with Stein. She hit the number for the morgue in her cellphone directory wondering if she should call Stein directly. Too late; after two rings Liz felt herself cringe as she heard the unmistakable voice say, "Medical examiner's office; Myers."

Liz instantly felt repulsed and angry with herself for not thinking to call Stein. *Damn*, she thought; *decisions. Just hang up or grin and bear it?* Never one to turn away in the face of adversity, Liz made the snap decision to bite the bullet and deal with the waste of skin and air she knew as Myers.

Liz steeled her nerve and spoke with her calmest, most authoritative voice. "Myers, its Jordan. I got a message to call Stein," she lied. "Is he in?" No surprise to Liz that she heard the definite sound of a gasp being muffled followed by silence. Liz could see with her mind's eye the pale, sinewy face, the clenched jaw, the thin, puckered mouth. She started to say *just cut the crap Myers, is he in or not?* But Myers beat her to the punch.

"Well, Detective Sergeant Jordan," she was told, "actually no, Chief Medical Examiner Stein is unavailable at present."

Liz felt her eyes roll and a sharp intake of breath that made her stomach ache. "Well, here's the deal Myers. Stein completed the post on Bishop, first name, Leah. Can you give me the basics over the phone? Please?" Silence. A beat. Two. "Myers, I said please and I don't have time to waste here." Myers exhaled a slow sigh. Liz asked herself why everything he did was slow and annoying.

"Here is the post mortem summary: Bishop, Leah. DOB is unknown at this time. Subject is between sixteen and eighteen years of age. TOD placed at thirteen hundred, Sunday afternoon. COD cardiac arrest due to extreme blood loss from severe head wound." Myers droned on, clearly bored and not happy to comply with Jordan's request. But then how could one tell? Myers always sounded bored and not happy. "Victim was hit repeatedly with a hard, flat object of roughly six to eight inches in diameter and one inch in width. Probably metal, stone or glass, however no trace found in wounds. Subject was in relative good health prior to death. Epidermis, head/body hair, teeth, and nails indicate good level of nutrition and med/dental care. Toxicology is negative for illicit drugs, substances, and/or medications. No indications on the body of same. Examination of external genitalia shows no indication of sexual assault. Trace amounts of vitamins and minerals present consistent with prenatal or postpartum combinations."

"What?" interrupted Liz. "Vitamins? She was taking vitamins? Stein mentioned she was in good shape considering she'd been on the street, but that's odd for a homeless girl."

Myers sighed slowly and loudly, then asked, "May I continue, Detective?"

Liz stopped thinking out loud and answered, "Yes. Sorry."

Myers continued reading Stein's summary. "No pathologies indicated on examination of internal organs. Organs of the internal reproductive system indicate that the subject experienced vaginal birth approximately three months prior to death. Condition of mammary glands, breast tissue and areolae indicate subject had lactated within three weeks of death."

"Wait a second, Myers. Stein says she had a baby three months ago? And she was lactating, as in breastfeeding, two months later? Could she have had a late abortion or a still birth?" Liz asked.

"Sergeant, are you asking my opinion?" asked Myers without much of an attitude, which caught Liz slightly off guard. But Liz was surprised enough by what she had heard that she needed to process the information, even if it was with Myers.

"Yes, I am, Myers. Please tell me what you think," Liz replied.

"We are unable to deduce from her physiology whether this woman gave birth to a live infant or delivered a full term or nearly full term deceased or stillborn fetus. We know, however, that she continued to ingest prenatal vitamins for several weeks after the birth. This would be the usual practice for a woman planning to nurse an infant and doing so would have been unnecessary if she had terminated or if the child had not survived the birth. We also know that she was lactating within a few weeks of her death so we can assume she was nurturing a live child whom she had delivered. Are you following my logic, Sergeant?"

"Yes, yes; makes sense. Go on. Please."

"Dr. Stein also noted indications that she was most likely pumping breast milk. The areolae, the area around the nipples in the common vernacular, were not toughened by the suckling of an infant. This is a significant distinction, as often surrogates or birth mothers giving up their infants for adoption will pump breast milk. The purpose is to allow others to feed the child and therefore bond with the infant, either in the mother's place or in addition to their own attachment with the child. In the case of adoption or surrogacy, the practice serves to make it easier to detach emotionally."

"My educated guess is, and I'm sure Dr. Stein's as well, that this woman delivered a live infant, and pumped milk instead of nursing the child herself. As to why she stopped I couldn't begin to guess. Perhaps if you find the child you will find the answer. This woman obviously cared enough about her own health and considered the infant's health important enough to attempt the best outcome. Alas, it was a tragic outcome for her, unfortunately. Perhaps the infant fared better. At any rate, the complete post will be available, of course. Is there anything further, Sergeant?"

Liz was stunned but managed to say "No," and thanked Myers before she heard the click at the other end of the call.

Chapter 14

Liz relayed the M.E. results to Connors, including the additional information from Myers. Connors paused for a beat, just long enough to ask, "Did you say that you conferred with Myers?"

"Yeah," said Liz shaking her head with wonder, "weird, huh? I needed the information and couldn't sit on it. Don't know what came over me. We didn't even exchange profanities. He was helpful, I have to admit."

Connors shared what he had learned from a call to the crime scene unit. "She died there, as we figured. Amount of blood at the scene confirms and there was no evidence that she was moved. No weapon at the scene and nothing much at the scene to print. Did the best they could collecting trace but the scene was rough. They found several fibers that may have been from her assailant, not consistent with her clothing. Lab checked for additional trace, i.e. saliva, blood, substances, etc., on her clothing. Some kind of herbal mint tea was on lower front of her flannel shirt. She may have spilled it or her assailant did. Lab said mostly water. Matched the fluid found near the body."

Connors mentioned that the alley was a frequent shortcut between Avalon and Beaumont. Someone may have seen something but so far they hadn't found anyone. Garbage cans and boxes in the alley had been searched, but yielded nothing.

Liz considered the news Connors had shared, and asked,

"Anything from her bags or the paperback book? Or that scrap of paper with the heart and the numbers?"

Shaking his head, Connors replied, "Nothing, Sergeant. But I'll check back with them. They're still looking."

"So, now we know there's an infant somewhere but we don't know if it's alive at this point." Connors began thinking aloud and jotting notes. "I'll start with hospitals; live births three months ago to young Caucasian women; adoption agencies, too. That gets tricky though. We may need court orders."

"We will, if it comes to that. We focus on Leah for now." Liz went on. "Check into shelters and community programs in the Tri Cities. Maybe we can get a line on her or someone who knew her from what we found in her pack." Liz took her phone out. "I'm sending you the photo of the numbers on that paper she kept. It must have been significant to her. Let's figure out why. If the numbers are a date, it would be October eighth of this year. Where was Leah in October? Check the intake information Mike has again. Check in with Kelly, too. Maybe there's something else."

"Also, I want you on site when the gal with the baby, Candy, comes back," Liz told Connors. "We have two young homeless women who knew each other at least briefly. They each had recently given birth and now one of them is dead and her infant, if it's alive, could be anywhere. That can't be coincidence, Connors. We need to know everything about her connection to Leah. And we need to consider her a person of interest until we can rule it out."

Connors nodded, writing down each point Liz was making as she spoke. Thinking out loud again, he said, "I'm thinking better to look for her now. Or at least alert patrol." Liz pulled on her coat, checked the time and realized it was after two p.m.

Liz stared at Connors and thought for a few seconds, blinked and said, "If she walks in here, Mike can't keep her here, nor can he interview her about Leah. Let's alert dispatch with a description so patrol can watch for her and notify us if she's seen. But we don't want her spooked. I'm going to talk to Mike, then head over to talk to Kelly's contact, Nyla. I'll be over at the Grayson Avenue Hotel. Notify me if you need to leave here. We're going to need to meet up before the end of the day."

Liz found Mike in the dining room. Liz told him that Connors was remaining at the shelter and could she speak to him alone for a minute. After following Mike to the shelter office, she closed the door and asked him if he remembered seeing Leah talking with anyone in particular, maybe another young woman? Had guys her age come by asking for her? She was careful not to lead. Mike's response was that after meeting with Leah for her intake on Friday, he hadn't seen her again until she was lying in the alley.

Liz made the snap decision to break protocol and share with Mike that Leah had most likely delivered a live infant three months ago. Out of what she considered to be fairness, she also shared that Leah was observed talking with Candy. And it had not been friendly, according to their source. Liz explained this was the reason Connors was staying on site. If Candy didn't return soon, patrol would have to find her and pick her up for questioning. "I'm hoping to avoid that, but at this point, talking to Candy is the best lead we have," said Liz apologetically.

Mike absorbed the information about Leah and Candy. He sighed and glanced at his watch, then said, "Candy Schinde has been here before. Last year. She was here for three weeks then disappeared. Two weeks ago she showed up and asked for shelter with a high risk baby. Candy is nineteen years old, according to her ID. But she's a scared, emotional kid. I can't believe she had anything to do with this, but it sounds like she may know something."

"Are you scheduled to be here this evening, Mike?" asked Liz. "I'm heading over to Grayson Avenue to interview someone who recognized Leah's picture. I was thinking we could meet up for a burger after. We need to eat, right? Maybe Kelly and Connors want to join us, too? We may need to share what we've learned. I've got to assess all the info we gather and that's the best way."

Mike exhaled loudly as if he had been physically exerting himself. "Hell, Liz. Yeah, I'll be here. I usually stay when we're locked down anyway. And I'm not going anywhere until I see Candy and her baby. Let's hold off on dinner plans just yet but we'll figure something out. If you're ready I'll let you out the door."

Chapter 15

Liz took the freeway north. She hit the power button on the CD player. Pearl Jam's "Even Flow" their song about a homeless guy, started to play. It was one of Liz's favorites, and the meaning hit hard today. Vedder could have been singing about one of the guys on the street, the ones Liz had been talking with over the last couple of days. She thought of Ty and Skip, of how rough their life was. She thanked Eddie for the reminder.

Listening to Pearl Jam on the drive over to Grayson Avenue, Liz thought about Mike, his staff, the residents at the shelter. She thought about Kelly and Connors, whom she now knew had a first name, Kyle. She thought of Fran, the nurse at the clinic. She thought about the incident with the kid named Malachi. She thought of how Skip stepped up and how Ty had his back. In her cop brain, she wouldn't eliminate anyone from suspicion unless she knew them well enough to trust them. She knew Mike. She knew Connors. She would trust Kelly for now as she had no reason to suspect her.

Liz mused over all that had occurred in the hours since the body of a young woman named Leah had been found dead in an alley. Liz's thoughts centered on looming details, such as the fact that Leah had carried a pregnancy to term and possibly given birth to a child. Her child and whom else's? They had learned that Leah most likely was known to Candy, also a new mother. But Candy and her infant daughter were alive. Why were they alive while Leah was dead? And what of Leah's baby? Was it alive? If the baby lived, where the hell was it? Liz thought about her conversation with Myers. How strange was that? And why did Myers know all that shit about births and nursing mothers and surrogates? Did *ALL* doctors and forensic medical pathologists know that stuff? Did Stein know that stuff?

Liz took the Grayson Avenue Exit from the freeway and waited at the light to make a left. Navigating around this area where Interstate 5 and Interstate 205 converged was awful and traffic congestion was particularly bad this time of day. School having let out, the streets were packed with school buses, minivans and huge SUVs loaded with kids. Adding to the traffic was a major hospital, three large medical facilities, the district's main firehouse, and several shopping centers with a variety of restaurants. Typical suburban glut, thought Liz, but when you wanted or needed those services, it was nice having them close. If only the sun would come out and dry things out a bit.

The registered voters within the limits of Columbia City had advocated for a mass transit line that would run from the north end of town to the south and link up with the very user-friendly public transportation system across the river in Portland. Unfortunately, the city dwellers couldn't carry the measure on their own and it was defeated by suburban constituents who, in their infinite wisdom, thought Oregon should help pay for it. The result was the daily migration by freeway of the tens of thousands who live in or near Columbia City but work in or around Portland. The migration had been going on for decades and was worse every year.

It made no sense to Liz, and the middle class urban commuters, warm and comfy in their private vehicles with no passengers on board, didn't seem to notice how fortunate they were. Ironically, the few transit lines available to commuters who used public transportation were packed. But the lines were used mostly by elderly folks getting themselves to appointments and young, working families, trying to get their little ones to school or care and themselves to work on time. Liz was all for supporting self-sufficiency but she knew that, for some, it was a matter of getting to a level of maintenance. Mike expressed it best, she thought, at a community meeting, speaking in favor of the transit line link up:

"How can we, as a community, in good conscience, cut off social support for our most vulnerable citizens, requiring them to work in the minimum wage jobs that no one else wants, and then make it damn near impossible for them to get here?" The saddest part was that desperate people sometime resort to desperate measures, especially with children to feed. If the desperate measures result in unlawful activity, that's when Liz goes to work.

Liz thought of Connors and his attitude of fairness, and the trust he earned from the folks on the street. Liz believed in equal justice under the law but often the underlying situations were not equal.

She drove down Grayson for about a mile and saw the Grayson Avenue Hotel on the right. The Grayson had been in business for thirty years as one incarnation or another. The building offered a total of thirty rooms on two floors. The larger rooms had balconies. The place had changed hands and been renamed several times after starting out as a B & B when a group of transplanted Californians tried to operate a winery north of town. It wasn't a bad idea. The hillside topography was okay for growing varietals but it rained too much. The spring growing season was too short and too late. So, the aspiring vintners lost interest and, taking a huge tax-deferred loss, sold to a corporation.

Liz knew that part of the story and that about five years ago, a Seattle billionaire who made a bundle on internet startups bought the place through one of his holdings. A native Washingtonian, the weather didn't bother him and he liked that the property was close to restaurants, services, a community college, and a branch campus of the state university. A total of no fewer than five brew pubs were within walking distance. Mr. Billions had refurbished the place keeping it northwest-rustic and once again called it the Grayson Avenue Hotel. It had become a trendy place to "weekend" between Seattle and Portland. What Liz didn't know was that Mr. Billions had a partner, a college buddy named Keith, who had been a linebacker at UW. After an injury sidelined his plans for the NFL, Keith used that business degree he had had the foresight to complete and went into the hotel business with his friend.

Liz parked, reported her location to dispatch and after looking through her notes, entered the hotel. The wooden double doors were new but made to look old-fashioned and heavy. There were groupings of comfortable sofas, end tables, and upholstered chairs arranged for private conversations. Nothing looked new but nothing looked either cheap or shabby, with lots of rough wood, deep colors, and iron decor. The desired effect was that one was welcomed by time warp into a hunting lodge of days long past. The lobby was spacious. The lobby ceiling met the roof above the second floor. The hallways leading to second floor rooms were open creating long, narrow lofts. The lighting was low but sufficient due to natural light from large windows that reached to the second floor.

The property on which the hotel stood backed up to an old industrial area. The BNSF railroad tracks were about two hundred yards beyond. Liz figured that that may be how Malachi came to have the business card and the number for the men's shelter. The Grayson wasn't the Four Seasons but it wasn't a dive either. She doubted he'd been a guest.

As Liz approached the desk, she was greeted by the largest man she had ever seen. The man was at least six foot six and would tip a scale at close to three hundred sixty pounds of muscle. The enormous man appeared to be of Samoan or Pacific Island descent, possibly Hawaiian, maybe Asian. Liz placed his age at early to mid-thirties, his skin the color of a caramel latte. He was attractive with a dazzling smile, killer-white teeth, and a head of longish, shiny, jet black hair, neatly tied back.

The man was attractively dressed in what Liz thought of as professional casual. He was wearing a pullover sweater, long-sleeved, silk with V-neck, in a muted teal green and deep grey wool slacks, sharply creased. A large diamond stud in one ear, a goatee, and a soul patch completed a package that Liz found beguiling. With some effort, she managed to pull herself together and remember that she was investigating a murder. In a deep voice the man said, "Welcome to the Grayson. How may I be of help to you?"

"I'm Detective Sergeant Jordan with Metro Police. I was asked to meet one of your employees here, a woman named Nyla," explained Liz, displaying her shield. Although rather tall for a woman, Liz had to look up about a foot to make eye contact. Liz was dwarfed and felt vulnerable, which didn't happen often. As a police officer and as a woman, it was a sensation she detested. She continued, "Will she be taking a break soon? I can wait, if necessary."

"Greetings, Detective," the man said as he extended a huge hand and as he and Liz shook, he continued. "I am Keith Akeuchi, owner and manager of the Grayson and Nyla's employer. Nyla informed me that you would be arriving regarding a matter of importance. Waiting won't be necessary. If you'll permit me a moment, I'll take you to Nyla." Keith turned, stepping halfway into an office area behind the registration desk. Liz heard him say, "Cover the desk, please, Amanda. I'll return in a few minutes."

Keith stepped out from behind the desk, and extended his hand toward an exit to the left of the lobby. In a gentlemanly manner, Keith offered to let Liz pass in front of him and said, "Right this way."

Liz looked him in the eye and said, "Go ahead, please. I'll follow you." Keith seemed caught off guard but quickly realized his error. A savvy officer would never turn their back on someone in an unfamiliar place.

He nodded and said, "Certainly. I understand. Right this way."

Liz followed Keith outside and down an exterior walkway to a door with a sign that read, "Housekeeping -- Employees Only." He opened the door and entered and Liz entered the room after him. The room was larger than Liz expected. It was also loud, warm, and damp in a clean, pleasant way with the aroma of fresh linens. Liz realized they were in the laundry room when she saw two sets of industrial sized washers and dryers, the source of the noise as well as the dampness.

A petite, thirty-something woman with short, straight red hair was sitting at a long table folding towels. There were stacks of freshly laundered linens and towels on the table. Liz glanced around the room. It was very neat, very clean and surprisingly comfortable. There was a small table and three vinyl-covered chairs to one side and a small sofa nearby. A pillow and neatly folded blanket were on the sofa. Over the table was a sign that read, "No Smoking at ANY Time. EVER. Thank you."

Beyond the washers and dryers, a large, wide counter ran along one wall under which were stored crates of cleaning products. There were two large laundry baskets on wheels. A smaller basket held stacks of neatly folded empty laundry bags, but Liz saw none filled with dirty linen yet to be washed. Nyla had been busy. Opposite the washing machines was a door that Liz assumed was a bathroom. Beyond the bathroom door stood three folding beds. "Detective Jordan to see you, Nyla," said Keith. "Let me know when you've finished. I'll be in the office. Take your time."

"Keith," the redhead said, "Thanks for this. I'll find you." She turned to Liz and said, "Kelly called to tell me she gave you my message and that you'd be coming. I'm Nyla. Nyla Garrity. Have a seat, if you'd like." Liz shook the hand Nyla extended to her.

Keith nodded toward Nyla. He looked at Liz with one hand on the door through which they had entered, and said, "Nice to have met you, Detective. Let me know if I can be of further help to you." With a slight almost bow, he turned and left the room.

Chapter 16

Liz watched as the door closed then turned to Nyla and sat down. Nyla glanced briefly at the detective's shield and ID that Liz produced but as Kelly had arranged the meeting, they were both good with dispensing with the formalities for now.

Nyla was a small, thin woman. Maybe five foot two and about a hundred pounds, she was thin but didn't look weak. Liz guessed her age as mid-to late-thirties but she'd been wrong before. Nyla had a pixie-like quality that reminded Liz of Peter Pan. Her red hair was almost boy short and it worked well on her. Her complexion was very fair with a few freckles and Liz was sure that summer sun would be rough on her. She had greenish-blue eyes, wore no make-up or jewelry, except a tiny hoop earring in each ear lobe. She wore jeans and a zippered sweatshirt with some sort of uniform polo underneath.

"How long have you worked here?" Liz asked.

Nyla answered, "Almost two years. I've known Keith for a really, really long time. Since back when we were both kids in the University district in Seattle. I didn't attend U-Dub but I had friends who did. I was an army brat. My dad landed at Fort Lewis my freshman year and I stayed in the area clear up until Skip and I moved here."

"Seems like a good guy to work for. Doesn't look like easy work though," was Liz's response.

"Keith is a friend and a good boss. Like I said, we go way back. We trust each other. I don't say that about many people from my past, especially men." Liz detected sadness in Nyla's words but had no reason to pursue it. "Anyway," Nyla continued, "I actually like the work, to be honest. There are four of us that work in housekeeping. Two don't speak a lot of English. They have kids in school so they both want to work the day shifts anyway. We all bust our butts but we got a system, you know?"

Nyla looked around the room. "Ana and Graciela are thorough and fast. A lot of days, they finish the rooms and just leave the laundry for me. They hate doing the laundry," she said with a smile. "I guess they do a lot of laundry at home or something. It works for me though. Amanda works with us a few hours a week. She has a shift in the office on Mondays so I figured we'd be able to talk alone. I value privacy 'cuz I don't have much, you know?"

Liz said that she understood and added, "I met Skip this morning at the clinic but I guess you know about that. I appreciated his help with the kid." Nyla responded with a nod of her head and a slight smile.

"Well, enough about me, Detective. You want to talk about the girl." Nyla took a deep breath and began. "We heard about a young girl dying. The folks on the street that we asked didn't know much. When I asked Kelly about it this morning, nothing rang a bell for me even though I spent several days in The Suite not too long ago. You know what that is, right? The women's room?" Liz said yes, she knew of The Suite. "Kelly reminded me that I was gone by then." Nyla stopped for a minute, looking at Liz. "I had pneumonia. I was pretty sick. The doctor at the clinic put me in the hospital for three days. I was able to get a bed in The Suite when I was discharged. It helped a lot not being on the street then, even though the weather wasn't cold yet."

Nyla continued with her story, trying to stay on track. "Anyway, sorry, there I go again. Kelly showed me the girl's picture. I knew it was her right away. No doubt. Around late summer, she was here. She had a room here for, I don't know how long, at least a few days. Keith can tell you exactly when. I thought her name was Leanne but I may have got it wrong. She was in 208 second floor, fourth door on the west side. She called and asked for towels once so I know what room."

Liz listened and took notes of everything Nyla said. Then Liz asked, "How many times do you think you saw her? And how many occasions did you have to talk with her?"

"Not many, not much. But I don't think the other housekeepers saw her at all. She didn't want housekeeping service, kept the *Do Not Disturb* on the door. Don't think she asked for anything else from us and of course she was gone when the room was cleaned after she left. It barely looked like she'd been there. She was easy on the place. Someone in the office must have talked with her though, right?" asked Nyla wanting agreement from Liz.

"You'd think so. I'll ask. What else can you tell me? Even if you think it's not important. Did she have visitors? Was she loud? Anything delivered?" Liz asked Nyla.

Nyla shook her head, "No, nothing that I know of. She was quiet. Barely went anywhere far as I know. Of course I wasn't here all the time. Here's what I remember that was odd though: there's a diner a couple of blocks down from here. Mickey's. Do you know it?"

Liz knew of the place. Not the most popular place and not the best food. Greasy spoon, really. "Yeah, it's been there forever," said Liz.

"I walk by it a lot," Nyla explained further. "It's between here and the bus stop. Sometimes Skip and I get coffee there. Anyway, I walked by one day on my way here and she was sitting at a table with another woman. I think it was the day after I took her the towels, because it struck me weird, you know. I thought at least she had a shower before her meeting. I guess on the street you think that way."

"Meeting?" asked Liz. "Why'd you think it was a meeting?"

"The other woman she was sitting with is a lawyer," said Nyla. "I know. You're thinking how would I know a lawyer, right?"

Liz looked at Nyla, feeling surprise but not shock. "Please go on, Nyla. I don't doubt you and you definitely have my attention."

"Here's why I noticed and why I remembered it." Nyla took a deep breath and waited a beat, then continued her explanation. Nyla's voice became a bit quiet like she was sharing a secret. "Skip got into some trouble after we moved here; nothing too awful. He was angry, thought he had a job, got screwed 'cuz he's not union, you know. It's a racket. Can't work without a union card but can't pay the dues without the job. Assholes. Anyway, he landed in the tank with a Drunk and Disorderly. The lawyer that got him released and credit for time served was donating time, you know how they do that. Skip thought she was okay, too. Anyway, it was her."

"And you're sure it was the same woman?" asked Liz.

"Oh yeah, it was. She looks the same. Her hair is longer, but same dark color. I recognized her right off. But what I especially remember is that car she drives. It's been my dream car since high school. A vintage Saab 900 Turbo. Slate gray, two door. Skip and I watched her get into it at the courthouse and drive away two years ago. She still has it. It was parked in front of Mickey's that day, too. Her name is Diana Harrison. Her vanity plate says "LADY DI JD".

Liz had met Diana Harrison a couple of times. She was a fierce defender and a tenacious advocate. If Liz ever needed an attorney, other than her police association rep, she'd want Harrison in her corner. Liz hoped to hell Harrison wasn't involved in Leah's death. But if she was, she was. And Liz would find that out.

"So, why did you think her name was Leanne?" asked Liz.

"She called this extension directly for the towels that day. I answered and I thought she said, 'This is Leanne in 208, can I come down for towels?' I said I'd bring them up to her and she said that'd be nice. I could easily have got the name wrong, like I said. The girl struck me as not having spent much time in a hotel. Asking to come down for towels, you know, like you would at a shelter or boardinghouse. But she knew a bit about service work. She even tipped me two bucks. Sweet of her."

Liz made notes accordingly and asked Nyla if she could talk with her again and was the hotel the best place to reach her. Nyla said to leave a message with Keith anytime, and that she usually worked afternoons. Liz had to ask, "If necessary, are you willing to repeat what you've told me either in court or in a statement for the record?" Nyla said that she would.

Liz thanked her and said if Nyla thought of anything else to please call her. Liz handed Nyla her card. She would try to get information regarding Leah's stay from Keith before she left the Grayson. Nyla stood and shook Liz's hand, thanked her for coming to the hotel to talk. That it was much easier for her and more private.

Liz was about to leave when she turned around to ask Nyla one last question. "Hey, Nyla, can I ask you a question? About Skip?"

The defensive reaction was immediate and unmistakable. Nyla looked Liz in the eye and said, "I guess. What's the question?"

"Skip must be a nickname. What your guy's real name?" Liz asked. "I'm not asking to check up on him. I have no reason to. I'm just curious, having met him. He seems a handy dude to have around."

Nyla grinned. She placed both hands on the table. Then looking up at Liz, she said, "Millard Lafayette Thibodeux. Don't ever tell him I told you because I'll deny it all day long. His folks were Louisiana French, I guess. Can you imagine growing up with a name like that? Jeez."

"Wow. That's some name, all right." Liz grinned back. "I'd go by Skip, too."

Chapter 17

Liz verified with Keith that he had been the one to handle Leah's check-in but hadn't seen her again after that brief encounter. Leah Bishop had been a guest of the Grayson for three nights, checking in on September the twenty-seventh and departing on the thirtieth. She had called the desk early the morning of the thirtieth to say that she was checking out. Amanda, the assistant desk clerk, had taken the call. There were no incidental charges to the room and no long distance calls placed from the room. The reservation had been made by credit card and the bill paid by same. The name on the account was Harrison and Gilliam, PS. At the corporate rate, the bill came to $396.00, including taxes.

Why would an attorney meet with a homeless girl and put her up in a hotel for three days at her own expense? Not just some homeless girl, but one who had given birth some six weeks earlier? A homeless girl who was then found dead approximately six weeks later?

Liz talked with Keith in his office and waited there while he made copies of the paperwork she requested. Not only was he very cooperative but he smelled really, really good. Maybe Perry Ellis or Ralph Lauren, she wasn't sure. But whatever brand of men's cologne he wore, she found it definitely appealing. While she waited, she put in a call to Harrison and Gilliam, PC. After identifying herself and explaining that she needed to meet with the lawyer regarding a current investigation, Liz was told she'd be able to talk with Diana Harrison at four fifteen p.m. The attorney was in court until then. Liz saw that it was just after three p.m. so that would work. And she'd have time to connect with Connors and might still have that burger break with Mike.

Keith returned and handed her the documents regarding Leah's stay. "I appreciated being able to speak to Nyla so quickly," Liz told him. "She was very helpful and so were you. Your help could speed the investigation along considerably. Nyla speaks highly of you, as an employer and as a friend."

Keith smiled. "That's nice to hear. Nyla has been a friend to me since we were both little more than children. She's had challenges, but then so have we all. She does a good job for us. I never have to worry." For the first time, Liz realized that Keith Akeuchi spoke English with the slightest accent, but she couldn't place it.

Liz remembered Malachi and the card he had on him. "Since I'm here, can I ask if you gave a business card with the men's shelter number to a young kid recently?"

"I see street kids once in a while," Keith answered. "It's rarely a problem for us. As long as my guests aren't bothered, I don't bother the kids. Most of them know to stay off the property. Occasionally, I direct them down the road but I've been known to give them bus fare and the number for one of the shelters."

"That's good of you to try to help the street kids, doing what you can. They can be a difficult group to help. Never know who they can trust. Have you ever had to call us with a problem?" As Liz asked the question, she realized that given Keith's size and obvious strength, few of the street kids would push him.

Keith's response was much different than Liz expected. "Detective, are you familiar with Vivekananda, the Hindu holy man and teacher?" Liz said that she was not and after a slight pause Keith continued, his large hands assuming a very natural posture, almost a prayer pose.

"Vivekananda was adamant that the social worker should never be motivated by a belief that you are actually improving the situation of another or of the world, which would be, after all, an illusion. He taught, instead, that service should be performed without attachment to the final result. In this manner, social service becomes karma yoga, the discipline of action, ultimately bringing spiritual benefit to the server, as well as to those served. These small gestures are good for my soul, but if the kids are helped, even briefly, so much the better."

For a split second, Liz wondered if Nyla's good friend and employer, Keith, was aware that she was homeless. If not, Liz was not at liberty to tell him of Nyla's situation. She remembered the small couch in the laundry room with the pillow and blanket. Instead, she shook Keith's huge hand once again and turned to leave. "Good day, Sergeant Jordan. If I may be of any further help to you, please let me know," said Keith. Liz smiled at him and nodded then walked out the door.

As she headed to her car, musing over Keith's words, Liz's cell phone buzzed and the spell was broken. It was Connors. "Detective, I'm still here at the Avalon shelter."

"Connors, I'm leaving the Grayson in a few minutes. I have information from the hotel as well as from Nyla Garrity. You know who she is, right? Her old man is Skip, the dude that helped me out this morning? Anyway, Leah was a guest here and not on her own dime. Apparently, she met with an attorney while she was here. That's who picked up the tab for the room; none other than Diana Harrison. I'm heading over to Harrison's office in about an hour." Liz stopped her narrative, took a breath, and realized it was Connors who had called her. She said, "Hey, sorry, Connors. What's up? Did you talk with Candy?"

"We've got a situation here, Sergeant." Connors was keeping control of himself but he sounded anxious. "Candy's gone. But she left her baby here. There's a note."

"Shit," said Liz. "I'm on my way. We'll talk on the road."

Liz headed back to Avalon by the reverse of the route she had taken to get to the Grayson, but she made the trip in half the time. For the few minutes she was in the car, she had Connors on speaker explaining what he knew.

Candy had returned to the shelter, as expected. Connors had been present when Mike let her in the front door, told her the shelter was locked down, and explained to her that Connors was wrapping up interviews of residents and wanted to speak with her. She asked if she could prep afternoon snack for the residents and lay baby down for a nap before she met with Connors. It wouldn't take long, she said, so Connors agreed. She took care of snack and then went to her room with her baby.

After about fifteen minutes, Connors asked Mike to see if she was ready for him. Mike asked another female resident to check on Candy. She returned a few minutes later, and told them there was a handwritten sign on Candy's door that said, "Baby sleeping; please knock softly." She had knocked, softly as requested, she explained, but Candy did not answer.

Mike thought Candy may have fallen asleep herself as she often napped along with baby in the afternoon. He and the female resident returned to Candy's door. Mike knocked, waited then called Candy's name. No answer. They opened the door to Candy's room. Candy's baby was asleep in her small crib. On the bed were the baby's clothes and diapers neatly folded and stacked, cans of ready-to-feed formula, clean bottles, pacifiers, and other assorted items for the baby's care.

There was a page of instructions regarding the well-baby exam completed at the community clinic that morning. Candy, bless her heart, even had a car seat. There was the note that Connors had mentioned earlier. But Candy was gone. Mike had no clue how she got out of the locked-down building. He was beyond pissed about that, but more worried about Candy and the baby.

Connors explained that Child Services had been alerted. They were, of course, incredibly busy and may not have a social worker there for a while because since Connors was on site, the infant's safety was not in question. Officially, the child was in the custody of Officer Connors until a worker arrived. The social worker would be there, hopefully within the hour.

"Sergeant, no one saw her come out of her room. No one saw her leave the shelter," said Connors. At this, Liz pulled up at Avalon, parked, told Connors she was there and hung up the phone. She hurried to the door and a young woman was waiting to let her in.

"Sergeant Jordan, I'm Lydia. Mike asked me to take you to him." Liz followed Lydia through the door that lead to resident rooms down a hallway. She stopped in front of an open doorway and pointed into the room. Inside the room, Mike and Connors were standing near the bed. Sitting in a rocking chair was Kelly Blevins, holding Candy's baby. The infant seemed somewhere between sleep and wakefulness, unaware that her mother had disappeared. Kelly was lightly holding a pacifier in the child's mouth as if to keep if from falling out. The baby intermittently sucked and stopped, sucked and stopped.

"I was here meeting with a couple of residents. I guess I walked in the door just as she started to stir," said Kelly softly, indicating the baby. "She knows Mike and me better than anyone, other than Candy, that is. She settled right back down. I don't have the heart to disturb her."

Mike and Connors both started talking to Liz in a loud, exaggerated whisper, so as not to wake the baby in Kelly's arms. Mike was faster and said, "Liz, she was in here. I would have bet my left testicle on that. I have no clue how she got past us. But she did." Mike placed his hands on top of his head, fingers laced, as perps are directed to do when they're under arrest. Then his arms fell to his sides, palms up, in resignation. "I can't believe any of this. I'll be in the dining room if you need me." He walked past them and left the room.

Connors began. "Sergeant, it was a total of forty-five minutes from the time she arrived back here until we discovered the baby asleep in here alone. Damn it if I can figure out how she slipped out. There's a few of Candy's things left here but not much. It looks to me like she may have been planning this. It'd be a lot to organize in forty-five minutes."

Connors handed Liz what appeared to be a sheet of paper torn from a spiral notebook. Liz took it from him. It was the note Connors had mentioned. "You've read this already?" she asked. Connors nodded yes. Liz looked again at Kelly and at the baby in her arms. She unfolded the paper and started reading:

> *Dear Kelly & Mike,*
>
> *I want to do the best thing. The adoption people they wouldn't take her cuz she's not healthy, they said. They said she was a drug baby but she's not! I never, ever used while I was pregnant. I can't keep her 'cuz I've got nothing. My family said no way they could help. Her Dad don't want anything to do with me anymore and he doesn't care what happens to her either, can't find him anyway. He's an asshole.*
>
> *I heard you can give a baby up at a firehouse or a church, no questions asked. I don't know if the shelter is like that but I hope so. I know you two will know what to do. I wanted to call her Caroline after my grandma. Please tell her new family. Maybe they will like it too. I really did try.*

The note was simply signed, *Candy.*

Chapter 18

Aside from baby things, the few items Candy had left behind were insignificant: a used, empty paper coffee cup, a bus schedule, a giveaway plastic pen. In the garbage however was one significant item: a business card from the law office of Diana Harrison, Attorney at Law. Liz bagged the business card and turned to Connors.

"So, looks like you're here until Child Services comes for the baby and who knows when they'll find a receiving home for her." Liz couldn't help but feel overwhelming concern for an already fragile infant with few adults she knew and trusted. The scenario wasn't unusual but in Liz's experience it was rare with infants so young. "Connors, Candy's note alludes to the Safe Haven law. I don't know if a judge will deem the shelter as such, but Candy knew that her baby would be in good hands with Mike and Kelly. She obviously gave it some thought, at least. Until we know otherwise, let's assume we may need to issue a warrant for abandonment. As long as you're here, keep asking if anyone else on site talked with her or saw her leave. I'm heading over to Diana Harrison's office."

Liz turned back to Kelly, still holding Candy's baby girl. "Are you able to stay here with Mike and Connors? Not because they need a woman here but she looks really content in your arms."

"I'm not going anywhere," replied Kelly adamantly.

Liz walked into the hallway and out to the lobby area of Avalon. Lydia was sitting in the lobby, still watching the door, Liz assumed. She smiled slightly when she saw Liz and Liz acknowledged her with a nod. She found Mike sitting alone at a table in the dining room with a cup of coffee. She sat down. Mike didn't glance her way, just sipped his coffee, lost in thought. Liz waited a few moments then said, "Kelly's staying with the baby until Child Services arrives. Connors has to stay here, of course," she told him. "Candy's baby is, more or less, in his custody."

Mike nodded but remained silent and didn't look at her as she spoke. "Mike," Liz asked, "I'm so sorry about this. I need to know: is there anything else you can tell me about Candy? Did you see this coming? Where might she go? Any friends or family she might reach out to?"

Mike shook his head. "I don't know, Liz. I know very little about Candy other than her last name, which is Schinde. I told you she'd been here before. She's had a hard time of things. Better than some but worse than most. I know she wasn't the most stable girl who has sought shelter here but she was never a problem as a resident. I can give you the copy of her ID, if you need it." Mike thought for a beat then continued. "I sometimes tell myself that this scenario would produce the best outcome for some of these young children. Right now, though, it's just sad. I'll get over it and stumble ahead, like always." Mike looked like he'd been trying to collect himself. "I need to check with Kelly. She may need a break herself. The baby knows me pretty well, too."

Liz had already shared with Mike that she had made a connection between Leah and Candy. She took the gut shot and decided to share more. "Mike, there's a clear connection between both young women and an attorney here in town. I'm headed over there now."

Mike looked intrigued but as he stood to go back to

Candy's room and relieve Kelly, Lydia entered the dining room accompanied by a tall, attractive young man with dark curly hair.

"Hey, are you Mike?" the man asked. When Mike answered that he was, the man extended his hand and said, "I'm Peter Denuccio. Kelly Blevins is my fiancée. Kyle Connors left me a message that he's here. Is that right? Kyle said Kelly wanted me to meet her here. She's all right, he said, but there's some kind of emergency. What's going on?"

They turned around as Kelly, still holding Candy's baby, and Connors came into the dining room. The baby was awake. "Pete, you're here!" said Kelly. "Let me explain." She indicated the infant, and said, "This is my little friend. I guess I should tell you I was working with her mom. I'll tell you what I can in a minute but right now, she wants a bottle." Kelly handed the baby over to Mike and gave Pete a quick kiss. Connors and Peter obviously seemed to know each other but Kelly quickly introduced Peter to both Liz and Mike.

"I told you I'd meet you at home but I needed to stay here later than expected," she explained to Peter. "I asked Kyle to get in touch with you. Sorry to worry you, Pete."

Peter was instantly enthralled. "Oh my Gosh, Kel, she's so tiny! Would it be okay for me to hold her? Do you think she'll let me?" Liz hadn't thought in terms of whether babies determined who did and who did not hold them. She watched in amazement as Mike held the tiny infant while both Connors and Peter hovered, amazed by the tiny person. Connors looked up, suddenly aware that a superior officer was watching, and blushed very red.

Kelly had moved over to the kitchen area, had filled a small bottle with infant formula and was warming it under the hot water faucet. Glancing back over, she said, "I'm sure she will, Pete. Just give her a few minutes with Mike first. Maybe you can give her the bottle I'm warming."

Liz looked around at each of them, obviously with the

situation well in hand, and said, "I've got to run. Nice meeting you, Peter. Mike, I'll be back as soon as possible. I'd still like to grab some food later but it may be quite a bit later. I'm guessing you'll be here."

Mike, holding the baby, looked up at Liz and said, "Yes, I'll be here. Food will be good for all of us."

Before Liz headed out she looked at Connors and said, "Try to pull yourself away from the baby and ask around about Candy."

Chapter 19

Liz arrived for her four-fifteen appointment at the law offices of Harrison and Gilliam with about two minutes to spare. She'd even had time to grab a double skinny latte and an energy bar at Dutch Bros., her usual mid-day meal of choice when working. The coffee and the snack, especially the coffee, made her feel almost human. She explained to the receptionist who she was and why she was there. Luckily, it was the receptionist Liz had spoken with when she called earlier from the Grayson Hotel. Not only was Liz expected but she was pleased to be told that Diana Harrison would be with her very shortly.

Within a couple of minutes, a dark-haired woman of about Liz's age came into the reception area. She held her hand out to Liz and said, "Detective Jordan, I'm Diana Harrison. Please follow me back to my office. We'll talk there."

Diana Harrison was attractive, with dark hair pulled into a rather loose but neat chignon. Her face held the slightest traces of makeup. She was wearing a simple suit on her slender, fit frame consisting of a fitted pencil skirt and single button jacket without lapels or collar, made of dark wool with an almost undetectable plaid. The attorney wore an off-white collarless blouse under the suit jacket; her black shoes were low-heeled pumps. The only jewelry Liz saw was one strand of small pearls at her neck and a smartwatch on her wrist. Harrison walked briskly and as Liz followed her to the end of a short corridor, she realized that she was not, as was usual, the faster walker.

They entered an office and Harrison directed Liz to a visitors chair, then closed the door and took her seat behind the desk. She was obviously a busy officer of the court. Files and papers were stacked neatly on the credenza on the other side of the desk from Liz. The office was typical of attorneys whom Liz had had occasion to speak with: nice office furniture, PC, window with a street view, reasonably comfortable for a face-to-face. The requisite diplomas indicating the lawyer's degrees were hung on the wall. Liz noticed an undergrad degree from UCLA, law degree and Juris Doctor from Stanford. Impressive. There was a closed file on the top of the attorney's desk and a blank legal pad and pen ready for notes.

As Diana Harrison took her seat, she started their meeting by asking Liz if she cared for anything to drink. Having just gulped down a double latte, Liz thanked her, but declined. "Lynda indicated you wanted to see me about an open investigation, but that's all she could share. What can I help you with, and I believe its Detective *Sergeant*, am I correct?"

"Yes, it is, thank you," Liz answered, "and we've actually met before, professionally. In court a couple of times, nothing too memorable. And I was in the audience when you spoke to the Officers' Association a few months ago on the rights of victims of violent assault. Good information for officers."

Harrison accepted the assessment with a slight smile and a nod and Liz continued. "Yesterday evening, the body of a young woman was found in an alley in the Beaumont district, near the Avalon Street shelter. We've determined she may have a connection to you. Do you drive a Saab, dark grey with vanity plates?"

The attorney studied Liz, and replied. "Yes, I do. Why? What's this about?"

"Ms. Harrison, we've tentatively identified the young woman as a Leah Bishop. You were seen with Ms. Bishop in a cafe near the Grayson Hotel in late September. You and your car were identified by our witness." Liz paused as Harrison took in breath, obviously shocked. "Registration records from the Grayson show that you booked and paid for a room occupied by Leah Bishop during that same period of time. I think you'd better tell me all you can."

The attorney took a moment to process, but she collected herself quickly, not missing a beat. "I heard news reports that a woman was found dead last night but hadn't heard that an ID had been made. I've been in court since early this morning," the attorney said with a sigh. She reached for her phone and when Lynda, the receptionist answered, Harrison said, "Please reschedule my five fifteen call, Lynda. Apologize for me. And don't wait for me to finish up. Lock the office when you leave. We'll be awhile." She hung up the phone.

"Are you sure it's Leah?" she asked. Liz explained that the woman had been identified by her photo ID and that she had recently been a resident at the Avalon shelter, which was how police had obtained the picture. Liz pulled out the ID photo and the attorney looked at it, nodded yes, that it was the young woman she knew as Leah Bishop.

"Positive ID and family notification are pending," Liz told her. "I'm hoping you can help with an ID, Ms. Harrison. That means a visit to the morgue. You aren't a relative, but if you knew her in a professional capacity, as counsel, it would be allowed. Do you know Leah's date of birth? I'm still trying to confirm her age."

"Yes," the attorney said as she turned to her computer and found the file she wanted. "Leah turned eighteen in June," she said and then asked Liz, "I wasn't aware she was in town. I thought she had returned to her mother's home when she left the Grayson. Do you know what happened? Do you know when she died?"

"We're investigating the death as a homicide. The medical examiner ruled COD as cardiac arrest from blood loss due to blunt force trauma to the head. She died early yesterday afternoon." Liz gave the woman a few moments to absorb then added, "I need to know whatever you can tell me about Leah. But I'm afraid I also need to ask if you're acquainted with a Candy Schinde?"

"Yes, I know Candy. Is she all right? Is her child all right?" Harrison's voice sounded alarmed as she asked about the other young woman.

"I have no reason to think she has been harmed," Liz told her, "but I don't have information as to her whereabouts at this time. Your business card was found in the room she had occupied at Avalon." Liz waited a moment before she continued. "Ms. Harrison, Candy disappeared this afternoon and left her infant daughter at the shelter. The child appears to be fine. I have an officer on site and Child Services has been called. She left a note indicating that she hoped the shelter fell under the Safe Haven law. She mentioned the shelter manager and a county homeless advocate as people she trusted." Liz's point was that Candy had been acquainted with the attorney but didn't consider her an ally or resource. Liz hoped to learn why.

The attorney looked surprised, sad, but not stunned. She leaned back in her desk chair and took a deep breath. "This is all a lot to take in… please, call me Diana," she said. Harrison looked at Liz, shaking her head, she added, "Poor, poor Leah. And poor Candy, as well."

Then the attorney asked Liz, "Are you aware that Leah gave birth in August, to a baby boy?"

"Leah's autopsy indicated that she had delivered a child approximately three months ago, but the post mortem was unable to determine whether the child was alive at birth," answered

Liz. "The information I received was that she had been taking vitamins and was lactating within three weeks of her death. Those facts indicated that she had delivered a live child and provided nourishment for it, as well as having had resources to consider her own health and the child's."

"Lactating?" Diana Harrison stared at Liz for a second or two, assessing the situation and deciding where to go from here. A quick thinker, she needed only a few moments to choose her course and begin her story.

"Leah Bishop was officially a client of mine. And it wasn't pro bono. I was retained by cash payment of five dollars. A copy of a receipt with her signature is included in her file," she began. "Detective, I should give you a ration of bullshit about ethics and confidentiality, subjects I believe in strongly. But if Leah Bishop is dead, I feel compelled to assist you. And I won't be a shit and ask if we can speak off the record." Liz wasn't easily impressed, and although she already held the counselor in high esteem, she'd just scored a few more points.

"Initially, I was contacted by Leah's mother, who lives in Richland, one of our Tri Cities. This was late August," Harrison checked the computer again. "August twenty-eighth. Leah's mother, her name is Connie Bishop, inquired about legal assistance for her daughter who had been in and out of her home for the last couple of years. A single mother since Leah was very young, Ms. Bishop had worked in maintenance and janitorial at the Hanford Site, but when the plant moved from power production to closure and clean up, the full time positions were cut. Ms. Bishop explained that she didn't have much in the way of funds to pay for legal services but that her daughter needed help, nonetheless."

"I sometimes work with homeless shelters in the southern part of the state, mostly along the Columbia River and up the Gorge; predominately women's shelters for victims of domestic violence. Services for the homeless, especially legal, can be difficult for them to find. Pro bono assistance to people in need reminds me of why I went to law school in the first place. It keeps my ire up." Liz thought back to what Keith Akeuchi had shared earlier, of how social work must personally impact the provider to be authentic. Liz felt out of touch hearing the same idea from two diverse sources in one day. *Maybe I should read more*, she thought.

"Anyway, Leah's mother was given my name at a shelter in Richland. As I said, Leah had been in and out of her mother's home. Attended school when she was home, excelling in studies and making up for what she'd missed. Sharp girl. Not many friends, didn't like authority, you know of kids like that, I'm sure, Detective."

"Leah's pattern was to take off for a couple of months. Then she'd ask to come home, a complete mess; sick, dirty, all of it. Things would be good for a while, a few months. Leah would rest, get healthy, and give her mom some hope. Then she'd take off again."

"Do you have any clue as to why Leah ran in the first place?" Liz asked.

"Not that she shared with me. I think her reasons were a mystery to her mother, as well," shared Harrison. "Anyway, after having been gone for several months, Leah went home to her mother's in February. She was pregnant. She figured about three months. She would never say who had fathered the child and refused to discuss him. She didn't want to terminate the pregnancy but didn't think she could raise the baby either. Connie Bishop assured her that she would help her, that they could raise the child together. Leah decided to place the child for adoption and once that decision was made, she didn't waiver."

The attorney continued. "There are only a few paths by which children become available for adoption. In Leah's case, she decided to make private arrangements, which was her right as the birth mother. Her official paperwork claimed that the child's father was unknown, although whether that's true, we may never know. Anyway, Leah contacted a resource that handles private adoptions. She got the name off a bulletin board on the wall in the same shelter where her mother got my name. At least, that's what she claimed."

"Leah asked lots of questions, especially about how adoptive parents are screened. She was impressed initially. She liked that the adoption service used an LCSW -- licensed clinical social worker -- to advise them as to the fitness of the applicants to be parents. But shortly before Leah delivered in August, she learned that the service was paying the LCSW but not following the recommendations. Basically, Leah learned that people, sometimes very wealthy people, were adopting children after being refused for consideration by mainstream or public adoption services."

"Do you know how Leah learned that information?" asked Liz.

"No, I can only guess. And the more questions Leah asked, the more she learned that she had made a terrible mistake. Before she could reverse her decision and find another agency to handle the adoption, she went into labor and delivered the child."

"That's bad timing. If that's what happened, I feel for her," said Liz. "Can you tell me when her baby was born?"

"Yes, that's in my records. Let's see," Diana consulted her computer. "Here it is. She delivered at a birthing center in Pasco on the tenth of August."

A thought occurred to Liz as she looked back through her notes regarding the case. "Do you have the time of day Leah delivered her child, by any chance?"

"I do," said Diana. "Two twenty-three p.m." Liz found the notation she was looking for regarding the slip of paper that was found in Leah's things. The numbers surrounded by a heart were 10/08 @ 1423. If the notation meant the tenth of August, as dates are often written with the day first followed by the month, it was her child's date and time of birth.

"Detective, have you heard of an attorney by the name of Carl Ridgeman?" Liz thought that she may have heard the name but couldn't place it. She answered Diana's question and confirmed the spelling for her notes. Diana continued, "You may be more familiar with other names under which he does business; maybe CER Legal Services or Sinai Ministries?"

That rang a bell. "Not CER, but I believe that Sinai Ministries is one of the sponsoring agencies keeping Avalon's doors open. It's listed on the sign in front of the shelter. I remember thinking I wasn't familiar with the name. Please go on," said Liz.

"Sinai Ministries is an evangelical organization with a hand in many of the benevolent programs here and in other counties in Washington. Carl Ridgeman provides legal counsel for Sinai and he serves on the governing board. In fact, just this past Saturday evening, I was present at an annual event honoring many in our community doing such work. Mr. Ridgeman received recognition for his "charitable contributions of legal expertise." As Diana talked about Sinai and Ridgeman, her face held an expression of unabashed disgust. Then she took a breath and her tone softened slightly. "Carl Ridgeman practices law in partnership with his daughter, Helene. Ridgeman's son is on staff at CER."

"Are you less than fond of the organization, Sinai Ministries, or just of Mr. Ridgeman?" Liz asked the attorney.

"I have no problem with Sinai, per se. Like most benevolent groups, they have the best of intentions. I'm aware of significant efforts they're involved in locally. I understand how important it is for non-profits to make use of donated services, especially those that would incur big expenses." Diana paused, appeared to be measuring her words, and deciding just how she wanted to continue.

"Carl Ridgeman and I are both members of the Washington State Bar Association. We both base our practices here in Columbia City. We both offer pro bono legal support as we each deem appropriate. I hope to heaven, Detective, that that's where the similarity ends. Carl Ridgeman has been under investigation for one reason or another for years. He has racked up many, many complaints with the ethics division of the Bar. Ridgeman is vindicated and his name and businesses come out clean every time."

"Okay, I hear you saying that the guy's a shyster and I don't doubt you," said Liz. "But how does this connect with Leah Bishop or her death?"

"Because the private adoption of Leah's infant was handled by CER Legal Services. CER stands for Carl Edward Ridgeman, Detective. He has handled many, many adoptions over the years, and I am sure that many of them were managed appropriately and ethically. But Ridgeman crosses lines and does so often enough to have raised suspicion many times."

"You see, it's legal to relinquish your parental rights and place a child up for adoption. It's even legal to enlist the help of professionals and for professionals to provide that help to make it happen. It's legal for potential adoptive parents to provide for the birth mother insofar as basic needs, health care, even reasonable monetary support, et cetera, for the term of the pregnancy. It is, however, illegal to provide to the extent that may be perceived as compensation because this can, and has been perceived, as payment for the purchase of the child. That, as you know, would be human trafficking, which is a crime."

Diana continued. "Our state's Attorney General and many in the legal community, including myself, are certain that Ridgeman essentially buys babies from young, desperate pregnant women. He sells them to the highest bidder, but no one has been able to prove it yet. There's no money trail. I'm convinced that's how they'll catch him. But so far, they've been unsuccessful."

Chapter 20

Liz absorbed the information she was hearing from the attorney. She certainly seemed to be on the correct course for finding the person or persons responsible for a young woman's death. Careful to reserve judgment, she asked Diana to go on.

"After speaking with Connie, Leah's mother, I arranged to meet with Leah while I was in Tri Cities on other business." The attorney consulted her file and added, "This was on September tenth. She told me a lot of what I've conveyed to you. I didn't share with her the extent of my suspicions regarding Ridgeman or the complaints against him, but I didn't have to. Leah was a savvy young woman with good intuition. And she was a good judge of character."

Diana paused briefly in thought then smiled and shared with Liz, "I even told her once that she should consider law enforcement as a career, Detective. She might have impressed you. Anyway, I was unable to return to Pasco so I brought Leah here for a few days. We were preparing to sue CER for fraudulent practice. Because Leah had reached her majority, she was able to seek the judgment on her own behalf, and on behalf of her child. Leah completed her deposition while she was here. I filed the papers with the court a month ago. The last time I talked to her she had returned to Richland. At least I assumed she had."

"Leah received information that supported her suspicions

from someone and she refused to have her source named in the lawsuit; for their protection, she said." Diana Harrison had an expression on her face that Liz assumed was usually saved for opposing counsel or hostile witnesses. "We discussed that it would support her case if we could obtain the information directly. I even offered to depose with anonymity. Leah wouldn't involve them directly. My best guess is that it was either the social worker who was making the assessments or someone else employed by CER.

Liz made notes of all the information from Diana Harrison. She nodded and switched the conversation to Candy. "So...Diana, we found one of your business cards in Candy's room. What can you tell me about her?"

"Candy came to see me. Leah asked her to. Candy and Leah met up somewhere in the eastern part of the state. Both were homeless and pregnant and trying to figure things out alone. Candy was having CER handle a private adoption for her child, as well. Unfortunately, here is where Ridgeman's true colors really show. Candy's beautiful baby girl was not healthy enough to pass muster for the family that had planned on adopting her. They refused to take her and Ridgeman let them out of the agreement."

"Candy claims she was sick throughout her pregnancy, really sick, but that she never used drugs or drank. She delivered a low birth weight baby at thirty seven weeks, or about three weeks early. Candy was adamant that her baby was fine developmentally and just needed to catch up. At least she's been assured of as much by the doctors that examined her. Candy was distraught but she wasn't ready to give up on the idea that her baby would be found "acceptable." She was still hoping to work with CER so she was hesitant to go on record to help Leah. And she didn't trust me."

If Harrison was being straight and Liz suspected she was, that explained why Candy threw away her card. The poor girl didn't realize that Diana Harrison might have been the best ally she could have hoped for.

Liz thought for a few seconds about the information she'd received from Diana Harrison. She knew the facts the attorney had been able to provide were significant and pointed the investigation in a clear direction -- toward Carl Ridgeman. But Liz knew better than to expect things to fall into place easily. Even if Ridgeman was guilty of fraudulent practice, or had harmed or was behind the harm inflicted on Leah Bishop, it was a painstaking process to build a case -- a case that would lead to an arrest. And if she and Connors completed their part of the process, the trial would be a whole different ball game. Liz had seen cases fall apart. She knew better than to make assumptions. That's how cops miss details. And we all know, she told herself, the devil is in the details.

Liz asked if Diana had seen Leah since they met during her deposition visit. She had not. Had she talked with Leah? Yes, she had notified Leah that the papers to sue had been filed. Harrison checked her records and added, "Papers were received by the court on October 14. I notified Leah the same day."

Liz ended their meeting by asking if the counselor would be available over the next few days if other questions came up. Then Liz told the attorney, "I appreciate your time and all the information you've been able to provide. May I ask if it's possible for you to identify the body this evening? Then we'll ask local authorities in Richland to notify Leah's mother."

"Yes, of course, Detective. Is it best for you to accompany me?" asked the attorney.

Liz answered, "I certainly can. Let me contact the M.E.'s office and let them know we're coming and why."

"Detective, if this is a way I can help, I can handle the sad task of the ID alone. I'm sure you have many other things to do regarding the investigation into her death. I'd feel better knowing that you were spending your time moving the case forward and not babysitting me. If I identify Leah, and neither of us have doubts that it's Leah lying in the morgue, maybe I can be of help to her mother through this."

Diana took a breath, sighed, and continued. "I've met Connie Bishop. I've talked with her. She's a strong woman and she's been through a lot in her life. And she'll go through a lot more now that her daughter is gone." Liz was taken aback by Diana's mix of compassion and pragmatism. The attorney was willing to do whatever she could to help the investigation because by doing so, she was still able to help Leah. Liz knew exactly how she felt.

Liz nodded as she listened to Diana's words and explained the process. "We will contact the Franklin County Sheriff. A representative from their department will notify Leah's mother in person after the official ID. They will ask to contact a friend or family member to be with her. The sheriff's department will explain that we are investigating and will want to talk with her as soon as she feels able." Liz continued, "And actually, I've been hoping to meet with the officer working the case with me, as well as others who are assisting us. We need to debrief. So, if you're sure, I'll let the M.E. know to expect you and that you're there for Leah."

Liz glanced at her watch. It was after five thirty p.m. "If you could contact me after the ID, we can decide how to meet up to contact Connie Bishop. But it'll need to be soon."

"I'll be in touch this evening, Detective Jordan," responded the attorney.

"Please, feel free to call me Liz," she said, as she handed the attorney her card.

Chapter 21

Liz reached Dr. Stein by phone at the morgue from the road and informed him that Leah Bishop's attorney, Diana Harrison, would be coming down for positive ID of the body.

"Harrison ID'd her from the photo but she agreed to make the official ID," Liz explained. "She was representing Leah and is acquainted with her mother. Harrison has asked to assist Leah's mother after the ID. The mother is in Richland, Tri Cities area. Also, Harrison had a DOB for Leah. She was eighteen in June. Apparently, she delivered a baby boy on August tenth. The infant was placed for adoption. That's how Harrison knew her. Leah was contesting the adoption on grounds of fraud."

"Well, you've been busy. I can't say I've ever had a kid off the street that had their own attorney. I met Diana Harrison once so I think I'll recognize her when I see her and I'll alert the front desk to expect her. Good to know more about our girl. I feel for the mother, of course, and let's pray her baby is safe," said Stein. "Did you read the report from my post? I entered it hours ago. Wasn't sure you'd had a chance."

"Uh, no, I haven't read the full report yet," Liz told him. "I called earlier and got the basics over the phone. I talked with Myers."

"You talked with Myers, huh?" asked Stein. Liz could tell Stein had a grin on his face as he spoke. He was enjoying this.

"Yes, actually I did. He was very helpful. Who would have thought that Myers knew all those facts about births, breastfeeding, and nurturing," answered Liz.

"Myers is quite a resource on women's health concerns, particularly pregnancy, birth and postpartum care. Maybe you can ask him sometime about the two years he spent in Eastern Europe. He worked with birth centers and orphanages. He tells fascinating stories about it."

"Well, I'll keep that in mind. Maybe someday I'll ask. I'm headed over to Avalon to connect with Connors. I hope he's still there. We need to talk about this case. It's been a long day."

After Liz ended her call with Stein, she called Connors at Avalon. "Connors, I'm on my way back to Avalon. What's going on with the baby? Are you an honorary godfather or something by now? I've been gone for like two hours. That looked like long enough."

"No, I'm not, but she's a cute little thing, Sergeant. Actually, the baby just left with her emergency foster parents." Connors explained, "Child Services really came through. I can fill you in later."

"Good, and great timing. We need an hour or so to go over our info on the case. And I need to arrange for Leah Bishop's mother to be notified of her death. That can't wait much longer but I am waiting for the ID and the go-ahead from Stein as M.E." Liz asked if Mike was still around. She explained that they had hoped to sit down over dinner.

"Yes, he's here. Food's not a problem, Sergeant. Mike and I decided it was Pizza Night at Avalon. We went in together and bought twenty pizzas from Our Best Pies on Main. They deliver and they sell them to Mike at a big discount. Mike took half of the cost out of his budget. He said he could justify that. We each split the rest of the cost between us. We're feeding the whole place tonight. There's plenty for you. Good pizza." Liz thought it likely that Connors was eating pizza as they spoke.

"Pizza sounds great. I'm starving and I'll chip in. Maybe we can meet in the small room we used for interviews. Saves us time not having to go into the precinct," added Liz. "I'm not far out, so I'll see you shortly. Is the shelter still locked down?" she asked.

"Yep, until the girl with the ex from earlier and her kids are out of here in the morning, Mike insists on it. He still can't figure out how Candy got out the door either. He says talents emerge at odd times."

Connors met Liz at the door when she arrived at Avalon. As they walked back to the dining room, Liz noticed a difference in the room. Not that she was the best judge of the attitude at the shelter and the place had experienced a terrible tragedy with Leah's death, but there was a noticeable difference. It felt as though everyone had pulled together. It was dinnertime. Parents and their children were sitting together as families, and families were grouped together with other families, enjoying their pizza, talking, feeding children, sharing.

For human beings, sharing a meal with others can be a comfort, a fortifier to the soul as well as to the body, thought Liz. She wondered as well, if the residents felt safer knowing that the shelter was locked down. And, there was the fact that a personable police officer had been on site, in plainclothes, most of the day, with their safety and wellbeing and that of their children as his first priority.

Mike was sitting at a table in the dining room eating with the roughly sixty residents who were able to make it to dinner. Connors sat down a couple of places from Mike and dove back into the slices of pizza on the plate at that spot. Mike saw Liz and motioned her over.

"Liz, grab a plate when you're ready and have some pizza," he said. "There's water on the table, too. You're welcome to eat here in the dining room with everyone. I'm guessing you've had no break today so maybe you should take a few minutes and eat like a regular person." Liz knew that her friend was speaking from concern so she ignored the sarcasm.

Mike motioned to Connors and continued, "You and Connors are free to move to the small meeting room, if you'd like. I reserved it for you. I know you two want to talk. We have some details to share with you, as well." The pizza did, indeed, smell great. Liz decided to keep her jacket on, remembering the shield and side arm she wore under it. Connors was dressed casually but with a loose pullover, for the same reason she supposed.

Liz grabbed a plate, helped herself to two slices, and sat next to Connors. "Anyway, I was waiting for you," said Mike. "I have an announcement to make." Mike stood up and took his place behind the chair he'd been sitting in, placing his hands on the back of the chair as he began to speak to the room. "If I could have everyone's attention, for just a minute," he asked. Mike waited a few seconds as the parents directed their attention to him, trying to quiet their little ones. "I hope you are all enjoying the pizza. I know I am." A few chuckles were heard and a few heads nodded in assent.

"This has been a sad few days. It's been a frightening few days. For those of you with children, and that's most of you, it's been even more stressful than what you were already dealing with. I want you to know that it's been sad and scary for me and the other staff, too. So, I want to tell you that I appreciate that you've trusted us to keep you safe under the circumstances. That means a lot to us."

"A couple of families made the decision to leave Avalon and I can't fault them for doing what they think is best for them. But you know me and you know that I believe that your families are safer here at Avalon than on the street. That's why I'm here."

Mike paused for a moment, then continued, "But more than

all that, I want to acknowledge Officer Kyle Connors who has been here with us most of the day." At the mention of Connors, Mike gestured in the young officer's direction and the residents started to applaud. There were a few cries of "hear, hear," and even a whistle or two.

As they quieted, Mike went on talking. "I want to thank him for being respectful of all of us and in particular, for helping your kids understand that police officers are friends, which is a good reminder for us all, right?" There were nods and more clapping. "Having Connors here and the attitude he's chosen to have has really, really helped to make some bad situations better and safer for all of us here today. And…I want to be sure you realize that Connors chipped in for a big part of our pizza tonight. So let's hear it again for Connors."

There was a final round of applause, complete with high fives and fist bumps. As Liz sat enjoying her pizza, she applauded the officer along with the residents. Connors' face held an expression of humility mixed with embarrassment as he simply raised his hand in acknowledgement of the attention. Liz was very proud to be his superior officer. And to be honest, she was pleased that she had obviously tagged the right officer to assist her investigation.

As the pizza disappeared, a few residents began to clean up, wiping faces, folding chairs, and placing garbage in big plastic bags. The woman Liz knew to be Maria used a spray bottle and a kitchen towel and began cleaning at one end of a long table. Her son, little Javier, was nearby, engaged in chatter with another young child, whose mother was cleaning high chairs.

Connors and Liz moved to the small meeting room. As they sat and arranged their notes for review, Liz told him, "That was very cool out there, Connors. This is a tough house for a cop to play and you earned an ovation, man. Well done."

"Thank you, Sergeant," he replied. "I'm kind of used to talking with folks on the street, but the families living here in the shelter are different. These people are the Working Poor. They're all busy people as far as I can tell. They're trying to scrape together enough to get out of here and into a place of their own. At the same time, they've got kids to get to school, doctor's appointments, whatever."

Connors paused for a second then continued. "I keep my guard up, don't get me wrong. I've been as much a cop here today as I ever am, Sergeant. There's no doubt some sneaky shit going on around here, but they kept it away from me. Anyway, I believe a little respect goes a long way. It sure did today."

Liz nodded. "Okay, Connors, as you're the man of the hour around here, you go first. Then I'll tell you what I've learned. I want to know what you've learned about Leah and fill me in about Candy's baby. Are we sure no one saw anything? And when did Kelly get out of here? I assume she was here until they found a receiving home for the baby."

"Uh, yeah, she sure was," Connors began. "When the social worker from Child Services got here, a guy named Carlton Jackson, he was in a fit. He'd been looking for a temporary foster arrangement for the baby since the call went in and wasn't finding anything. Then Kelly went into a full scale argument about how this was a high-risk infant with medical needs that could not be placed in temporary home after temporary home; how she was at risk for failure to thrive, was low birth weight, all of it.

"She argued that the child had been seen by a doctor today, who recommended routine and continuity of care and she had the paperwork from the clinic to back her up. She was awesome, Sergeant. So was Pete. You met Kelly's guy, Peter. He's a buddy of mine, so when Kelly asked me to contact him, it wasn't difficult. I mean, I have his cell number in my phone. We play basketball together."

"Oh that's right. Kelly mentioned that to me," Liz answered. "She also said she knows you as Kyle."

"Well, not when I'm on duty...but anyway, poor Carlton was beside himself. He asked what Kelly would do if she was him. Then she blew us all away. She said, 'Have Pete and me cleared as emergency foster parents.' We just stared at her. Carlton balked at first, said that wouldn't fly with his department. But Kelly was relentless. She said she and Pete both had current background checks, FBI-cleared, hers with the state and his with the school district -- he teaches second grade. She just knew what to say to any response he had. She insisted that the child was familiar with her and waved Candy's note under his nose."

"Are you kidding me?" Liz was staring at Connors in disbelief and surprised that Kelly and Peter would feel comfortable with such an arrangement.

Connors continued. "Kelly and Pete both feel strongly about advocating for kids that need a champion. They both admitted that the request was unusual, but based it on the child's 'critical period of development' as Kelly called it. Placing her with strangers would be detrimental, if not outright cruel. She argued a strong case with Carlton that convinced him to put in paperwork to place the infant with them temporarily. He went straight to a family court judge with the request."

"The judge apparently feels that the shelter may fall under Safe Haven, and even took Candy's note into account as evidence that she knew she was leaving the infant with people she deemed, and the state has deemed, as responsible. Sergeant, they approved it. The baby went home with Kelly and Pete. Carlton went with them to do a required safety assessment of their home. It's a done deal. They thought it best to list Peter as the primary temporary guardian because he had no professional link to Candy; had never even met her."

"Pete has a couple of weeks off work soon for the holiday break. Kelly's going to work afternoons and evenings until next week." Connors grinned, chuckled and added, "Pete's mother, nicest lady you could meet, is heading up to help as soon as her background check is complete. They thought of everything. That's one lucky baby girl."

As Connors made that statement, he hesitated, deep in thought for a moment, and said, "And Sargent, I've checked in with patrol. No sign of Candy since she took off."

Chapter 22

It had taken Kelly about two minutes with Candy's baby in her arms to start figuring out how she could keep her out of a receiving home. It wasn't that Kelly was concerned about the quality of the possible placement -- she had confidence in the screening process -- it was the fact that a nine-week-old, vulnerable infant needed to be with someone she knew and trusted and be given time to get used to a new caregiver. Kelly was familiar with Failure-to-Thrive. She had seen it as an intern in college. As she read through the notes of the doctor who had examined the infant that morning at the clinic, she knew she had to try to intervene.

The baby was eating well and was gaining weight, was responsive to stimuli, and had passed sensory screenings as WNR, or within normal range. Candy had agreed to the first round of immunizations. But Kelly knew that staving off FTT was only one hurdle to jump. It was her belief that the baby's social/emotional development was as important as the physical, that they actually enhanced one another.

So, she'd had Connors contact Pete to please meet her at Avalon. Pete. What an amazing man. She had known he would agree with her, that advocating for and caring for this baby was something they could take on. When they discussed it, sitting alone in the dining room at Avalon, it was Pete who ran with the plan. He brought up the fact that he had time off work coming up, and could assume full time care. He said he could ask his mother to come help until then, knowing she'd never be able to stay away. Kelly thought of Alice Denuccio and smiled. She was the perfect grandmother. She had raised five children to be kind, productive, and responsible adults, one of which was her very own Pete. Her children and her eleven grandchildren loved her dearly.

Pete had asked her, "So Kel, how do you want to make this happen?"

Kelly stood up and with the tiny girl in her arms walked around the table to where Pete was sitting. She gave him a big kiss and said, "Thank you so much. I love you," and placed the baby in Pete's arms. Then Kelly Blevins went into the lobby to find Mike and Connors, ready take on Child Services, the State, a judge, and anyone else who got in her way.

After the judge cleared them as temporary foster parents, Kelly and Pete packed up all the baby's things, borrowed from Mike the crib she'd been sleeping in, and headed home with the baby to their little apartment. Carlton, a big teddy bear of a guy, followed them home. The judge had, as expected, ordered a preliminary assessment of the home for safety. Because the infant was not yet mobile there was less to check, but the basics were still required.

Kelly and Peter settled in for a quiet evening with their tiny charge and shared the pizza that Mike had insisted they take home. Carlton was thrilled.

Back at Avalon, Connors and Liz finally had the chance to share what they'd had learned. No one had heard from Candy, nor had she been seen. Mike had mixed feelings about whether the shelter would fall under Save Haven. He wasn't exactly opposed to it, but until it was more clearly included in the law, he wanted to be cautious. The shelter system would have the same responsibility as a hospital or fire house and would be required to immediately notify law enforcement and Child Services if a child was left with them. They would simply provide a safe place -- a safe haven -- for infants needing protection.

Liz wasn't surprised that Connors had come up with nothing from Nurse Fran and the other medical sources, and he wasn't able to uncover any information about BBQ Betty's, the restaurant whose takeout menu Leah had used as a bookmark.

Connors had not yet explored adoption resources, but he reported to Liz how he had contacted shelters and other agencies serving the homeless in the Tri Cities area. Shelter staff wanted to help, but it was difficult to make connections between the girl known in Columbia City as Leah and anyone they might have served in their part of the state.

Connors wondered if enlisting help from Mike or Kelly might be beneficial to the investigation. When he mentioned the idea to his Sergeant, however, she said it may not be necessary. Liz explained what she had learned from Nyla, leading them to Diana Harrison, and the attorney's cooperation.

Liz continued to share what she'd learned regarding the birth and private adoption of Leah's infant boy. She shared the meaning of the numbers surrounded by a heart on the slip of paper in Leah's things as signifying the baby's birth. Connors shared Liz's enthusiasm for the fact that Leah had retained Harrison and that she had suspected fraud by the adoption service and Carl Ridgeman himself. Liz added that Harrison was providing an official ID for the M.E., and had requested to assist with supporting Leah's mother following notification of her daughter's death. They discussed Harrison's allegations about Carl Ridgeman and the history of suspicion.

"Diana Harrison thinks that Ridgeman has been proficient enough at covering his money trail to avoid discovery," Liz explained. "You and I will speak with Mr. Ridgeman tomorrow morning but first we'll talk with a forensic accountant about our information and enlist their help. If we need to pursue warrants, we'll be ready for that, too."

Mike was in his office trying to get through some of his endless paperwork. He knew that Ada, a shelter assistant, was out front and usually answered the phone. So when the phone rang and kept ringing, he thought it odd, but tried to ignore it and concentrate on his work. When the phone started ringing for the third time and kept ringing, Mike put the work aside and picked up the phone.

"Avalon, this is Mike," he said into the receiver.

There was no response for a second or two. Then Mike heard a small voice say his name, like a question. "Mike?" It was Candy. Mike was suddenly overcome with sadness.

"Yes, it's Mike, Candy. It's good to hear your voice. Are you okay?" Mike thought to glance at the caller ID. The five zero three area code placed Candy in Oregon or meant she was using a cell phone with an Oregon number. Mike thought the connection sounded like a landline and he quickly calculated that in the time since she disappeared, Candy could be as far south as Roseburg.

"Yeah, I'm okay. You been in my room, right?" she asked. Mike detected sniffling and heard every exhale, as if her nose was plugged, like she'd been outside in the cold or she'd been crying.

"Yes, of course. We found her at about three o'clock. She's in good hands," he told her.

Mike heard a sharp intake of breath. "I'm glad," she managed to say. "Where'd she go, Mike? Are they nice?"

"Yes, Candy. They're very nice. They're great folks. You know I couldn't tell you more even if I wanted to." Mike was kind, but clear and firm.

Candy was quiet for a beat or two. "I gotta go, Mike. I just needed to check in with you and make sure she's okay. She went to the doctor today. Did you know? She's doing good, he said."

Mike was aware of noises in the background but couldn't place what he was hearing. Maybe traffic, maybe voices, maybe just static, he wasn't sure.

"Yeah, I know. That was good that you took her, Candy." Mike waited a second, asked her, "Are you sure about this, Candy?"

"Yeah, I'm sure. Thanks for always being cool, Mike. I won't be back up that way," she said.

Mike thought he heard a muffled, "Bye," and Candy was gone.

Chapter 23

Mike told Liz and Connors about the call from Candy. They both listened to him, but just nodded their heads. He guessed that since the baby was okay and they weren't pressed to find Candy and arrest her, they weren't too interested. But that wasn't fair, he told himself. They were busy with Leah's case and trying to stay focused.

"Anyway, I'll leave you two to it." Mike was exhausted. "We're staying locked down until ten tomorrow morning. I'm heading home soon. I may call Kelly and let her know of Candy's call. I think she'd like to know."

"We'll be leaving soon, too. Connors, you should get some rest. We have a game plan for tomorrow." Liz turned back to Mike and said, "I hope you get some down time. I'm expecting to hear from Diana Harrison any time. The sheriff over there is handling notification. Harrison and I will speak with Leah's mother together."

Mike looked at Liz with a blank stare. Liz asked him if he had a few minutes. After Connors left, she filled Mike in on what they had learned about Leah Bishop, her child, and her suspicion about his adoption. She didn't name Carl Ridgeman, however. She needed to hold that back. Liz agreed with Mike, that they had made progress. Unfortunately, they still didn't know who had killed Leah.

Liz got a call from Diana a few minutes later. She had ID'd Leah. The lawyer sounded subdued but that was to be expected. She had viewed and identified the remains of a young woman whom she had known in life, a young woman who had come to her for help. Not a walk in the park. Liz suggested she meet Diana at the morgue. Her office was nearby and they would have the privacy to call Connie Bishop from there.

"I'll meet you at the precinct, if that's all right?" asked Diana. "I'd like to get the hell out of here."

Ten minutes later, Liz pulled in to the parking lot at the justice center and saw the dark gray Saab, Nyla Garrity's dream car, parked in a visitor's spot. The vanity plate was proof that it belonged to none other than Diana Harrison. After meeting up with the attorney in the lobby, Liz led Diana through the squad room to her office. The contrast to Diana Harrison's place of business was not lost on Liz, but she didn't mind the differences. The lobby area was unobjectionable enough that civic leaders weren't embarrassed, but durable enough to handle an angry crowd.

The squad room was quiet, even for a Monday evening. A few cops were busy with paperwork or on the phone. A couple of uniformed officers with desk duty were in and out of the room. Liz grabbed an officer on phone duty and asked if a call had been received for her regarding the notification. The officer told Liz that she had spoken with a Deputy Evans with the Franklin County Sheriff.

Deputy Evans stated that she had notified Connie Bishop of Leah's death, and that ID was confirmed by the attorney, Diana Harrison. She stayed with the mother until her friend, a woman named Ginny arrived. Ms. Bishop was saddened, of course, but Evans thought she was dealing with it and understood that Liz would be calling.

They entered Liz's small office that was neat but pure business. There was little space for much besides law enforcement paraphernalia, except for a dark red ball cap emblazoned with the WSU Cougars logo and a twenty ounce insulated coffee cup from Dutch Bros. Liz offered Diana a chair and then she sat down herself. Their thoughts were already with Leah's mother, Connie.

With the phone on speaker, Liz dialed the number for Connie Bishop. After four rings, she answered.

"Hello?" the woman answered

"May I speak with Connie Bishop?" asked Liz.

"Speaking," the woman answered tentatively.

"Ms. Bishop, this is Sergeant Jordan in Columbia City. Deputy Evans told you I'd be calling, is that right?"

Oh, yes...that's right," she responded with grief in her voice.

"Connie, this is Diana Harrison. I'm so sorry about Leah," the attorney told her with compassion. "I wanted you to know I'm here with the police."

"Diana? What happened? I can't believe this," the mother said.

Liz intervened. "Ms. Bishop, this is Sergeant Jordan again. I'm so sorry for your loss. I'm sure you have many questions and I'll try to answer them...and Ms. Bishop, I need to ask you a few questions, as well. Did you think you're up to that?"

"You're a police officer you said? What was your name? And you're there with Diana?" the woman asked.

"Yes, I am. I'm Detective Sergeant Liz Jordan with the Metro Division in Columbia City," she repeated. "We contacted Diana Harrison when we became aware that she knew Leah. She's been very helpful to us and yes, we are here together. We are in my office and have you on speaker but there's no one else in the room, only Diana and myself. I do need to ask if I have your permission to include Diana on this call."

"Diana? Oh...yes, please, that's fine. Sergeant, what happened? Was there an accident? Oh, my God..." she processed. Then Connie was heard speaking with someone and told them, "Ginny, my friend is here with me. I'm so glad she was home, but if we're out in the evening, we're usually together. And Ginny knew Leah," Connie said. "Now, please tell me, what happened to Leah?"

Liz began. "Ms. Bishop, Leah's death wasn't an accident and it's been ruled out that she harmed herself. I'm sorry but we're investigating Leah's death as a homicide."

Liz heard the woman's intake of breath and was aware of another voice in the room with her, murmuring gently, but Connie Bishop was quiet on the other end of the phone.

"Ms. Bishop, when did you last see Leah? And when did you last speak with her?" asked Liz.

"She...was home with me for a few weeks... after the trip over there, to meet with Diana. Leah was so glad to have Diana to help her. We were going to find her baby." Liz waited patiently because she heard the anguish in Connie's voice, but the woman continued. "She said she needed to go back over there. This was more than a week ago. It was Tuesday last week. She let me know she was going, Diana. She didn't just take off like she used to."

It went unsaid, but they knew that Connie had considered this openness about her plans as a sign that Leah had turned a corner. "So, Leah was home with you until last Tuesday?" Liz asked to clarify. "From the time she returned to Richland after her trip to see Diana?"

"No, no, that's not right. I'm sorry. I need to get this straight for you. We talked about things on Tuesday, how she needed to make another trip. But she left on Wednesday last week. I know it was Wednesday because she stayed until I went to work swing shift. She wanted to take the train. I dropped her at the Amtrak station in Pasco," Connie said. "I expected her to call me, but I didn't hear from her until this past Friday. She said she had a room called The Suite."

Connie took a moment for herself, and continued when she

was ready. "We laughed at the name, The Suite. I thought it sounded really nice, like the place she stayed when she met with Diana weeks earlier. Leah laughed and told me it was okay, but not that nice."

"Do you have any idea where Leah was between Wednesday a week ago and when you talked to her on Friday?" Liz asked.

"No, I don't. We were doing so well I wasn't going to push her," replied the grieving woman. Liz quickly counted and found that there were nine days between the time she left her mother's and began her brief stay at Avalon.

"I need to ask, Ms. Bishop," warned Liz, "do you know of anyone that might have wanted to hurt Leah? Did she say why she wanted to come back here?"

Connie thought for a minute, said, "I don't know, I guess it's possible. Leah was so headstrong. Always was." At this, Connie sobbed. When she was able to speak, she said, "I think her feistiness helped her survive on the street. Diana, you know as well as me that Leah was so mad about the adoption. That's why I asked around about some legal help and we found Diana. But then she got really, really angry." Connie paused again, and continued.

"You see, Leah was pumping and freezing her milk and sending it by express mail to an address in Columbia City. She sent it, packed in dry ice, every three days. Someone was paying for her to do so, paying for everything she needed: equipment, shipping costs, even her prenatal vitamins. She agreed to that as part of the adoption. She was willing to continue to do so until Christmas. But toward the end of October, the money was cut off and her packages were returned. No word, no reason, just cut off. Leah was so angry. It was about a week after Diana called to say she'd filed those papers."

"Every three days? Leah sent a package every three days?" asked Liz. She looked at Diana, who shook her head and put her hands in the air, as if to say, *I had no clue.* "Then she must have sent a package while she was here in the city." Diana and Liz had the same thought; the recipient may have realized that Leah had sent a package from here, thinking she was still in Tri Cities, and not been pleased with the information. "I'll need that address, Ms. Bishop," Liz told her.

"It's right here. She had taken what she needed with her when she left to meet with Diana. She had to -- she was pumping several times a day. She stopped when the second box was returned. Leah left the pump, the bags and all the shipping supplies. When she left the second time she didn't need them anymore."

"It broke my heart to see her so upset. She was angry to begin with about having been lied to, and then to be dismissed like a servant with no notice. Here they are. The labels say 'K. Sutton, PO Box 960, Columbia City, WA.' They gave her prepaid shipping tags, too."

"Okay, that's helpful. Thank you, Ms. Bishop," Liz said as she wrote down the name and address. "Also, there was a takeout menu with a book in Leah's things. Have you heard of a place called BBQ Betty's?"

"Oh, sure... it's been closed for years. I worked there when Leah was little, as a cook. Leah's babysitter would meet us there. After my day shifts, she'd bring Leah to me and before my dinner shifts, she'd take Leah home with her. Leah always said she wanted to work there when she was old enough. We ate there a lot, I'm sorry to say. She loved the barbequed ham sandwiches. It was a happy time...except that I was broke most of the time," she shared.

"Is there anything else you think we should know, Ms. Bishop? Anything you want to tell me?" Liz encouraged, "Don't worry about whether it's significant or not, I'll decide that, okay?"

"Well, I appreciate your kindness. I'm glad to know Diana's there. It was good of the deputy to call Ginny for me, too." Connie turned to her friend and they heard her say, "I'm so glad you're here." Connie sighed and again, addressed Liz and Diana.

"There is one other thing you should know, Sergeant Jordan. She didn't want me to tell anyone, not even Diana, and I apologize for that now. But Leah said if anyone found out it would ruin her plans to find her baby."

Connie hesitated, but then forged ahead. "Leah wired some money to me. She wanted it put away in a bank account and kept safe. Until we needed it, she said. She told me to keep a copy of the wire slip from Western Union. It was for $16,000."

Liz and Diana looked at each other, shocked. Liz asked Connie when she had received it. Connie said she got the wire transfer from Leah, with her explicit instructions, two days after she left her mother's home on Amtrak, exactly one week before she died. Liz asked if the money was still in the bank. "Every cent," replied Leah's mother.

Chapter 24

Diana spoke with Connie's friend, Ginny Mathews, before their call ended. They made plans to bring Connie to Columbia City to claim Leah's body. Ginny would stay with Connie as long as she needed to and would accompany her on the difficult trip. They exchanged contact information and Ginny said she'd let them know when they would arrive.

The interview completed, Diana looked across the desk at Liz and said, "I don't know about you, but I want a beer."

Liz nodded her head very slowly, and replied, "That sounds really, really, good. Let me initiate a search with the post office regarding that address and I'm with you."

They decided on Callahan's, a neighborhood place that both women were familiar with due to its proximity to the courthouse and the justice center. Callahan's had been serving food and drinks to thirsty, hungry cops for years. In fact, the majority of the patrons were either cops or lawyers. Very few high-ranking officers or judges visited the place, so it was always comfortable for the working man -- or working woman.

Taking a booth toward the back, Liz ordered a pint of draft Scottish Red and Diana a bottle of Dead Guy Ale. Half their beers were gone before they came up for air and started to process the call with Connie Bishop.

Diana started the exchange. "Leah never mentioned to me

that she was sending breast milk. I know that's become common with adoptions, but it never occurred to me she'd offered or had been asked to provide it," Diana said. "I'm really hoping the trip over here, at my request, didn't alert the wrong people that she was back in town."

"Well," said Liz, "we should know by mid-morning who that post office box is registered to. You don't know of anyone named Sutton, first initial K?"

"I don't, but I'm sure you can search that out, correct, Detective?" the attorney replied.

Liz's thoughts were in that direction. "Yes, and it may be a fake name or a flunky for the adoptive parents or for someone else that's had a part in all this. I'm thinking the post office box is a better hit. We need to know where the billing goes."

"Okay," said Diana, as she motioned to the server to bring two more. "Let's talk about the wire transfer. What the hell? I told Leah, same as I shared with you earlier, that following the money was the way to get Ridgeman. She told me she was to receive compensation for her 'expenses and cooperation' as they put it, but to my knowledge she hadn't yet received anything. Her primary motivation was finding her baby, and as her attorney, it had to be mine, too."

Diana stopped for a minute, thinking about how to continue. Then she said, "I've been thinking a lot about Leah's baby, actually about the whole case -- Leah's suit, her death, all of it."

"Legal actions brought before the court are usually nullified upon the death of the plaintiff. But Leah's suit against CER and Ridgeman was not for her benefit alone, but for the benefit of her infant son, who is still alive, we hope."

"Hear me out, Liz, because my argument may take a circuitous route." The attorney took a drink of her brew and then continued. "Leah retained me prior to her death, so I will probably be allowed to serve as executor of her estate, on behalf of Connie

Bishop. At least I can petition the court for that appointment, with Connie's permission. If that's granted, I may be able to be named as guardian ad litem for Leah's baby, when and if we find him."

Liz was listening to what Diana was saying and although a cop and not a lawyer, she actually followed the legal logic. "So, executing Leah's estate would involve finding a custodial guardian for Leah's minor child, should her petition to nullify the adoption be successful, correct?" Liz asked. "And any funds in Leah's accounts would go to the care of her minor child, I would think. If we find him, and I think the chance of that is good, maybe Connie will want to raise him herself."

"Yes, I agree with you on all points. Plus, as attorney for her estate," explained Diana, "it would be my duty to see any current litigation or actions concluded. So, it would be remiss of me not to seek judgment in Leah's lawsuit. And in doing so," Harrison clapped her hands together once then held them palms up like a magician, "we'd finally have Ridgeman by the balls."

"But," Diana continued, "Evidence must show the source of the money that Leah wired to her mother. We need the wire transfer receipts at each end, showing when Leah wired the funds and when Connie received them. But that alone doesn't prove the money came from Ridgeman, from CER, or from adoptive parents, or that Leah's accepted them, based on fraudulent information."

Diana was on a roll, but Liz interjected. "What we need, then, is to follow the money back to Leah receiving it directly from Ridgeman and then back to who directly paid Ridgeman himself. If it's the same people who adopted Leah's baby, it would clinch it."

"Right," Diana said. "You've got it. But it isn't going to be easy. He's a slippery son of a bitch."

Liz's thoughts diverged in another direction for a moment and she had a question. "You never asked me who it was that saw you with Leah. Aren't you curious?"

"Yes, a bit. But it doesn't matter. It was me," she replied.

Liz asked for the check and pulled her wallet out of her bag to pay for the beers. Diana waved her away, saying the drinks were her idea, so she'd get them. "Thanks, Diana. I should get some sleep. Connors and I are paying Ridgeman a visit tomorrow. We have many, many questions that he needs to answer. I've also requested a warrant to complete a forensic accounting of CER's finances. And we'll see what the post office tells us, too. We'll connect the dots. It may take time, but if you want to find what's rotten, you follow the stink."

TUESDAY

Chapter 25

Kelly was having coffee Tuesday morning and thinking about the night the three of them had had. Peter was up and off to his classroom of second graders at the usual time, having slept well after their early evening. From her conversations with Candy, Kelly had expected the baby to sleep on and off during the night. The tiny girl awoke twice, had a bottle of formula and a fresh diaper each time, and went back to sleep. Pete insisted on giving her the bottle and handling the second diaper change, although Kelly hung nearby for support.

"We need to get to know each other, Kel. You two will have all day together while I'm at school," he reasoned, "and if you need to go to work in the evening, I don't want to be a stranger."

While he was giving the baby her bottle, Kelly brought up the idea of what to call her. "I'm tired of calling her 'the baby' That's not a name, Pete. What would you think of calling her Caroline, just here, between us? Candy mentioned in her note that would have been her choice, her grandmother's name."

"Sounds like a good idea." Pete looked at the baby in his arms, looking back at him, sucking on her bottle, and asked her, "Little One, do you want to be called Caroline? Yeah, okay? Yes, it's a very pretty name, a pretty name for a lovely, smart girl."

Kelly sipped her coffee, recalling the earlier scene. Caroline, as they were calling her, had been sleeping for the past forty-five minutes. Pete had enjoyed a little play time with her before he left, and had her smiling at him with that precious, toothless baby grin.

Kelly reviewed the paperwork from the clinic again. She was watching the infant for any discomfort or reaction to the round of immunizations Caroline had received the morning before. So far, Kelly didn't see any issue, but was grateful for the tiny bottle of liquid acetaminophen that the clinic had given Candy, and it was still in the baby supplies unopened.

Kelly's thoughts turned to Candy. Mike had called last night to let them know that Candy had called him at Avalon. She was relieved that Candy had no idea that Caroline was with them. They had managed to pack up and leave the shelter without drawing too much attention to themselves. Mike seemed to think that the residents present at the time weren't aware that Caroline had gone home with them. Carlton, the social worker from Children's Services, had followed them home to check the apartment, so it was just as possible that he had left with the infant himself. It wasn't that Kelly had concerns or was secretive, but foster families always need to consider safety and security, not to mention privacy.

Candy had been a challenging client for Kelly, but she had spent significant time with her and her infant daughter. She tried to recall their conversations and Kelly had reviewed all of her notes, gleaning every iota of information about Caroline that would help Kelly and Peter care for her. She was concerned about Candy, but had placed that concern on a back burner when she assumed responsibility for Caroline. The infant deserved no less from her.

Kelly and Pete had talked about how long Caroline might be with them. Initially, Kelly's objective was to avoid having Caroline subjected to repeated adjustments to new caregivers. Babies can be very resilient but Kelly knew that they need time to attach to new caregivers, and even though they can develop attachments to a handful of people, at least one primary relationship should always to be consistent. The many facets of development, Kelly thought, social, cognitive, and even physical, are built upon strong attachments, or trust relationships, with caregivers.

Kelly explained to Peter that because Caroline was familiar with her and trusted her to some degree, she couldn't in good conscience see her placed with complete strangers, however wonderful they might be. Yes, she knew that Caroline would most likely attach, little ones usually do. But what if the foster system asked that of her again and again? Kelly simply hoped to help avoid that from happening. Kelly asked herself about boundaries but decided to ignore the concern. Wanting to support this one tiny girl in a very personal way, because she could, was a first for her in her professional life.

In the end, Kelly and Peter decided to commit to caring for Caroline until a long term, preferably a permanent situation, emerged. Kelly picked up the phone and called Carlton to begin the process to become foster parents for Caroline, not just emergency caregivers.

Again, Carlton was thrilled.

At the precinct, Liz and Connors met up early Tuesday morning to prep for their visit with Carl Ridgeman. After completing a number of data searches, they had learned a lot.

Carl Edward Ridgeman was sixty-one years old. He was originally from Salem, Oregon and had earned a law degree from Willamette University in his hometown. Ridgeman had been married once, for over thirty years when his wife, Amelia, died five years ago. Amelia and Carl Ridgeman had had two adult children. He had no grandchildren, and no other living relatives.

Ridgeman had lived in the same home, on Cheltenham Drive, for twenty six-years. He was a long-standing, active member of Faith in the Savior Church. He drove a Lexus sedan, silver. He rarely traveled, had a full time housekeeper, was a registered Republican, and had a license for an eight-year-old blonde Labrador retriever named Coulee.

Ridgeman was mentioned dozens of times in local news articles, mostly for his benevolent work with a non-profit named Sinai Evangelical Services. As Diana had mentioned, he had received an award of appreciation at a community event this past Saturday evening.

And Diana was correct about something else. Ridgeman had been under investigation many, many times due to complaints lodged with the Bar Association's ethics committee. Liz counted nineteen complaints dismissed due to no evidence of wrongdoing. Another three complaints were currently pending decisions. The most recent was filed by Diana Harrison, JD, on behalf of one Leah Bishop. Not once was Helene Ridgeman listed as a party to any complaint, which seemed odd although Liz was not sure as to why.

At any rate, Ridgeman was likely aware that he was named as respondent in a civil suit, and had yet another complaint filed with the Bar, both actions due to his professional association with Leah. Interesting.

Ridgeman's daughter, Helene, aged thirty-one, was an attorney and member in good standing of the Washington State Bar. There were no red flags in her Bar Association file. She was listed as a partner with her father in the law firm. She had earned her law degree at Willamette, as well, and had an address that Liz recognized as a high-end condo near the river. There was a Mercedes coupe registered in her name. No marriages, divorces, annulments, or domestic partnerships on file.

Ridgeman's son, Brad, twenty-seven, had earned a law degree from Gonzaga, in Spokane, but had not yet passed the Bar. His listed residence was an apartment on the east side of town, not far from his father's home. DMV listed a ten-year-old SUV in his name. He was currently on staff at CER Legal Services, the firm his father owned that had handled Leah's private adoption. Like his sister, Brad Ridgeman had not been married, divorced, or otherwise.

CER Legal Services had an office on North Main. Ridgeman's law firm was located on the sixth floor of the PacWest Building. It was Liz's plan that she and Connors would speak with Mr. Ridgeman at the office of the firm. She wasn't sure how much time he actually spent at CER's place of business.

Liz had a message from the United States Postal Service. The post office box to which Leah had been directed to send packages of frozen mother's milk was rented by an individual named Kathryn Sutton. The box had been in her name for eleven years and the rental charge was paid annually. As proof of residency, Ms. Sutton had produced a rental agreement for a residence. Liz was familiar with the address. It was on Cheltenham Drive.

Chapter 26

Before grabbing Connors and heading out, Liz updated her notes to reflect the new information she and Connors had learned. As she was finishing her updates, she took a call from the forensic analysis unit. The Specialist III who was calling was a seasoned veteran of the unit named Alan Gibson. Although Liz had confidence in the entire crew of specialists, she was always happy to learn that Gibson was handling evidence for a case she was working.

"Good morning, Sergeant Jordan," was the greeting she heard.

"Hey, Alan. What do you have for me?" she asked.

When she heard the voice on the phone, she made the mistake, for just a moment, of thinking it was Dr. Stein. It had happened before. It was the similar tone of their voices and the fact that the gentlemen were of about the same age, she guessed. But it was the formal address that clued her in. Gibson never failed to address Liz as Sergeant Jordan, even though the two had worked together for many years.

She tried for a long time to get him to call her Liz. Gibson would respond with a nod of his head and a slight smile, and an "Oh, yes," and then the next time they had occasion to speak, he would, once again address her as Sergeant Jordan. Liz finally gave up. At least, he didn't call her Ma'am. Now, that would be unnerving.

"I'm calling with some additional information regarding the Leah Bishop case," Gibson told her and then he asked, "Do you have a few minutes?"

"I do. I have about ten minutes, as a matter of fact," Liz said as she checked the time.

"That's great," said Gibson. "I've had a substance analysis come in as complete and haven't had a chance to document yet. The fluid substance found at the scene, on and near the body was herbal tea. Mint, with honey."

"Okay, thanks for the call. One mystery solved, huh, Gibson?" said Liz as she jotted down the information. "Anything else, by chance?"

"Actually, yes, and it's pretty interesting. I'd like to show it to you personally if you can spare just a few minutes." If it had been anyone else, Liz may have balked, but for Gibson to make the request and claim to be *pretty interested* in whatever he had discovered, intrigued her. They needed to have that sit down with Ridgeman, but having more details pinned down prior to that conversation could be to their advantage.

"I'll be right there, Alan," Liz told him, "and thanks."

Liz wrapped up her notes in a flash. She grabbed what she needed, threw on her coat, and walked out of her office. As she walked over to Connors' work station, she saw that he was on a phone call but gestured that he was ready to head out, as well. She held up her empty Dutch Bros. travel cup, indicating she planned to fill it. Connors hung up the phone, stood and grabbed his jacket all in one motion.

"Sergeant, that was Ty Phillips," he told her. Liz was already walking toward the break room and the coffee maker. The name rang no bells for her.

She halfway turned to look at Connors and asked, "Who? Tell me why I need to know about this phone call?"

Connors told himself to slow down, but there was an art to it so as not to make his superior feel dim-witted. "He's the dude who found Leah. I think he talked to you at Avalon and again at the clinic yesterday, right?" explained Connors, making it sound like Liz already knew.

Liz remembered him, of course. She thought of Ty and the help he had provided but hearing his last name threw her off. She had heard Ty's last name only once, when she had taken his statement. Liz recalled not having known Connors' first name. Liz asked herself, *what is wrong with you? That you don't know people's full names?* Then she craved caffeine even more. Her thoughts returned to Ty, last name Phillips. No wonder these people feel invisible, she thought. Liz gave herself a mental kick in the ass, vowing to do better.

Liz slowed her pace, chastising herself. "Oh, yeah?" she asked. "He's on task early. Any updates we can use?"

"No, Sergeant," Connors continued, "he was calling from the men's shelter. He and Skip are making plans to visit Malachi and wanted to know if we could assist. I told them it was iffy, depending on where the kid is with detox. They're thinking he was detoxing on the street before the incident at the clinic, that's why he was so agitated and sick yesterday. Ty said both he and Skip know the drill, know they'd be searched, and that the visit would be closely monitored. They're good with all that. He said Mike offered to go with them."

"What did you tell him?" asked Liz.

"I told him that as soon as med staff cleared it, it would be good with us," Connors replied.

Liz thought of the kid Malachi, and of how Skip and Ty were such help during the incident. She knew it could have gotten out of hand if the two homeless men hadn't intervened.

"It's fine with me, especially if Mike's on board. It's nice of them. I hope the kid appreciates the effort they're making. But it's not like they need our permission to visit the kid. I wonder why they thought to call us," she mused.

Connors grinned as he put the top on a paper to-go coffee cup. "Well, I think you scored points with them yesterday by sending the kid for some help instead of jail. I think they like you."

Liz thought about Connors' comment for a moment but just said, "Huh...okay. We have a quick detour before heading over to Ridgeman's office," Liz told him and explained her call from Alan Gibson. Connors also was intrigued, but he simply listened to his Sergeant and muttered an affirmative okay.

As he prepared to follow her out of the squad room, he added, "Sergeant, I talked with a crew patrolling downtown a while ago. Ridgeman's Lexus is parked in the lot at his office. They'll try to notify me if he leaves. Depending on how exciting their morning is."

Liz and Connors then left the precinct for the five-minute jaunt to the forensics wing of the Justice Center. Connors was curious and when he asked, Liz assured him she didn't know what Gibson had discovered. She was as in the dark as he. However, she didn't doubt that it would be significant, she said.

Liz asked if he had spoken to Kelly or Peter. Connors said that yes, he'd heard from Peter. His buddy told him that the three of them had had a good night and that he was hoping to play basketball in the evening tomorrow, as usual, but it would depend on Kelly's work schedule. Then he added that his buddy was having a ball with their tiny houseguest.

Walking into the forensics unit was like walking into a cloister housing a group of experimental scientists. Liz always thought it looked weird and it sounded weird and often, even smelled weird. Crime Scene Specialists tended to be a trendy lot, young and hip, whereas the forensic folks were somewhat older. They were best described as middle-aged, very smart nerds.

Alan Gibson was no exception. Mid-fifties, slight with a wiry build and a government-issue buzz cut, Gibson wasn't bad looking, just rather ordinary. He had worked in law enforcement forensics since leaving the Army as a young man. Gibson wore trifocal glasses, perpetually chewed gum that smelled of cloves, and even had a pen protector on the pocket of the lab coat he wore.

Regardless of appearance, Liz knew that Gibson was the best in the lab for recovering weird, off-the-wall detail from crime scenes that the department would use as evidence. She had observed Gibson testifying in court and watched cases crumble as he explained away theories. And when his evidence was attacked on cross examination, he was unflappable.

Finding Gibson in his usual workspace, Liz greeted him and explained that Connors was assisting her. Then she asked, "So, what have you got for us?"

Alan Gibson began to explain, "I'm sure you remember the paperback novel that was taken into evidence." He continued, "Well, it did look like it had seen better days, well worn, well loved. But it seemed peculiar to me that it would have been mended with cheap packing tape. Librarians, or sellers of books, even used books, wouldn't use that kind of tape. And the inside of the back cover looked odd to me. Oddly thick. So, I took a closer look. Of course, I documented each step, Sergeant Jordan."

Liz didn't doubt Gibson for a second as she and Connors listened and watched. Gibson described using a variety of methods to discover an envelope concealed under the packing tape. "The envelope is just your garden-variety, white, moisten-to-seal item. And yes, it was sealed, with saliva from our victim. Also, her prints were found on the flap of the envelope where one would hold it as it was licked to seal." At this, Gibson pantomimed holding such an envelope, and licking the pre-treated edge.

"I wasn't able to remove the packing tape from the front of the envelope. The adhesive on that product is too caustic. I didn't even try that route. So, the tape covering the envelope front is intact, as you found it. Visually, from the inside of the back cover of the book, it appears white or blank. However, I was able to do the reverse from the other side, and remove the paperback cover from the back of the envelope where, of course, there was no tape. Once the back cover was removed, it was easy to open the envelope."

Gibson had a look on his face that told them how much he enjoyed his work. He could have been explaining to them how he uncovered the Holy Grail. But Gibson knew that to Liz and Connors, working to find Leah Bishop's killer, this discovery could be important.

Gibson took a step toward his work space and produced three small, transparent evidence bags. All were carefully labeled and numbered. He showed the first to Liz and Connors. It was the paperback copy of Wuthering Heights found in Leah's things. The back cover had been removed but was included. The second evidence bag contained a small white envelope with clear, shiny packing tape covering the front. There were tell-tale signs of print dust and traces of reagent to indicate that the seal had been swabbed for DNA. Gibson reached over to his workstation for gloves, essential to handling pieces of evidence, and put them on. From the third evidence bag he carefully extracted three pieces of paper.

The first item was a Western Union receipt given to Leah for the wire transfer of funds to her mother for $16,000. The second item was a photocopy, front and back, of a check payable to Leah Bishop for $18,000. The check was issued by a bank in Columbia City and drawn from a joint checking account of

Cyril Benedict and Lenora Martin Benedict. The third item was a second photocopy, front and back, of yet another negotiable item. A money order issued by a bank in Portland, Oregon. It was paid to CER Legal Services. There were no names or other indications except for the date it was issued. The money order was for $32,000.

Chapter 27

"Sergeant, I need to make sense of all this," Connors told Liz, as they left Gibson's lab. "Can we take a few minutes to process what we've got before we move ahead?"

"Good idea," she told Connors. "We need to catch our breath and be sure neither of us has missed a detail before we talk to Ridgeman. We may decide to question him at the precinct instead of his office, and I'm not sure how much of our hand we want to reveal yet. Let's head back to my office. We can review and document what we learned," then Liz added, "and adjust our game plan before we talk to Ridgeman."

Sitting in Liz's office a few minutes later, they began to go over the evidence of the case. "We know that Leah Bishop was a troubled kid from the Tri Cities," Liz began. "We may never know why she chose to run and live on the streets. She shows up back at her mother's home early this year, pregnant. We don't know who fathered the child. At some point, she connects with Candy Schinde, also a troubled kid, homeless and pregnant herself. Leah and Candy decide to place their babies for adoption. After learning of a private adoption resource called CER Legal Services which is affiliated with Sinai Ministries through a system of homeless shelters, they each contacted the firm. Ridgeman is connected to CER and Sinai."

"Leah is happy with her choice at first, but becomes suspicious that they're not being truthful about their screening of potential adoptive parents. Her mother, Connie Bishop, seeks out legal support for Leah and finds Diana Harrison. Diana's veracity as a legal advocate for Leah is verified by her mother, by Nyla Garrity, who saw her meeting with Leah, and by the legal documents filed with the court and the Bar on Leah's behalf."

"Leah changes her mind about having CER handle her adoption but before she can stop the process, she delivers the baby at a private birthing center in Pasco. We can assume that baby was placed with the adoptive parents after his birth. They may be a couple by the name of Benedict, who may or may not live here. We know they bank here, at least, and thanks to Leah, we have a copy of a check they wrote to her for eighteen grand. We need background on them."

"So, Leah accepts their check and agrees to supply breast milk for the infant, at someone else's expense, probably the Benedicts as the adoptive parents. She freezes and overnights the milk every three days, to a K. Sutton, at a post office box here in Columbia City. K. Sutton, we know, is Kathryn Sutton and she listed her physical address with the post office as Ridgeman's home address on Cheltenham. She had a rental agreement to back it up. But who the hell is Kathryn Sutton? We need to know. If there's a connection to Ridgeman, we can establish that Sutton was in collusion with CER to defraud Leah, otherwise it's circumstantial."

"Leah stays at the Greyson, information verified by our witness, Nyla. She stays there at Harrison's expense while she is in town for her deposition. All is verified by hotel documents and by Keith Akeuchi, the Owner-Manager. If she stayed true to the routine, we can assume Leah sent a package during her stay at the Greyson. We can't verify it, but if she did, someone may have discovered she was here and not in Tri Cities."

"At some point, she wires her mother 16K, tells her not to tell anyone, not even Diana, but to keep proof. Leah returns to her mother's home in Richland. Diana notifies her there that papers have been filed, including one more ethics complaint against Ridgeman. A few days later, Leah's packages of mother's milk begin to be returned to her. She's even more upset than she was before and tells her mother that she needs to return to Columbia City. She leaves on the train from Pasco and nine days later, she puts in for a bed in The Suite."

"Leah tells her mother that she's at Avalon. We don't know if she knew that Candy and her baby were already there or if that was a surprise -- for either of them. But they knew each other, and Maria overheard their tense conversation in the corridor."

Connors finds the notes, "Here it is. Maria heard Leah say 'It's not over yet' to which Candy replies 'Yes, it is over, just go back to Richmond, at least he was straight with you' to which Leah replies 'How can this be straight?' We thought she said Richland, like, just go home. Maybe she said Ridgeman. Just go back to Ridgeman? Like, to explain? Why?"

"And Connors, there are three people named Ridgeman. If Candy meant 'go back to Ridgeman' did she mean Carl, his daughter, Helene, or his son, Brad? Maria heard them talking on Friday evening. We don't have any reports of where Leah was from that time until Ty finds her dead in the alley. And remember, she was somewhere for nine days between leaving her mother's and landing at Avalon."

"We may not be able to find out where she was the whole time, but let's see if an attendant on the train can tell us where she ended her trip. If she traveled straight from Pasco to Columbia City, she may have been seen or she may have stayed somewhere, or with someone," said Liz.

"She died Sunday around one p.m. after she was hit on the head with a heavy object," said Connors. "Let's see, the M.E.'s report says 'glass, stone, or metal; no trace or fragments;

approximately one-inch thick and oval shaped or round, six to eight inches in diameter.' It sounds disc-like, thick and heavy."

"What else are we missing, Connors?" asked Liz. "What else may implicate Ridgeman, in the adoption fraud and in Leah's death?"

Connors thought then he said, "The money order. It was paid to CER but isn't linked to the Benedicts, not like the check paid to Leah. And as for the money Leah accepted, we can account for all but a few hundred dollars, including the seventy-something she had hidden in her things and the price of the Amtrak ticket."

"That's where a thorough financial search comes in," was Liz's response. "We need to link that money order to CER and to Ridgeman, and for more than the appropriate cost of legal expenses."

"Yeah, you're right," agreed Connors. "And what about Candy taking off and leaving her baby daughter? She was aware of Leah's plans to have CER handle her adoption, as was Candy herself. But the adoption of Candy's baby didn't go according to plan any more than Leah's although their outcomes were very different."

Liz considered what Connors said. "Maybe Candy knew more than we think she did. Maybe she knew more about Leah's death. She may have been frightened into leaving. She may have left her infant as a last ditch effort at what she saw as protection."

"But if that's true," asked Connors, "who did Candy want her infant to be protected from?"

"If we discover that," said Liz, "we'll probably discover who killed Leah Bishop."

Chapter 28

"Here's what I'm thinking," Liz shared with Connors. "Ridgeman doesn't have any idea what direction we're taking. He may suspect that we know about Leah's lawsuit but he won't know for sure. So, let's not go that route. We will have a conversation about Leah's death, which is our primary investigation, and see what he has to say. We can't appear to have made any assumptions, of course. And the adoptive parents have as much to gain by Leah's death as the adoption lawyer, regardless of any fraud. I'll be interested to see what Ridgeman has to say about the Benedicts. In fact he'll find me very interested so maybe we'll get lucky and he'll share more than he means to."

Connors checked in with patrol. Ridgeman's Lexus was still parked at his office. As long as he was in the building, they could wait as long as it took for him to make himself available to them. Having detectives hanging around was something most people wished to avoid.

"Okay, let's do this," said Connors, ready to move ahead. "Are we bringing him here?"

"No, let's play it like this," she said. Liz picked up the phone and dialed. When the call was answered at the other end, Connors heard her explain, "Yes, Good morning to you. This is Detective Sergeant Liz Jordan with Metro Police. This is a courtesy request.

We need to speak with Mr. Ridgeman as soon as possible, regarding a current investigation. We should be on site within the hour. Please let him know that we appreciate his cooperation, as always. We won't take any more of his time than necessary and will try to avoid disrupting his schedule."

Liz paused to listen. "Great. Yes, thank you." Liz ended the call and with a grin told Connors, "My kiss-ass tone worked with his receptionist. She said, 'Absolutely, Detective. I'll let Mr. Ridgeman know. We'll be expecting you'." They walked out of the precinct and down to the car. With Liz driving, they headed to Ridgeman's law office. It wasn't far but with traffic and parking, the trip would take a few minutes. Liz had a thought. She connected with Diana Harrison's office, the phone on speaker so that Connors could hear.

"Harrison and Gilliam; how may I help you?" the receptionist inquired.

"This is Detective Jordan with Metro Police," Liz answered. "Is Ms. Harrison available, by any chance? I just have a quick question."

"Can I ask you to hold for just a moment?" the receptionist requested.

Before Liz could respond, she was placed on hold. Before she had a chance to hope it wouldn't be for long, she heard her name. "Detective Jordan, this is Lynda, Ms. Harrison's secretary. Diana is with a client at present, but I've been instructed to assist you if I can, and if necessary I'm to interrupt her. She's only unavailable to you she said, if she's in the courtroom."

Liz was taken aback by her sudden elevation in status. Nice, she thought. "And Detective," explained the secretary, "I'm to mention that, as Ms. Harrison's employee, any conversation with me is strictly confidential."

"Okay, that works for me," responded Liz. "Don't interrupt her. And you need to know we're on speaker and I have another officer here with me. Let us run it by you and we can decide if I need to talk with Diana later." Liz decided how to phrase her inquiry, and went for it, considering she had only a few minutes. "My question is regarding an attorney by the name of Helene Ridgeman. Are she and Diana acquainted? How well do they know each other professionally? I just want a sense of Ms. Ridgeman, from Diana's point of view."

"Yes, Ms. Ridgeman is an acquaintance. She and Diana are on good terms professionally. I wouldn't say they are friends outside the legal community, but I would say they respect each other. No incidents come readily to mind when they've sat as opposing counsel."

"That helps, thank you. I just needed an idea, an overall impression," said Liz. She glanced over at Connors, riding shotgun. He appeared to like what he was hearing.

"Detective Jordan, can I add something else?" asked Lynda. "An impression of my own, but a point Diana would agree with... but may not share with you?" Liz was intrigued. She looked over at Connors, who was spinning his hand in the gesture that meant *keep it going, by all means!*

"Yes, please. What would you like to tell me?" said Liz.

"Diana is a few years older than Helene. She's been practicing law longer." Lynda paused for a beat. "There's a kind of unofficial league amongst the female attorneys in town. I'm sure women in law enforcement have the same kind of unspoken support for each other."

"Oh, yes, I know exactly what you're saying," replied Liz.

"Diana is well respected by the majority of the lawyers in Columbia City, male and female. Anyway, what I'm really trying to say is that Helene Ridgeman looks up to Diana. She no doubt considers her a role model," shared Lynda, the secretary.

"Thank you, Lynda, and thank Ms. Harrison for making you

available to us," said Liz and she added, "Please, let Diana know we spoke and that I'll be in touch."

"Very good, Detective. I'll let her know." The call ended as Liz pulled into the parking garage of the PacWest Building.

Chapter 29

The lobby elevator took them to the sixth floor, where they found the Law Firm of Ridgeman & Ridgeman. Liz and Connors approached the receptionist, identifying themselves.

"Yes, Detective," the receptionist said. "We appreciated your call. We have a meeting room reserved and Mr. Ridgeman will be with you shortly." A professional-looking young man in suit and tie appeared just as the receptionist finished greeting them. She continued with, "This is Mark Hopkins, one of our Associates. He will show you to the meeting room."

They acknowledged the young attorney with a nod of their heads and followed him to a corner conference room furnished with a beautiful table, the top polished to a glassy sheen, and six comfy chairs. The large windows spanned two sides of the room and offered a panoramic view of the west side of town, reaching to the lake. To the south, the view took in the river and the Interstate 5 Bridge.

Mark, the associate, said it shouldn't be long and asked if either of them would like something. When they declined, he indicated the tray at the table center and mentioned there was water available if they needed it. He then excused himself. In full cop mode, neither Liz nor Connors took a seat. Always best to be on your feet at the beginning of an interview, in Liz's mind.

"I want Ridgeman to feel that he's in control of this meeting.

If he's hiding anything, that approach will keep him a bit off guard. No good cop-bad cop ruse. I want him to feel that we appreciate his time and any help he can provide," explained Liz.

"I want to gauge his reaction to being questioned by a woman. Other than the obvious point of rank, I want us to approach Ridgeman on equal footing. You'll ask about Candy and her adoption falling apart. We'll find out what he knows about Candy's whereabouts and leaving her infant at the shelter. But I'll address the aspects of the investigation involving Leah first, of course. That's the priority. We'll mention the M.E.'s report but we'll keep the crime scene evidence, including the hidden copies, to ourselves."

Connors nodded that he understood and said, "Sounds good. I have my notes with me. I hope to add to them."

They stood at the window, admiring the view of downtown, when the door opened and an older gentleman of average height and build entered the conference room. He was impeccably groomed, clean shaven, dark hair turning silver, glasses shielding dark eyes. His suit was high-end Armani, dark wool with the slightest suggestion of pattern. The white dress shirt looked fresh out of tissue wrapping. The Hermes tie was black with minuscule red markings, held in place by a collar pin.

Moving quickly and with purpose, he extended a hand to Liz saying, "Carl Ridgeman, Detective Sergeant. I'm pleased to make your acquaintance." Ridgeman extended the same hand to Connors and said, "Officer Connors, my pleasure." Then addressing both of them, he said, "So sorry to keep you waiting. Please sit down and tell me how I can be of help to you."

"Mr. Ridgeman, thank you for seeing us on such short notice. We won't take any more of your time than necessary." Liz began with as much courtesy as possible and without condescension. "Sir, we're here about the death of a young woman in the Beaumont district. She had been staying at the Avalon shelter. I'm sure you're familiar with the shelter through your affiliation with Sinai Ministries. Actually, the manager of the shelter is an old friend of mine, since college. He speaks highly of the support Avalon receives from Sinai," she lied.

"I'm sure you refer to Mike Dwyer, Detective. Yes, we've met. We don't always agree in theory, but he's always impressed me. He doesn't have an easy job, by any means." Ridgeman paused before continuing. "The death of a young woman, you said; how sad."

"Yes, her name was Leah Bishop. Do you recall hearing the name before?" asked Liz.

Ridgeman appeared to mull over the name. If he had heard Leah's name before, he was hiding the familiarity very well. "Not that I remember, off hand, but I'd need to check records," Ridgeman replied. "Might she have been a client, Detective? Is that what you're thinking?"

"We're unsure at this point, Sir. You could check your records and let us know what you discover," Liz answered.

"How did she die, Detective? Was she ill?" he asked.

Liz deferred to Connors, who answered, "No, Sir. Actually, we are investigating the death as intentional. Ms. Bishop died around one p.m. Sunday. Her body was found in the alley behind the shelter."

"Oh, goodness, that's a shame. A young woman, you said." He sighed and seemed genuinely sad. "The evidence must suggest something more sinister than an accident."

Connors provided some details. "She was eighteen, from Tri Cities. Her mother still lives there. She had been on and off the streets for a couple of years. Blunt force injury, Sir. It wasn't an accident."

"Tragic." The attorney nodded thoughtfully, and asked, "Does this young woman's death involve the shelter or Sinai directly, somehow? Is this why you thought I could help, as counsel for the agencies?"

"No, Mr. Ridgeman," Liz said. "We have reason to believe that Leah was represented by another legal entity which we have traced to you: CER Legal Services." Ridgeman's face immediately lost all expression. Liz wasn't sure if it was a defensive tack or confusion, real or feigned. "Leah Bishop gave birth to a child in August of this year," Liz continued. "Apparently she had engaged CER to handle the adoption of her child."

"That's possible. CER handles many adoptions. Again, records would confirm or dispute that." Ridgeman was momentarily lost in thought. Then he suddenly asked, "You're not thinking her death is connected somehow to the adoption, are you? We're extremely careful, Detective. Birth parents and adopting families are almost never placed in touch. We protect privacy at each juncture. I've been doing this for a long time. Anonymity is essential to success, especially for the adoptive parents, who are, in all honesty, the more likely to be victimized."

Ridgeman stopped himself for a moment, and continued. "I'm sorry, I don't mean to sound judgmental, but there have been a few cases of a birth parent, either mother or father, or a family member, having a change of heart or a regret that the arrangement wasn't, shall we say, more appreciative."

"What would you be able to tell us about the adoptive parents? If, that is, Leah's adoption was handled by CER?" asked Liz.

"Files are sealed, Detective. They would be subject to subpoena," Ridgeman answered. "I'll cooperate fully, of course, but to show my own effort to maintain confidentiality, I'd like a subpoena on record. Please understand that I weigh that statement against the urgency of a murder investigation." Ridgeman hesitated once more, and asked, "I wonder if I might ask you both if we can take a brief break? I'd like to see if my daughter is available. Would you be agreeable to her joining us? She is my counsel as well as my partner in the firm and she likely may know more than I about the present state of things at CER." Liz and Connors had no objection to this. Ridgeman picked up a phone and asked the receptionist if Ms. Ridgeman was available.

Chapter 30

Mike Dwyer walked off the elevator on the fourth floor of the Columbia Community Medical Center. The fourth floor was where addicts were taken to detoxify from drugs or alcohol. Mike knew about detox, the process of ridding the system of a substance, and he knew it can be painful to endure. This kid named Malachi would be monitored closely. He may experience intense chills alternating with sweats, hallucinations, nausea, and vomiting.

If the addiction is severe, he may convulse, his heart could stop, liver or kidneys could cease to function. If the drug of choice is opiate-based, he may suffer from serious drug-induced constipation as the part of the central nervous system controlling the bowel is lulled into a stupor. So, it is not uncommon for an addict in detox to experience frequent, painful bouts of cramping and diarrhea that can last for days. This, of course, can lead to dehydration.

Mike knew all this. He had seen it before. He knew it wasn't pretty to watch and he knew the kid named Malachi would need as much support as they could muster. But in the end, the addict would have to do it himself. It wasn't like the old saying about being born alone and dying alone. Most addicts start using with "help" in the form of encouragement or pressure from some other user. But getting off the stuff can be a lonely, sometimes deserted road. If all goes well, after detox will come recovery. That's when Malachi may need daily, almost constant support.

Ty and Skip knew all this, too, as they got off the elevator with Mike. Mike knew a lot about Ty's journey of staying clean. He knew it had been years since Ty had used, as it had been years since Mike had had a drink. Mike didn't know Skip, but he trusted Ty. And Ty seemed to know Skip pretty well.

The two homeless men had shared with Mike about the incident at the clinic, about how Liz had seen the value of sending the kid to detox instead of jail. They hoped that some additional support from them on top of that big break from Sergeant Jordan would be the right set of circumstances he needed. But they all knew better than to place bets. The three men, one known in the community as the manager of the Avalon Shelter, a fierce advocate for people in need, were addicts the same as Malachi. They just hadn't used in a while.

Mike talked with the nurse at the desk, explaining why they were there. She said a doctor would be available to speak with them shortly. The men had few possessions with them when they arrived. Anything they had with them could be subject to search. If they were allowed to see Malachi, it wouldn't be for long and the visit would be monitored. The conditions were not only for the patient's benefit but for the safety of the visitor.

After a few minutes, a young physician, the resident on duty, approached them. "The admitting nurse said you were here to see Malachi Evanson?" They told him they were and the doctor asked them to follow him. He led them down a short hallway to a stark room with four tables, each table with several chairs. There was a phone on one table. There were windows high up in one wall. The windows had iron gratings covering the panes.

"I'm Nate Lewis, the attending physician on the floor this morning," the doctor offered as introduction. Interesting that he gave his first name, instead of calling himself "Doctor Lewis," noted Mike. Also, Mike thought it curious that Dr. Lewis shook hands with all three of them, asking their names. Mike was pleased that Dr. Lewis was as polite to Ty and to Skip as he was to him. It wasn't often the case.

They each took a chair. When Mike introduced himself, Dr. Lewis said he knew of him and was pleased to finally meet him. "Many of the patients I see here mention Avalon, and they all mention you," he said. "I see patients at the Beaumont clinic when they are in a bind. I can't contribute more time there right now. Funds have been reallocated so I'm working twelve hour days here right now."

"How is Malachi?" It was Ty who spoke up.

Lewis addressed Ty directly, as he had been the one to ask. "I can't tell you much without his permission, except that he's stable, which is good, of course," Lewis answered. "I'm going to tell him you're here and ask if he'll see you. I think he will. I'm developing a treatment plan that will continue with him to in-patient treatment. He should be out of the woods enough for medical discharge by Thursday. If he wants it, I've arranged for a bed for him at Columbia Shores."

Skip, Ty, and Mike were all familiar with the treatment facility. It was a decent place. Small, good staff. They looked at each other, nodded.

"I'll have to have the guard come in to frisk and search. Sorry, but it's mandatory. Do you each agree to that?" he asked them. They all said yes, that they expected it. "But none of you are family, correct?" the young doctor asked.

"No, we aren't relatives or anything." It was Skip who spoke up now. "We were with the kid yesterday when he decided to admit himself. We told him he was making the right move and told him we'd visit." Skip made it sound like Malachi had been in control of the situation at the clinic, when in reality it was Skip who kept it from escalating.

"Okay. It's nice that you kept your word. That doesn't happen often here. Sometimes family members visit but sometimes that's not for the best, at least not at first." The doctor continued, "You'll have fifteen minutes. If Malachi wants to end the visit early, it's his call. Don't upset him emotionally and don't physically touch him. The guard, Steve, will be right in."

Nate Lewis didn't add that Officer Kyle Connors had called the Nurse's Desk before the three visitors had arrived. Officer Connors offered his support for the visit, if the doctor deemed it appropriate and allowable. And he had personally vouched for the three men.

After being asked to empty pockets, the three were patted down by Steve, the guard, who wore latex gloves. Steve left and said someone would be right with them. Barely a minute later, Dr. Lewis himself, pushed a wheel chair into the room, and in the wheel chair sat Malachi.

They barely recognized him as the worked-up kid from yesterday. First of all, he was clean, as in cleaned up. In fact, he looked as if he had soaked in a hot tub with bubbles, playing with toys as they had as children. His hair and nails were clean as was the scruffy facial hair that wasn't really a beard. He seemed smaller, as if cleaning up had diminished his size by removing dirt, grime, and sweat. His eyes were clear although red-rimmed, as though he may have been crying recently.

Malachi wore cotton hospital garments, similar to scrubs, with a thin cotton robe and slippers. It was hard to believe this was the same filthy, whacked-out kid that had threatened to throw a chair at the clinic yesterday morning. He seemed subdued, but the visitors knew that he was not allowed coffee or tea at this point. The order of the day for Malachi was no stimulation.

Skip and Ty sat down near the kid but not so close as to be in his space. Mike, a stranger to Malachi, hung back slightly, waiting for an introduction. "Hey, Malachi, do you remember me from yesterday? I'm Skip. This here is my bro, Ty. He was there yesterday, too."

"Yeah man, I know ya." Malachi hadn't yet met their eyes. He looked at Skip from mid-chest to his own lap and back to mid-chest. As they talked to him, it occurred to them that the kid could have been suffering from any sort of serious illness. They could have been visiting him as a patient in any hospital.

"There was a lady cop. Is she gonna send me to lock up when they let me outta here?" Malachi asked, genuinely afraid. "I've been to jail coming off the shit before. I almost died. I was so sick I wanted to die."

"Can't speak for her," replied Skip. "Her name is Liz. She's pretty cool, though. If I had to guess what she might say, it's that it depends on whether you wanna clean up or not."

Ty took it from there. "How they treating you, kid?"

The care in Ty's question overwhelmed Malachi and he started to cry, although because he was dehydrated, he produced no tears. After a pause to settle a bit, he answered. "They're nice to me. Dr. Nate comes around a lot. He says I'm doing okay. He talks to me about baseball. I used to play ball a long time ago."

"We've all been there, bro, and actually, you're looking good," replied Skip.

"Malachi," said Ty, "this is Mike. Mike's a good friend of mine."

Mike took a step forward and extended his hand to Malachi, saying, "Good to meet ya, kid." Malachi, with great effort, reached up to shake Mike's hand. There was little more than a slight grasp and almost no movement in the handshake. Mike remembered too late that he wasn't to touch the kid but then thought, *to hell with it; it's what people do.*

Ty continued, "We asked Mike to come with us. He's a good guy for you to know. You know Gary at the men's shelter, right?"

Malachi thought, and then nodded. "Mike does the same kind of work with folks."

"...and I've been in your shoes." Mike added. "You feel like shit and you know why but if you had a hit you'd do it in a flash. That's how I felt."

Malachi looked like he could dissolve into tears again. "Anyway," said Skip, "we can't stay long but we wanted to see how you're doing. Do you need anything? Is there anyone we can call for you?"

Malachi just shook his head slowly and said, "I sure ain't ready for that, man. Nah, I don't need nothing. I just wanna know if I'm going to jail."

Mike sat down. "Listen kid. It just so happens I know the lady cop who sent you here instead of lock up." He chuckled and continued, "I've known her since we were kids. She's a pain in my ass sometimes, but she's a square person, you know? From what I hear, she told you as long as you stay in treatment and work on cleaning up she wouldn't send you to jail, right? I'm telling you that you can believe that. But I know her and she is a cop, man. If you cross her she'll hold you to it. And I sure as hell won't tell her you called her 'that lady cop'."

Just then Dr. Nate came in. "How we doing, Malachi?" He handed Malachi a paper cup. "Here's water. Every half hour, remember? We don't want to try another IV. It didn't work, you know."

Malachi took the cup and sipped. He swallowed, sipped again.

"I wanted to ask you while your visitors are still here," said the doctor. "If you want it, like I told you, there's a bed at in-patient for you, as early as tomorrow or the next day. If it's okay with you, Malachi, I was going to ask that one of the guys here might make the trip over with you. Help you settle in. No visitors for the first week but you can spend a few minutes on the way over and in the lobby when you're ready to check in. A familiar face would be good. What do you think?"

Skip and Ty shared a glance, looked at Malachi who was staring at his hands, then at Dr. Nate. Ty spoke up first. "I could do that. If you want me to, kid."

Malachi said, "I don't know what I want or what to think, I never done this before. Before, I even start to get clean, I use. But why are you doing this, for a crackhead like me?"

"Because we were there yesterday," answered Skip. "I figure, if you didn't want help you wouldn't have put that chair down. You wouldn't have come outside for a smoke with us."

Dr. Nate smiled and asked, "May I get a message to you, Ty, through Gary, about when Malachi is ready to roll?"

"Yep," answered Ty. "Maybe I'll try to stay there tonight, if there's room, and wait for a call from you. You okay with all this, Malachi?" The kid nodded.

Skip told the doctor he was on board, as well, but it might be harder to reach him. He'd try to connect with Ty about the plan. What Skip was actually thinking was that Ty would be a better help to Malachi, as he had been sober longer. But Skip was drawn to the kid, unsure of why.

Malachi looked at Ty and at Skip and said, "Thank you, man." Ty responded with a fist bump.

Dr. Nate then knelt down and whispered something to Malachi. Malachi listened, and then nodded his head very slightly. "My man, Malachi here, wants to tell you something," explained the young resident, "something about a girl."

Chapter 31

Mike, Ty, and Skip stared at the doctor. "I'll be outside. Malachi seems to be doing well and I just didn't think this could wait."

"No, Doc, can you just hang?" asked Malachi.

Dr. Nate stayed where he was. "Sure," as he sat down. "Just repeat to them what you told me."

Malachi took a ragged breath, as deep as he could manage, then began. "There's this chick I know, see. She's a runner, too… smart chick though…don't use shit. I see her now and again. She moves around but she knows people here. Anyway, we got mutual friends."

Malachi paused and looked at the faces of his audience. They were listening intently but only Ty said, "Okay, man, go on."

"I used to party with a crew. One of the dudes, older than us, you know, always had money, always had a ride. We called him Bee. We used to call out when we saw him, 'Hey, hey, float like a butterfly, sting like a BEE'. You know, like Ali used to say," Malachi told them.

"Like Ali, huh? Black dude?" asked Ty.

"No man, white guy. But we called him Bee. Don't know why. Older, like I said, but always with us young 'uns, you know. Anyway, this chick I'm talking about, she was around a lot. First time I met her was with Bee. He said he knew her from school or something. She used to stay with him. He was hot on her, man.

Then she'd take off. I'd see him and say, 'Hey where's your lady'? He'd be all sad and shit, say 'she gone'."

"So, I was in the park and saw them. Hadn't seen her in a while, that's why I noticed. They were down the block a bit but I know Bee's ride, you know. They were sitting in his ride...just sitting there... both of 'em talking. Mad. She got out of the car. He drove off. She was mad, man. I was gonna wave 'hey' to her but off she went," he said.

"You were in the park? On the Beaumont side or the river side?" asked Ty.

"Beaumont," answered the kid, "sitting at a picnic table near the shrubs by the bathroom. I sit there sometimes." Ty and Skip shared a look and nodded. They knew the spot.

"I didn't think much of it. Folks fight, you know? I forgot about it. I hooked up with a group and looked for a place to crash. I woke up the next day. Bee was nudging me. I didn't know he was there. He's nudging me and says, 'Come on man, I need your help. Let's go'."

"You saw your buddy Bee the next morning? He found you where you crashed and woke you up?" asked Ty.

Malachi's hand went to his chin. He nodded and continued his tale. "Bee was dressed really nice, like he'd been to some swanky place and hadn't been home, you know. He had a long coat on. Nice. I told him to just give me that coat I'd do anything for him." Malachi smiled slightly at his own joke. "Bee says, 'I need you to help me. I need to talk to her.' I said 'Who, man?' He said, 'Leah. I need to talk to Leah'."

It was the first time in Malachi's narrative that they'd heard the girl's name. Malachi had mentioned it without being asked or prompted. And Dr. Nate was there to hear it. They were unsure of where the story was going but Malachi had their attention.

"We sat outside the Coffee Shack and drank coffee. Bee is always good for a big java with a ton of sugar, you know. I didn't tell him I saw them, him and Leah, I mean, when she was so pissed. Bee said he saw Leah go into the Avalon shelter the night before. He couldn't get in touch with her there. He said she wouldn't talk to him anyway. 'She mad,' he said." Malachi paused for a moment, remembering.

"He wanted me to watch and if I see her, for me to tell her to please call him. He didn't wanna wait all day 'cuz he was beat and needed to crash. I told him I'd tell her if she showed up. But she's a tough one, I said. I can't make her call him, you know?"

No one noticed Mike's reaction, but when Malachi mentioned Avalon, he felt a jolt in his chest and his stomach tightened, like a physical attack. Malachi went on. "He took off. I walked down to the corner of the park. The bathroom was open. I took a piss and came back out and sat on the picnic table."

"After a while, I saw her. She was walking down the street right at me, with a coffee cup in her hand. I waved 'hey' at her. She walked over and gave me a high five. She sat down next to me. Asked me how I was. Said I looked pretty shitty. We laughed. I told her I was enjoying my java. Love my coffee. She said she switched to tea. Mint tea. I told her I couldn't handle that, man."

Malachi paused. Dr. Nate had excused himself and returned with more water for his patient. "I told her I had a message from Bee. She wasn't happy about that and looked around the street. 'Was he around?' she asked? I said, 'No, he took off.' I just told her he wanted to talk to her. She said, 'Oh well, too bad. Folks in hell want ice water.' I asked why she so mad, that he was always good to her, to me. She said it don't matter. She stood up and said she gotta go, for me to take it easy. Said I should go see Gary at the men's shelter. She walked up the street and turned into the alley."

Malachi took another sip of water. Swallowed. Dr. Nate asked him, "Are you sure you want to go on right now?" Malachi took a breath. Mike, Ty, and Skip were amazed by the kid's fortitude as well as by what they were hearing.

"Yeah, Doc...I do," he said. "A little while later, I finish my java. I'm still sitting on the table in the park. I turned to toss the cup in the garbage can and I see Bee's car parked up the street. Almost same place he was parked when I see him and Leah. Only facing away, you know. I watch him pull out and drive away in a big damn hurry. It was all too weird, man. I watched him walk away after we had coffee. I swear I didn't see his car there before."

Malachi was lost in his thoughts. But then he continued, "I looked over to the alleyway where Leah was headed. I don't know why, I just had to head over there too. I walked up to the alley entrance and saw her. She was laying there, man." Malachi would have cried, had he been able. It was difficult to watch the kid as he made himself relive it. "She was still. I could smell her mint tea, spilled all around her. I couldn't see her face but I saw blood near her head and I freaked."

Ty spoke up and said, "It's okay, Malachi, you had to tell somebody. I'm glad you trusted us. What did you do then?"

Malachi struggled as he remembered the horror. "I booked, man. I freaked out! I got outta the alley, back the way I came in. I didn't wanna run into anyone and explain what I was doing there." Malachi paused, thought for a moment. "I headed back to where I crashed, where Bee woke me up. If Bee came back I wanted him to think I was there the whole time, you know. In case he'd seen me talking to Leah at the picnic table. I was scared shitless, man. What if somebody saw me come out of the alley?"

"I knew Leah, too. I knew her from Avalon. I work there," said Mike. Mike didn't mention he ran the place. "What day was this, Malachi?" Mike asked.

"It was the day before yesterday. I know 'cuz I got high. Last time I got fucked up, man, after I saw that. I was so messed up yesterday with what I saw and the shit I did, that I went to the clinic. I needed help, man. That's when I ran into you there."

It was Ty who spoke next. "Malachi, can you tell Liz, the cop, what you told us, the whole thing?"

"Yeah, I think so, man, sure." Malachi stopped, thought about it and then looked Ty in the eye. Then he said. "Yeah, I can. I can."

Chapter 32

The phone in the conference room at Ridgeman's law firm buzzed and Carl Ridgeman picked up the receiver. "Yes," he answered, listened and then said, "Good. Yes, that's fine." Ridgeman hung up the phone. "My daughter, Helene, is on her way back to the office from a meeting off site. She'll be here very shortly. I'd like to move our meeting to my office, if you don't mind. Lorraine reminded me that this room is needed by one of the associates." He stood up and motioned to the door. Liz and Connors followed him out to the corridor. A woman, maybe Lorraine, went into the conference room as soon as they vacated, probably to tidy it up for the next meeting. Liz asked to please be excused as she headed to the lobby to check messages. She directed Connors to stay with Ridgeman.

Connors followed Ridgeman into a large inner office, occupied by Carl Ridgeman, down the hall from the conference room. Ridgeman's office held a large desk with a credenza behind it. The desk was positioned so that the view from the window, the same view as from the conference room, was to the right. To the left were two winged chairs and a small sofa arranged with a coffee table between. The room was large enough to hold a smaller version of the polished conference room table with four of the identical comfy chairs, to the right side of the door. The wall space was nearly covered with assorted diplomas, commendations, and accolades.

Near the sofa and winged chairs was a bookcase with glass shelves. Connors walked over to the bookcase and remarked on the objects held there. Ridgeman seemed happy to pass a few moments chatting with him about this award or that acknowledgement. One particular item held Connor's attention. It was a commendation from a local benevolent group for Ridgeman's donation of legal counsel. The piece was polished black granite, about an inch wide, oval shaped, and about eight inches across horizontally. The inscription read, "To Carl E. Ridgeman, Esq. for donation of his time, energy, and extensive legal expertise to the organization known as Sinai Ministries to assist with furthering the good work provided to our community." The last line of the inscription was the date of the commendation. It was recent, just this past Saturday. The day before Leah Bishop died.

"This is a beautiful piece, Sir. And you received it recently, according to the date." Ridgeman focused on the piece of granite sitting in the brushed metal stand.

"Oh, yes, thank you. I think so, too, Officer Connors. I received this at a dinner event this last weekend," Ridgeman explained. "Both of my children were in attendance with me. Lucky for me, Helene was there as well as my son, Brad. You see, I felt ill toward the end of the event." Ridgeman seemed embarrassed, but continued. "I enjoyed a rare glass of wine with dinner and sometimes it doesn't agree with a certain medication I take. I should have known better. I left with Helene and hadn't wanted to make an unnecessary scene collecting the award before I left. I didn't want to appear ungrateful either. Luckily, we reached Brad. He was still at the dinner. He took it with him when he left for the evening. He brought it by this morning. I wasn't sure I was going to like it positioned on the glass here, but I've decided that I do."

As Liz entered the room, she and Connors shared a glance. Connors decided that either Ridgeman was an excellent liar or a kind, elderly man. Or, he thought, he's an excellent liar playing the part of a kind, elderly man. Connors laughed at himself privately for how much that sounded like Liz, but he wanted to keep Ridgeman on topic.

He turned to Liz and said, "Mr. Ridgeman and I were talking about this award he received recently and he mentioned his son, Brad." Liz took notice of the black granite piece and returned her gaze to Connors, with a nod of acknowledgement. She took the cue, but decided to wade in slowly.

"Yes, your son. I was just going to ask about him when we decided to wait for your daughter." Liz hoped she sounded nonchalant. It was not easy for her to put up a front so different from her nature. And she was mindful that the man she addressed was a skilled attorney. "Brad Ridgeman, your son. I believe he's also an attorney."

Ridgeman thought for a moment, and then responded. "Brad has completed his law degree. He is waiting to take the bar exam and be licensed to practice."

"He's listed on the staff roster for CER Legal Services. How does that work?" she asked.

"You're correct, Detective. Brad is on staff at CER. He functions much like a paralegal or intern." There was something odd about the way Ridgeman explained his son's situation but Liz couldn't put a finger in it. Ridgeman continued. "Brad knows the law but until he is licensed, he isn't able to practice law independently. Either Helene or myself is the attorney of record for all motions or filings."

Liz looked at Connors, nodded and said, "I think I understand, like a rookie officer." Liz smiled as she said this and Ridgeman returned the smile. Connors wanted to roll his eyes but he resisted the impulse. He was following his Sergeant's lead.

"I thought to consult with my son about your questions regarding CER, when you asked about their services earlier. Brad mentioned to Lorraine this morning that he would be in meetings all day. That's why I opted for including Helene instead." Liz did not miss the proffered excuse from Ridgeman for a request she had not made.

The door to Ridgeman's office opened and in walked Helene Ridgeman, attorney at law. The details provided by Lynda, Diana Harrison's secretary flooded back to Liz as she faced the young woman. Helene extended her hand and introduced herself to Liz and then to Connors. She walked toward her father and, for a moment, Liz expected her to kiss his cheek, normal for a daughter, but odd for a business partner. And odd for an attorney at an interview with police. Instead, to Liz's relief, Helene slightly touched her father's arm and speaking to the three of them, said, "I'm sorry to keep you waiting." Liz wondered, *why does everyone always say that?* Sometimes, she knows damn well, people do intend to keep others waiting. Has the phrase become a social nicety in lieu of a greeting? Or do self-important people want to convey how busy and important they are?

"I asked Lorraine to bring us coffee. I'm not sure you'd want it, Dad, or that you'd care for any, Officers, but I need some caffeine after the morning I've been having," she said.

Helene sat down at the table and invited the others to join her. She was very similar in looks to Diana, although a few years younger, as Liz had expected. Her hair, make up and professional attire were similar to Harrison's look except that while Diana had dark hair, Helene was very blond. She wore it pulled tightly back in an ornate clip. Her complexion was fair. She was tall, about the same height as Liz. Helene was professionally dressed, as Liz would expect from an attorney, but the suit she wore had a bit more color than Diana's, the skirt a bit shorter, and the heels of the pumps a bit taller.

Coffee arrived and Lorraine offered to serve them. Helene waved her away, saying she would handle it, knowing the receptionist was busy. Liz wondered if Lorraine hadn't been busy when Helene had requested she bring the coffee. At any rate, Helene poured a cup for herself and for Liz, while Connors and Ridgeman chose to drink water.

"So, please, bring me up to speed here," requested Helene, as she sipped her coffee. "I'll help in any way I can." Liz decided to ask Ridgeman to summarize their earlier conversation for his daughter. Liz was curious about which details he may leave out as well as any he might subconsciously include. To her ear, his summary was spot on. She had tried to trip him up and had failed. Was her failure to Ridgeman's credit or had Liz simply underestimated his cunning?

After listening to her father, Helene responded slowly and thoughtfully. "I recognize the name, Leah Bishop, and I'm so sad to hear of her death," said Helene. Liz's cop brain wasn't ready to believe that her sadness was genuine, but she had to admit it sounded sincere. "I'm familiar with most of the paperwork my brother prepares for clients of CER. Legally, I'm required to be, of course. I'm sure my father explained that Brad hasn't yet been licensed to practice. He does good work for us behind the scenes, so to speak, for now. The only files I'm not involved with are those which my father or another associate here at the firm are handling. But off hand, Detective, there hasn't been a case of that sort in months."

Liz directed her next question to both attorneys. "We understand that there's a means to determine fitness of potential adopting parents; a sort of vetting. Could you describe that process?" Helene Ridgeman glanced at her father, a gesture of deference more than uncertainty. Ridgeman responded by urging his daughter to explain.

"Yes, clients are thoroughly interviewed," Helene stated.

"CER has a contract with a Clinical Social Worker to complete studies of the families and their homes. It's quite an extensive process. Incidentally, birth mothers also are interviewed. We are careful to examine their motives for relinquishment and ability to make decisions, as well."

Liz made notes and then continued further in this line. "A Licensed Clinical Social Worker; if my research has served me well, that refers to an MSW who has received a license to provide counseling, correct?"

"An MSW or a Doctorate in Social Work, with a counseling certification, but yes, that's correct, Detective," said Helene.

"Sounds like a thorough process, indeed," said Liz. "We'd like to speak with the social worker who interviewed Ms. Bishop."

"Certainly," replied Helene, as Ridgeman nodded his assent. Helene jotted down a few notes and appeared to contemplate how to continue. "I'd like to suggest a couple of ways to move things along faster for us all. First, I'm going to have Lorraine locate Brad and let him know you need to meet with him as soon as possible, Detective Jordan. I think there were aspects of the adoptions, certainly information on the parties involved, that only Brad can address." She looked to her father as she finished and he nodded assent. "He may be in meetings, as we were this morning, but he may be able to rearrange something or possibly there was a cancellation. It does happen."

Helene picked up the phone and told the secretary to get an urgent message to Brad Ridgeman to contact the office as soon as possible. She didn't, however, ask that he be told why. "Also, there are a couple of points I'd like to discuss with my father privately for just a moment. Is that agreeable to you, Detective?" Liz nodded yes, and Helene asked her father, "Dad, can you join me on the other side of the room?" As Helene and her father each stood and walked over to his desk, Helene said, "We will be quick, and I thank you."

Connors and Liz watched them closely. They spent a few moments in murmured conversation, then returned to the table and sat down again. "Out of respect, I wanted to run something by my father. Thank you both for your patience," began Helene. "I discussed with my father, and he agrees, that under normal circumstances, we could expect to wait for subpoenas to release sensitive records. But an investigation into a death, maybe a homicide, is hardly a normal circumstance. So, whatever information you need is at your disposal."

"That will certainly speed things up, Ms. Ridgeman. We appreciate that level of cooperation," said Liz. "How long has Brad been involved with the planning of open adoptions at CER?" Liz was careful to address the question to both Helene and her father.

"He finished his law degree two years ago." She paused and looked at her father for a slight moment. If Liz hadn't been watching carefully she would have missed it. "Since finishing school he's been working at CER, studying for the bar exam."

"Two years ago," repeated Liz. "Could you narrow that down?"

It was Ridgeman who answered. "He finished course work two years ago in June, but was clerking for a judge in Spokane through October of that year. He moved back to Columbia City after the holidays. So, he's been handling preliminary paperwork and appointments since then, about eighteen months."

"Can you give me an idea how many adoptions have been arranged by CER in that time period?" she asked. "I just want a ballpark number."

This time it was Ridgeman who looked to Helene. His hands made the gesture that universally says *I haven't the foggiest idea.* Helene jumped in and said, "I can find the exact number, of course, but I'd guess that we handled about thirty adoptions in the last eighteen months." She paused, added, "It doesn't sound like many but it's a time-consuming process because it's an important process."

Liz's questions continued. "And can you give me an idea of what the fees run for an adoptive family that engages CER?"

"Well, it differs depending on the needs of the birth mother and the child, or necessary travel expenses incurred due to where the family is located," Helene explained.

"That's okay, just a ballpark number again," said Liz.

"Expenses covered for the mother and child, usually medical, however sometimes temporary living expenses, can run between, oh, $5,000 and $8,000." said Helene. "Legal fees for handling the adoption run between $10,000 and $12,000."

Liz listened, using the calculator app on her phone. "So, fifteen to twenty grand on the average, is that correct? Let me see...so that comes to roughly 300 to 360K in revenue, if you subtract the birth mother's expenses. That's factoring in thirty private adoptions in the past eighteen months," she concluded.

"That sounds correct, Detective. Not having financial information in front of me at the moment, but, yes, that's a good estimate," agreed Helene.

"Okay, thank you. I'm sure you have a reasonable explanation for this, but I have to ask," continued Liz, directing her query to both attorneys. "What can you tell me about the complaints that have been filed with the ethics committee regarding CER?"

Liz and Connors heard a reaction from Ridgeman that was between a moan and a growl. Before he could respond, Helene said, "I'll address that subject, as it riles my father to even think about them. It's not uncommon in any professional field for there to be complaints, but realize it's very common in law because argument itself is our mainstay. I try to remind him of that." Helene smiled at her father, an effort to calm, then continued, "About a third of the complaints were due to misunderstanding on the part of a member of the birth family, and usually not the mother, regarding the terms of the relinquishment. Usually a third party is brought in to further explain the details, to the complainant's satisfaction."

"Another third are, and let me be frank, filed by professional entities that seek out former clients with the intent of causing issues with private adoptions because they don't agree with the practice. Also unfortunate, however, it happens. The remaining complaints, honestly, are due to Brad's learning curve, you know, inexperience in addressing clients and timelines, things of that sort."

"Okay, thank you for your honesty," said Liz. "Just a few questions more, then we're finished here. Do either of you know a person named Kathryn Sutton?"

"Kathryn? Of course," Ridgeman blurted out in surprise, then chucked. "She's my housekeeper. She's been in my employ for years. We call her Kay. Why on earth would knowing Kay be relevant?"

Liz deferred to Connors. He explained the post office box and the packages sent from Leah Bishop to K. Sutton. "Your housekeeper has a rental agreement that shows her living address at your residence, Mr. Ridgeman. That's how she obtained the post office box."

"That's most extraordinary! Oh, not the rental agreement, I'm aware of that." He waved his hand in the air and offered further, "It's recommended to have an agreement in place when a portion of compensation is paid in lodging. But the packages, my goodness, what was in them?"

"I'm not at liberty to say at this time," Connors replied. "But we'll need to talk to Ms. Sutton. She may not know what was in them, depending on how they were handled."

"I'll inform her as soon as possible that you'll be in touch," said Ridgeman, with resolve.

"What is Ms. Sutton's relationship with Brad?" asked Connors.

"Friendly. She's known him since he was a teenager," said Ridgeman, "since his mother was alive." Connors was rolling. He quickly moved on to the next question.

"Do either of you know of a woman named Candy Schinde?" He spelled the last name. Ridgeman's expression was blank. He looked stunned, uncomfortable, and slightly pale. He slowly shook his head and turned to Helene.

Helene met her father's eyes and then answered Connors. "Yes, I know the name. An unfortunate story. CER was arranging for the adoption of Ms. Schinde's infant. The adopting parents backed out of their agreement. Ms. Schinde was devastated. It was the first time this ever happened in my experience."

Ridgeman was outraged. "Why was I not made aware of this? What was their reason?" His color had returned.

"The adopting parents felt they had been misled as to the physical condition of the mother and the child. They expressed concern that Ms. Schinde had abused drugs during her pregnancy; however, her prenatal records disproved this. She had a difficult pregnancy and delivered the child early. But she was fine and baby was healthy, small but healthy."

"My God! They were adopting a child, not buying a used car!" Ridgeman was furious at the notion that adopting parents would be so callous.

"Dad, this is why we didn't tell you. We knew you'd be livid," said Helene.

"Please tell me we have not placed another child with these people," said Ridgeman.

"I put my foot down and refused to work with them further," Helene said, then realized the implication of the statement, that if she had not been involved, her brother may have simply offered up another infant. "We returned their fees to them and covered the mother's expenses ourselves."

"Thank God, Helene," said her father. "And what of the child they refused? Were we able to place her with a family?"

"Let me explain what we know about that." It was Connors who spoke up, and due to his presence at Avalon that day, Liz was happy to let him tell the story. "Candy Schinde knew Leah Bishop. We aren't sure how or where they met. Apparently, Candy still hoped to work out an adoption through CER, but gave up. Before we could question Ms. Schinde about Leah, she disappeared, leaving her infant in her room at Avalon. She left a note hoping to invoke the Safe Haven law. A judge felt she had a legal point about safe haven, but it's moot now. We have no idea where she is. The infant is in state custody, placed with foster caregivers. She's doing well."

Carl Ridgeman and Helene listened in silence to Connors' words and were silent for a few moments when he finished. Finally, Helene exhaled audibly, but it was Ridgeman who spoke, quietly and with heartfelt meaning. "I appreciate you providing us with that information, Officer Connors. I know that you didn't have to do so."

"Yes, Sir," said Connors. "We'll want to talk to the social worker that handled Candy's interview, as well."

As Liz looked through a few of her own notes, she came upon a detail, an important one that had not yet been approached. "Are either of you aware that Leah Bishop was suing CER?"

Ridgeman was mortified. "What?" He was clearly unaware that the firm bearing his initials was named in a lawsuit and that the plaintiff in that lawsuit was dead, mostly likely murdered.

Helene was obviously shocked, as well. She looked at her father, then at Liz, then Connors. "Oh, my God," she said. Helene took a moment to process, and then continued. "I was aware that litigation had been filed. Brad told me. He was extremely irritated by it, claimed it was a scheme for extorting money. I asked to see the papers but he said we hadn't received them. He claimed he did not know the name of the plaintiff." Helene paused briefly, then looked at her father, touched his hand and said, "I'm sorry, but I don't believe that now."

"The suit would be a matter of public record. My information is that it was filed last month," Liz told them. "The attorney of record for Leah Bishop is Diana Harrison."

"Then it's not a scheme, as Brad said. I know Ms. Harrison. Diana wouldn't be involved in a frivolous venture," concluded Helene. Ridgeman was unsettled but trying to appear stoic and poker faced. Poor man, thought Liz. She was still unsure of either his or his daughter's lack of involvement in their case but she doubted any complicity on their parts. But Liz wasn't ready to believe anyone. Evidence, she told herself. Believe the evidence.

Connors paused for a moment, then speaking directly to Carl Ridgeman, said, "You have been cooperative, Sir. We realize that some of this information has been difficult for you to discuss. We have one last detail to share with you. As we mentioned, Leah Bishop was killed by a blow to the head. This was on Sunday, Sir. No weapon has been recovered. The M.E. has determined that we're looking for a heavy item, possibly stone or metal, oval or round, about one inch thick."

Helene looked at her father, obviously confused. "But why would you need to know that, Dad?" she asked.

Ridgeman looked at Connors. He had one arm crossed over his stomach, a hand tucked under the other elbow. His upper hand covered his mouth, body language indicating self-protection and a failed attempt at stoicism. The attorney's misery was palpable. Then Ridgeman closed his eyes and nodded his head. "Take it with you, Officer Connors. It's safer in your hands than mine."

Liz stood up and said, "Mr. Ridgeman, Ms. Ridgeman. You'll need to notify us when you hear from Brad. Please don't question him or confront him. There's still much we don't know; information that we need him to provide, if he can." Connors stood up, as well. He picked up the notebook he used to jot down his own case notes. He removed the small evidence bag kept there and walked over to Ridgeman's glass bookshelf. Using a sheet of paper, he picked up the polished granite award and placed it in the evidence bag along with the paper. Connors sealed the bag, made notations on both the bag and the attached slip, which he handed to Ridgeman as a receipt. He thanked them both, and then followed Liz out the door.

Chapter 33

Connors and Liz let themselves out. As they passed through the lobby, the receptionist, Lorraine, gave them a strange look. They thanked her as they went out the door and made it to the car before they shared a word.

"Connors, I know you're on to something with that award, something more than the size and shape. Tell me," she said.

"I think it's the murder weapon. Ridgeman said he just received it the day before Leah was killed. Ridgeman volunteered that his son left the dinner event with it, as a favor to his dad, on Saturday night, and that he brought it by the office just this morning. So it was in Brad Ridgeman's possession from Saturday night until this morning."

"Okay, that's significant, but..." said Liz, following Connors logic.

"It was Ridgeman's idea to move to his office. We didn't ask to enter the room. He freely talked with me about the award, sitting there in plain view, and the timeframe of its return to him. If Ridgeman had been personally involved in Leah's death, none of that would have been offered freely. I just don't see that. He had nothing to gain by subterfuge," said Connors adamantly.

"Whoa, Connors, that's a big word, man!" said Liz, surprised. "But I agree. Interesting that he told you it was safer with you. The man is an attorney and he seemed clearly outraged by some of what he heard regarding CER. I mean, shit, Connors, the place even bears his name; how humiliating!"

"Sergeant, I don't think he wanted the award in his office when and if his son returned there," replied Connors. "I think he wanted it safely into evidence. When this case is solved we may realize that it turned on the fact that Carl Ridgeman has a lot more integrity than we initially suspected."

Liz thought about that and said, "Maybe, but nice work, Connors. You secured possible evidence," Liz told the young officer. "Get it to forensics as soon as we get back to the office. Call ahead now. I want Gibson to handle it." Connors put the call in to Gibson for a heads up.

"Okay, here's what I've got," she said, switching gears. "When I left the room to check messages, I had five. Three of them were from Mike. I tried to reach his cell but it went to voice mail. The shelter staff that answered when I tried there hasn't seen him either. One call from him, maybe, but three is just weird. I'm thinking it's important."

"He was going to visit the kid in detox. Mike, Ty, and Skip were all headed there. But they must have left there a while ago," said Connors.

"Right," said Liz, thinking about the kid named Malachi and her hand in his fate. "Then, I got a message from Diana Harrison. She wanted to see if we had other questions regarding Helene. Her secretary filled her in about my call earlier. Also, she wanted us to know that Connie Bishop and her friend are arriving this afternoon. Diana is helping with funeral arrangements and for the transport of Leah's remains back to Richland."

"The last message was from Miles Carey, the financial investigator. Remember that I did a quick calculation, and Helene agreed, of revenues at CER of about 360K? Carey says it's closer to three times that, over a million bucks. Some of the money is traceable to an account in the Cayman Islands but it's not all turning up. He thinks someone may be paying big debts in cash, maybe drugs or gambling. Or is just hiding it somewhere he hasn't found yet."

"Well, we know Leah received eighteen grand and we have the name of the couple who presumably adopted her son. The Benedicts," Connors said, checking his notes. "And Leah hid the copy of that money order paid to CER for thirty-two grand. If it was purchased by the Benedicts for the adoption, we need to know why they agreed to keep it secret. And why would they agree to pay triple the norm for a private adoption? I'm almost afraid to find the answer to that."

"We need to move cautiously, Connors. I feel as bad for Helene Ridgeman and her father as you do, but we have to believe the evidence." Liz continued, "We're good at being cops so it figures that two experienced lawyers would know how to manipulate facts. They would be adept at using drama and emotion to persuade. Let's keep open minds."

"You're right, Sergeant, absolutely. I don't want to miss anything," responded Connors.

"After you leave the award with Gibson, alert Stein's office that we may have a weapon. If Gibson finds no trace, we may need Stein's opinion as to whether it could have been used in Leah's murder. Then research the Benedicts. Find out whatever you can. I'd like to see what Carey can find in their finances. I'll bet he can trace the money order to them."

"Got it," answered Connors.

"I'm going to keep trying Mike and I'm going to have a talk with Ridgeman's housekeeper, the infamous Kathryn "Kay" Sutton. That will be interesting, I bet," Liz told Connors, so he would know what she planned to handle herself. "Then I want to look into the social worker or workers who contracted with CER. Leah's mother, Connie, mentioned that someone close to the process clued Leah in about possible shady handling of things.

If it was a licensed counselor, maybe that's why Leah trusted them…" They pulled into the parking lot at the justice center, parked. Liz turned to Connors and said, "…and I should return Diana Harrison's call. I want to be there when she takes Connie to the morgue." Then they went their separate ways in pursuit of evidence against a killer.

Chapter 34

When Liz tried again to reach Mike on his cell phone, he picked up on the first ring. "Hey, I was in a lengthy interview," she apologized. "I tried to reach you. It sounded important. What's up?"

"I went with Ty and Skip to visit your kid in detox," replied Mike. "I suggest you talk to him, Liz, as soon as possible. He knew Leah, called her by name. And he says he saw her, talked to her Sunday morning."

"Well, yes, that is a development. But he's a messed up kid, Mike. How can I use anything he tells me? Maybe he's the killer I'm dogging," she said.

"I doubt it. But if that's true then you need to talk to him anyway." Mike sounded like himself, Liz noted, more than he had since Leah's death and Candy's disappearance. "I'm not exactly a novice in this area, but you're the cop. This guy Malachi, his last name is Evanson. He knew Leah and according to him, he saw her with a mutual friend on Saturday. And he saw this same friend, some dude he calls Bee, around the park late Sunday morning."

Some guy he calls "Bee," she thought. Was that a street name for Brad? She made a note of the possibility and of Malachi's last name.

"Sounds like I need to head over there. He's on the fourth

floor? And how is he doing, in your opinion?" Liz had to concede that this was more Mike's area of expertise than hers.

"He's okay. The worst of it has passed. He's got a young doctor that still gives a shit; has a bed waiting for him in in-patient. I think you can use what he tells you but you'll be the judge of that," he told her.

"Will Malachi talk to me if I show up by myself?" she asked. "Will he freak?"

"Well, my guess is he'll be okay with you. We talked you up, reminded him that you gave him a big break. Ty and Skip were both good with the kid," explained Mike. "Call ahead and ask for Dr. Nate Lewis. Nice guy, by the way. He was present when we talked to Malachi. He kind of prompted it, thought it was important."

"Okay, I'm on it, thanks, Mike." Then she asked, "Are you still in lock-down?"

"No, our gal and her kids are on their way south. Busy day though," Mike told her.

"I'll let you get to it then. Tell Ty and Skip thanks for me, too," offered Liz.

"Tell them yourself," Mike replied. "They're probably down the street."

After ending her call with Mike, Liz put a call in to Diana Harrison. Connie Bishop, accompanied by her friend, was due to arrive in a few hours. Liz would meet them at the morgue. Liz contacted Stein, who was on site at the morgue and said he wanted to be present for the viewing. And Stein personally would see to the release of the remains when authorized. Liz was relieved.

There was something prodding Liz's brain that she couldn't exactly define or even quite put her finger on. It wasn't really a poke in the brain; it was more a feeling in her gut. She wasn't sure why but her reaction was to arrange for eyes on both Carl and

Helene Ridgeman. Was it her bullshit meter? Was it a concern for their safety?

Knowing that investigators would be watching both attorneys, Liz felt better able to focus on interviewing Malachi. Before leaving, she placed ID photos in her walking file of Leah Bishop, Candy Schinde, Carl, Helene, and Brad Ridgeman, Kathryn Sutton, and Diana Harrison.

Liz arrived at the medical center and made her way up to the fourth floor. She identified herself and asked to speak with Dr. Nate Lewis. Liz spent a few minutes talking with the doctor and heard much the same details and conditions as the visitors had earlier. Soon, Liz was cleared to have a conversation with the young man identified as Malachi Evanson. A records search had indicated Evanson was nineteen, originally from Bellevue, near Seattle. He had had a couple of minor run-ins with law enforcement, drugs and loitering but nothing violent, no convictions. Records indicated he was a runaway who had been in various youth shelters.

Before meeting with his patient, Dr. Nate again explained to Liz his expectations for her conversation with Malachi. As with the visit earlier, the doctor felt that Malachi was well enough to talk, but if he became agitated or if Malachi chose, the meeting would end.

Liz met with Malachi in the same room where he had had the visit with the guys earlier. She asked Malachi how he was doing. Told him he was looking better than yesterday when their paths had crossed at the clinic. He was near tears when he talked about how grateful he was that she sent him here instead of jail. Liz responded that she was hoping it would make a difference for him. She told Malachi that she was glad that Skip and Ty were around and that he chose to listen to them. Malachi nodded silently, and then mentioned that they had been to see him. He said the visit meant a lot.

Liz mentioned the other man that visited, Mike Dwyer. Liz shared that Mike called her, suggesting she talk with Malachi, that he may have information she would find relevant to a current investigation. Liz explained that she was there in an official capacity, investigating the death of Leah Bishop. Malachi waived his right to an attorney but wanted Dr. Lewis present, if possible. Malachi agreed to let Liz record their conversation. She explained that it was for Malachi's protection and that the recording would be transcribed. She asked if Malachi knew what transcription meant. He thought for a moment, looked at Dr. Nate and said it meant it would be written down, what he said. Liz said yes, word for word. In addition, she explained that it was possible that the transcription of what he said could be used in court. So, if he was still okay with it, he should remember that as they talked.

Liz began the recording by naming the parties present. She stated her name and rank, Malachi's full name, and the doctor's name and title. She added that Dr. Lewis had authorized the meeting, aware of his patient's condition and capacity. Malachi Evanson recalled for Liz the same information he had shared with Mike, Ty and Skip. Dr. Nate was present for most of the interview. The doctor excused himself once, as he was needed by another patient, and when given the option to wait, Malachi chose to continue.

When he finished the account, Liz changed directions. She told Malachi that she needed to ask a few questions, wanted to show him a few ID pictures, and wanted to continue recording. He agreed. Liz took the ID photos from her file, unnamed and numbered for identification and asked Malachi one by one if he could identify them. He identified photo number one as Leah Bishop. He thought he had seen the person in the second photo, Candy Schinde, around on the street but didn't know her, didn't know her name, and had not seen her in Leah's company. Of the other five ID photos, he only knew the person in photo number six. Malachi Evanson identified Brad Ridgeman from his ID photo as the friend he knew as Bee. Liz's recorded Q and A with Malachi continued:

Liz: How long had you known Leah?

Malachi: On and off a couple years.

Liz: How long have you known Bee?

Malachi: Longer. I knew Bee first. That's how I met Leah.

Liz: How many times did you see them together?

Malachi: A lot, probably a dozen times. They were like a couple, you know?

Liz: You said Bee told you they met at school. Did he say where? When?

Malachi: Nah, I don't think so.

Liz: When Bee woke you on Sunday morning, how did he seem? What kind of mood was he in?

Malachi: He looked like he'd been up all night; still dressed up, like for a party. Tired; wanted to talk to Leah, but not bad enough to keep from taking off. He wanted to crash.

Liz: Did you see Bee drive off?

Malachi: No, he walked off; didn't see his car until later.

Liz: After Bee walked off, how long did you sit drinking coffee before you saw Leah?

Malachi: More than a few minutes but not like an hour or something.

Liz: You talked with Leah and then saw her head down the alley. How long before you noticed Bee's car?

Malachi: More than a few minutes, but not that long.

Liz: And you didn't notice his car parked up the street before you saw it drive away?

Malachi: No, Ma'am. I don't think it was there long. I woulda' seen it.

Liz: Did you see Bee approach the car?

Malachi: No.

Liz: Did you see Bee get into his car?

Malachi: No.

Liz: But you're sure it was Bee's car?

Malachi: Oh, yeah, it was; I been in that car lotsa times.

Liz needed to ask Malachi about seeing Leah's body lying in the alley. She was aware of his situation and didn't want to see him upset, although so far he had managed well. Liz had to push herself to push him. She told herself to get tough. They were pursuing a killer, after all.

"Okay, Malachi, you saw Bee's car drive off." Then she asked, "What made you walk up the alley?"

The kid thought for a moment. "It was weird, seeing Bee's car up the block driving off," he said. "It didn't make sense. I watched him walk off, said he was beat, just wanted to crash. I had just talked to her, gave her his message. I guess I wanted to ask her if she talked to him." The explanation seemed reasonable to Liz.

Liz moved on carefully. "When you saw Leah in the alley, Malachi, did you touch her?"

Malachi thought back and started to cry silently, but he maintained control. "No, Ma'am. I did not. I couldn't… I just had to get outta there."

"I know you were freaked out, but did you see anyone near the alley or running away?" Liz asked him.

"Not that I remember. I think I woulda' noticed," he responded. "I felt kinda' hyped. Scared." That statement seemed reasonable to Liz, as well.

"Okay, Malachi. Just a couple more questions." She tried to calm him. "From the time Bee woke you until you saw Leah's body lying in the alley and you ran off, did you get high? On anything? You're not in trouble no matter how you answer, but I need an honest answer, okay?"

"I didn't, I swear," Malachi replied. "I'm into java in the morning. But...that's why I ran off. I needed to get fucked up after that. I spent the whole rest of the day on the low down and loaded. I just didn't wanna think about seeing her like that." Malachi held his face in his hands for a moment. He took a ragged, deep breath, covered his mouth with his hand for a second, regained control, and continued. "And I was freaked, really scared. That's why I ended up at the clinic the next day, you know? I was in a bad way after all that. And Leah was dead. And I was too scared to do anything."

Chapter 35

Dr. Lewis rejoined them just as Liz finished her interview with Malachi. Liz thanked the doctor for allowing her to interview Malachi while under his care. She shook his hand. Liz thanked Malachi. She knew it was difficult for him. Malachi said he was okay, that he wanted to help, he hoped he had.

"You have helped. You've helped establish a timeline. And you may have identified another person who knew her." Malachi nodded, listened while Liz continued. "You had no reason to think she was in danger, no one did, except the person who killed her. You saw her lying there. You have to live with that, but we both know it was too late. You were scared for yourself, it's what people do. Fight or flight, it's called. You were too scared to fight so you flew." Malachi looked miserable. But he nodded again.

"So, are you going to take the bed at inpatient?" Liz asked. Malachi wiped his face with his hands and took a breath, calmed himself, again. Good survival skill, thought Liz.

"I am. I don't wanna go to jail. And anyway, I might not get a chance like this again. Dr. Nate's been nice. Ty said he would go with me, help me get checked in."

"Yeah, I can see that. He's a good guy to know," Liz said. She shook Malachi's hand and left.

Back in her car, Liz entered Ridgeman's address into GPS, and reached Connors by phone as she pulled out. She told the young officer about finally reaching Mike and how it led to the interview with Malachi.

"He ID'd Brad Ridgeman, Connors," Liz exclaimed. "He stated that he knew him, knew Leah, and that Ridgeman and Leah knew each other. And other than her killer, the kid may have been the last person to see Leah alive. Connors, the kid puts Brad Ridgeman in the Beau on Sunday morning."

"And the kid agreed to be recorded? And the Doc agreed, too? Amazing break for us," stated Connors.

"Not for us. It's a break for the investigation," she corrected.

"Do you think he sounded credible? I mean he is in detox and under doctor's care." Connors was skeptical.

"He did sound credible, Connors, and the physician was present, as well. And lucky for me I'd never laid eyes on the kid before I offered him detox instead of jail after the incident at the clinic. I'm sure some wily defense attorney would try to claim I'd set the whole thing up," she said.

"That's true, and you've got a host of witnesses, including clinic staff. And Kelly was there, too, right?" Connors had a thought. "You know, Sergeant, if you'd been more of a hard ass and sent Malachi to jail, you'd probably never have had the occasion to interview him. Weird, huh?"

Liz thought about the situation, and about what Connors had said. She knew his observation was correct. She was amused by his choice of words, but tried to sound serious. "What are you saying? That I'm regularly a hard ass?"

"Well...here's how I see it. The kid did present a threat to a clinic full of staff and patients. He may have deserved to be placed in custody and sent to jail. But you didn't leave him on the street either. Look at it this way. If he had had a knife instead of that chair in his hands and stabbed himself, we'd be obligated to ensure he received medical care before booking him, right?"

"I see your logic, Connors. Even though the need for care was due to his own choices, he still needed care. And I made it clear at the time, either treatment or jail."

Liz pulled into the drive-through at Dutch Brothers. "I'm on my way to talk with Kathryn Sutton. We need to locate Brad Ridgeman for interview as soon as possible. Any word from him?"

"Not that I've heard, Sergeant," answered the officer.

Liz confirmed that they still had eyes on Carl and Helene. She didn't mention the feeling in her gut because she still wasn't sure what it was telling her. She asked that Connors make a request for cops on the street to keep a look out for Brad. "I assume the award you took into evidence at Ridgeman's office is in Gibson's lab?" she asked.

"Yes. He's rushing it," Connors assured her.

"And what have you found on the Benedicts, the people who adopted Leah's baby?" she asked.

"Nothing terrible. The searches show that Cyril, or Cy Benedict, is sixty-three years old, twenty-two years older than his wife. Third marriage for him, second for her. They have an address north of town. Neither have other children." Connors was reading from his notes. "Lenora Benedict is forty-one years old, has been treated for breast cancer and ovarian cancer, both now in remission. And she's diabetic."

"How did you come across the health information? That can't have come up in a search," Liz said.

"Lenora Benedict was interviewed for an article last year in a local woman's health publication. She was pretty forthcoming about her issues. The tone of the article was to inspire other women going through similar situations," Connors continued. "The article doesn't mention their intention to adopt a child, but efforts to adopt through traditional means might have been thwarted due to Lenora Benedict's health problems, and the age of her husband."

"Okay, I've got about another minute. What about their finances?" Liz asked Connors.

"I put Carey on that. Man, he's fast, Sergeant," answered Connors. "They're comfortable but not loaded. He's a Financial Planner. On staff with a firm here in Columbia City that handles a lot of corporate work, meaning retirement plans for employees. Both divorces cost him. She works for an interior design firm in Portland. She didn't gain anything when she divorced five years ago. Carey found a closed Roth IRA in her name, cashed out in September. The cash out, after fees, was forty-seven grand. Almost enough to cover the total on the receipts Leah had hidden in her paperback novel."

"Well, that's interesting, how the pieces fit," said Liz.

"Carey's trying to tie the Benedicts' accounts to the money order for $32,000." Connors added. "He says that's tougher to do, but not impossible."

"Good. Keep me informed. Okay, I'm at Ridgeman's. Notify dispatch I'm here," she said, "and as soon as Brad Ridgeman sticks his head up, I want to know."

Chapter 36

Liz rang the bell at the front door of Carl Ridgeman's home on Cheltenham Drive. A few moments passed and the door was opened by a woman who appeared to be in her fifties. Liz thought she recognized Kathryn Sutton from her ID photo, although it had been several years since it was taken. She was of medium height with a not-so-thin figure concealed under the typical uniform dress worn by domestic workers in upscale homes. She wore her silver hair at a mid-length, the curls sprayed to keep them firmly in place, making Liz recall the Aqua Net ads of the 1960's. Her eyes were framed by dark lashes, her face surprisingly smooth, make-up skillfully applied. She appeared to be a middle-aged woman who had always taken pride in her appearance and continued to do so.

Liz identified herself and said she was looking for Kathryn Sutton. "I'm Kathryn Sutton. Please come in, Detective. Mr. Ridgeman was kind enough to let me know you wanted to see me." She stepped back from the door and as Liz entered the foyer, she closed it behind them. The housekeeper studied Liz's shield and ID for a few seconds. "Would you mind if we talk in the kitchen? I have bread for this evening in the oven that I really must watch."

When Liz replied that this was agreeable to her, Kathryn nodded her head once and led Liz through the foyer and down a long center hall. Liz noticed an office or study followed by a large dining room on the left side of the hall. The long dining table would accommodate a party of twelve. It was a beautiful room. On the right side of the hall was a formal parlor that looked to be rarely used, but often cleaned, followed by a large, neat, comfortable-looking den. Liz noticed a broad hallway off to the side of the den, perhaps leading to bedrooms.

The kitchen was behind the dining room, separated from it by a large pantry area and obscured by a double doorway. The aroma of fresh bread filled the room. The kitchen area included a nook that overlooked a private, well-manicured lawn and extensive shrubbery. An older gentleman wearing work clothes and knee boots was trimming shrubs. A large, light-colored dog reclined nearby. "Please find a seat and I'll join you shortly." As Kathryn said this she stepped over to the oven, turned on the oven light and peered inside without opening the oven door. Satisfied with what she saw, Kathryn Sutton walked over to the nook and gestured to Liz, who was still standing, looking out to the back grounds, and asked, "Shall we sit, Detective?"

"Yes, thank you, Ms. Sutton. You live on site, I believe. It's a beautiful home."

"Yes, it is. My room and private bath are through there," she said, indicating a doorway to the side of the expansive kitchen.

"How long have you worked for Mr. Ridgeman?" Liz asked her.

"Thirteen years," the housekeeper replied. "Mrs. Ridgeman hired me. I worked for her eight years before she died. She was a wonderful woman. I enjoyed working for her." Liz noted the calm of the housekeeper's demeanor. If Kay Sutton was concerned about speaking with the police, her affect didn't show it.

"And you stayed on after she died, obviously," noted Liz, aloud.

"Oh, yes. Mr. Ridgeman has been a wonderful employer, as well. I worked more closely with his wife, I guess you'd say. There was no question of my staying on following her passing." As she spoke, she smoothed the lap of her dress.

"Tell me about their children, Helene and Brad. How well do you know them?" inquired Liz.

Kathryn thought for a moment, answered, "Helene was in school in Salem when I began working for the family. Not terribly far away, but I didn't see her often until she moved back to Columbia City. That was when she joined Mr. Ridgeman's firm."

"And Brad?"

She smiled and looked at her hands. "Brad was a teenager when I came here. Fourteen, I think. Still in school so he was here in the home until he went off to college. I saw him on a daily basis for a few years. Nice young man, always polite to me. Of course, he's grown up now."

"How often do you see them, Helene and Brad?" Liz asked.

"Once in a while, not often," she answered. "They're adults with their own lives, you understand. Special occasions and holidays, they come home."

"How do Helene and Brad get along?" The housekeeper was decidedly uncomfortable with the question.

"I'm not sure what you mean, Detective. They're the offspring of my employer."

"I'm asking for your impression, Ms. Sutton. Are they friends? Are you aware if they spend time together?"

"Well," she hesitated still and finally responded, "Helene is a few years older than her brother. They work together at Mr. Ridgeman's other legal office. They don't share with me if they spend time together outside of that. They're very different people."

"How are they different people?" Liz asked, but she was thinking, is one a killer and the other not?

"Miss Ridgeman, Helene, is driven, very dedicated to her career, works all the time. Brad is a good person, but he enjoys himself. He enjoyed the college atmosphere, I think," she continued. "He would talk about it when he was home from school. I don't think I'd be out of line by saying that he is just starting his career whereas Helene has been involved in hers for years."

"Okay, thank you. That's helpful, Ms. Sutton." Liz paused and appeared to review notes. "It's come to our attention that you have a post office box. Do you receive your personal mail there?"

Liz expected a different reaction from the housekeeper, but there was no surprise or suspicion at being asked and she merely replied, "Most things, yes, Detective."

As Liz studied the woman seated across from her, she felt a fleeting sensation, a subconscious nudge. The feeling soon was gone but Liz made note of it, nonetheless. She took a breath and assessed the situation. Detecting no alarm from the cop part of her brain, Liz decided to forge ahead with her questions for Kay. "Do you ever receive mail or packages for the Ridgemans at your post office box? I'm referring to items of a business nature, for either the law firm or for CER?"

"Yes, I do, once in a while, for CER. As a favor, you see. They handle some sensitive cases and it's been explained to me that anonymity is so important." Kathryn looked worried. "Is this wrong of me?"

"Probably not," answered Liz. "It would depend on other circumstances that I'm not curious about right now. When there's an item for CER, how is it handled?"

"They're usually small packages. I'm notified when they are to arrive at the post office and I'm asked to pick them up that day and take them directly to the receptionist at CER," she said.

"Have you ever opened a package intended for CER?" asked Liz. "How do you determine if an item is for you or the legal services office?"

"Oh, no, I've never opened one that wasn't for me. And I would know because I would be notified it was coming. Also, the package would be addressed to K. Sutton and not my full name or even to Kay, as I'm called." The housekeeper seemed sure of herself and clear on the procedure.

"And Ms. Sutton, you have no idea what might have been in any of the packages?" Liz asked.

"No, I assume it's not my business. They would include me in the information if needed, but I can't imagine why I would want to know." Liz wanted to mention that legally, the items were addressed to her and coming to a post office box rented in her name, but she let it go, in favor of other details.

"How long ago did this arrangement begin?" Liz asked the housekeeper.

"A few years ago, and I've been happy to help. It's no bother." Unless you're helping a killer, thought Liz, or, at least, a dishonest attorney.

"And your employer, Mr. Carl Ridgeman, asked you to enter into this arrangement?" asked Liz.

"No, not Mr. Ridgeman, Detective ... but he's aware of the situation ... I'm sure. Why wouldn't he be? It's his business, after all." Kathryn looked confused, almost perplexed, that Liz was interested in the post office box. Liz recalled that when they talked about the post office box with Carl Ridgeman, he reacted as if he knew nothing about it.

"Then who asked you to handle this arrangement for CER?" Liz was sure of the answer. CER was primarily Brad Ridgeman's enterprise. And it was making him a lot of money.

"Why...it was ...Ms. Ridgeman," she answered. "Helene."

As she mentioned Helene's name, the door to Kathryn's private quarters opened and into the kitchen stepped Brad Ridgeman. Liz was sure of the young man's identity from the ID picture she had shown Malachi. But whether it was Brad standing before her or not, Liz wasn't taking any chances.

Chapter 37

It was Liz's cop brain that made her instinctively reach back for her side arm when she heard the door from the housekeeper's quarters open. Liz drew her service weapon. Brad's hands were raised and they were empty. "You need to stop, right there, and identify yourself. Now," Liz commanded.

"I'm Brad Ridgeman," he responded. "Are you Detective Jordan?" he asked.

Liz wasn't ready to answer any questions. "Do you have ID?"

He answered, "Yes."

"Turn around so I can see your hip pocket. Keep your hands raised," Liz said and the young man did as he was told. He wasn't wearing a jacket, but Liz wasn't completely sure that he did not have a weapon. "Now, don't turn around yet. Reach back and take your wallet out of your pocket. Hand it to Ms. Sutton." He did that, as well. Kathryn Sutton didn't look surprised at Brad's being there, just surprised that he had come into the kitchen.

"Ms. Sutton, remove the ID from the wallet and hand it to me," she told the housekeeper. Kay did as she was told. Sure enough, the ID was for Bradley Glenn Ridgeman. The address on the license was the apartment near his father's home, the one that had come up in the previous search. The ID photo was the one she had copied to show Malachi.

"Ms. Sutton, if you were aware that Mr. Ridgeman was on

the premises and this turns ugly, I will hold you responsible," Liz told the housekeeper, sounding as convincing as possible.

"Yes, of course, I knew Brad was here," she responded calmly. "It's not going to turn ugly, Detective."

Liz told her plainly, "You need to tell me right now, if there's anyone else in the house."

"No, there's no one else, Detective. Henry's working outside," she replied. "That's all."

Liz directed her attention back to Brad, boring a hole through him with her look. "Okay, Mr. Ridgeman, move that chair back from the table and sit down. And don't move."

Liz took her phone out and called Connors, eyes and service weapon peeled on the man. When Connors picked up, she said, "I need you here at Ridgeman's home. Brad Ridgeman is here." She paused. "That's right. Take an unmarked and bring another officer along. No siren or lights. Just inform dispatch." Liz paused. "Yeah, I was surprised too." She paused to listen again. "No. Not at this time."

"Are you Detective Jordan?" he asked again.

"Yes," was Liz's one-word answer.

"I saw her badge and her ID, Brad. She's Detective Jordan," Kay assured him.

Brad Ridgeman was of similar height and build to his father, but instead of the dark hair and eyes, Brad's hair was a wavy, strawberry blonde, worn a bit longer, and his eyes a lighter, almost golden brown.

"I got an urgent message from my father's office this morning," Brad explained, "to contact the office as soon as possible. Then I got a strange message from my father a short while later. He said to come here, to his house, and wait here. He wanted me to talk to an investigator, a Detective Sergeant Liz Jordan, regarding CER and a young woman."

"I'm aware that your father's office was to get a message to you." That much Liz knew was true.

"I arrived a few minutes before you. I was sitting here in the kitchen with Kay, explaining to her what Dad said. I wasn't sure what to do when you rang the bell, so Kay shooed me into her room. It happened so fast. I'm sorry if we broke some protocol." He was excited and talking over his own words, but even the coolest heads can do that when faced with an armed law enforcement officer. Kay, on the other hand didn't seem bothered. She even remembered to take the bread out of the oven. "I don't think I've broken a law here, Detective, and neither has Kay, unless I'm under arrest. She's a resident of these premises and I have her permission to be here."

"All that is probably true," said Liz. "And no, you are not under arrest. Yet."

Connors arrived with a plain clothed officer named Cryer a short while later with no fanfare. They searched Ridgeman as well as the rest of the house, and while Cryer assumed a decidedly authoritarian stance with Kay in the kitchen, Liz and Connors talked with Brad Ridgeman in the front parlor. Without saying names aloud, Liz asked Connors to check in with the eyes they had on the other two persons of interest.

"Let's start with this, Mr. Ridgeman. Why would your father want you to talk to me?"

"I'm not sure. My father is a smart man. I'm guessing he has his reasons and he must have trusted you after your visit to his office. I certainly hope he's right about that because there's a lot I need to tell you."

"Okay I'm listening," she said.

"I know you're here about Leah Bishop. And CER. My father didn't mention her by name but he didn't have to. I know she's dead." He stopped for a moment. Swallowed. "I didn't hurt Leah. I wouldn't. We...were...I'd known her for a long time...we...were close." He paused. "You're asking Kay about the post office box, but that's all she knows and she doesn't know much about that. Helene tells her to do something, she does it. It's that simple."

"Okay, let's start at the beginning, Brad. Tell me about Leah. How did you know she was dead?"

"I heard the announcement on the local news. I knew a woman was found dead and heard she'd been identified as Leah." Brad paused, sighed. "I met Leah in Spokane. I was in law school at Gonzaga, second year. It's grueling, law school. We used to cut loose on weekends just to feel normal for a few hours. We were at a party off campus. I knew she was young, too young for me, but we just hit it off. We really clicked. I'm kind of young for my age, I guess, and Leah was wiser than her years. I guess we connected somewhere in the middle. We spent a lot of time together before she told me she was sixteen and a runaway from Tri Cities. By that time, I cared for her a lot. I offered to help in any way I could. Not that I had much to offer, but at least I wasn't living on campus. Leah would stay with me for a while then she'd take off." It sounded similar to what Leah's mom, Connie, had to say about her staying on the move.

"She'd keep in touch so I knew she cared. She wanted me to concentrate on law school and finish," he said. "When we were together, it was great though. We were a good couple. She made it easier for me to work. She didn't distract, you know? She was supportive."

Liz nodded. "Go on."

"I finally finished law school and completed an internship clerking for a judge. He was an asshole, but I finished it, with a letter of rec. I moved back here. Dad put me on the payroll at CER. Mostly paperwork any para could do but it's a paycheck until I pass the bar. I haven't yet." His account of law school and the bar exam matched his father's. Liz gave the guy points for honesty, at least about that.

"Anyway, Leah spent time here with me, on and off, but we weren't into the family thing. She never met my Dad or my sister, or Kay. Kay's like family. I never met Leah's mom but she told me a lot about her. We just hung out, spent time together. We would hang out with friends. I was happy to be with her on her terms. Then she'd leave again. And she would, I knew that. How would I explain that to my Dad, anyway?"

"After I moved back here and worked at CER a few months, I started seeing some weird shit I couldn't explain. I'd ask Helene and get ridiculous answers. She really thinks I'm an idiot wastoid. I'd take notes and make copies of questionable items. I tried to ask my Dad a few times, if he was aware of how Helene was running things. He'd say, 'That's interesting because Helene says you're running things, Brad'."

"Describe what you mean by weird shit at CER," Liz asked him.

"The accounting was messed up. I'd see receipts off the charts but couldn't match them to deposits in the corporate account. Then I started reading odd correspondence from Michelle. She was asking why we were bothering to contract with her. I couldn't explain any of it."

"Michelle?" asked Liz

"Michelle Porter," he answered quickly. "She's a social worker with a counseling practice here in town. CER contracts with her for home studies, interviews of birth mothers and adoptive families and recommendations based on her findings. Her number one objective is to determine fitness of adoptive parents, and number two, ensure that birth mothers make informed decisions about relinquishment. She said it came to her attention that CER was placing infants without regard to her recommendations and sometimes in direct opposition to them."

Brad continued, "I called Michelle. She was surprised to hear from me. She had left many, many messages for Helene and been blown off. Not one call returned. Michelle was actually drafting a letter to dissolve the working relationship between her practice and CER. When I confronted Helene, she had the nerve to tell me that she 'wasn't finding Michelle's recommendations all that necessary anymore'."

"Okay, this is all good info and I want to hear all of it, but let's get back to Leah," Liz said.

He took a deep breath, resumed talking. "Leah...shit, man..."

"Are you okay, Brad?" Liz checked. Brad's eyes teared up and his lower lip trembled. He was obviously having a hard time continuing but he insisted.

"Yes, I'm okay. It's all tied together, Detective, all of this." He paused for a moment. "So, I'm sure that by now you've discovered that Leah had a baby in August. She didn't even tell me she was pregnant, Detective. She just said she needed to go home, wanted to spend some time with her mother," he said. "We didn't see each other for months."

"I have to ask," Liz said. "Brad, is the child yours?"

"Yes." He was struggling to hold it together and was managing, somehow. "I didn't know she was pregnant until early summer. Leah knew where I was working, that CER was my father's business. She knew what kind of legal services CER provided: private adoptions. She contacted CER from Tri Cities and began the process. Maybe she trusted us because of me. Jeez, how can I live with that? Anyway, when I found out, I begged her to reconsider. I offered to take care of her and the child, but she refused."

"Leah said she always felt so sorry for her mom, struggling to raise her. She felt guilty that her mom had such a difficult life and she didn't want her child to go through that. Leah wanted me to study, pass the bar and practice law. She said I had worked too hard to not see it happen and an instant family wasn't in that game plan."

"Did Michelle Porter interview Leah?" asked Liz.

"Yes. When I read Michelle's report on Leah's it was so typical of her: strong, decisive, and in control. She knew what she wanted to do. She never named the father of her child. When I finally was able to reach Leah by phone, I asked her, again, if anything I could say would change her mind. She was adamant. She didn't want me to intervene. Said it would be worse for all of us in the long run. Most of all, she didn't want my family to know that the baby was mine. She said if I told them they wouldn't take it well and I'd never forgive myself."

Brad paused, thoughtfully. "But Leah sounded different in some way and became really curious about things. She asked me about my father's business practices, about Helene, about CER. Then Leah asked me if I trusted Michelle."

"Do you believe that Michelle Porter will back up what you're telling me?" Liz would need to speak with her soon.

"I don't know why she wouldn't. She's always been straight, very professional. And, as far as I know, she and Leah were honest with each other," he said. "So," he continued, "Leah had made up her mind and wouldn't be dissuaded so I backed off. I consoled myself by remembering that, at least, I'd know where the baby was and would actually have a hand in choosing the best family for adoption. It wasn't much consolation but I was trying my best to deal with it. Then Helene made a decision on a family for Leah's baby," he said coldly. "The Benedicts."

"Yes, I have some information on them. Go on," said Liz.

"Michelle was livid. She said she was not in agreement with the decision, and knew that Leah would feel the same. Paternal age and maternal health history, she said. Helene just said 'Too bad.' I tried to reason with Helene. My bitch of a sister told me to butt out, it was a decision 'above my pay grade,' and why did I care anyway? Soon after, Leah delivered a healthy baby. A boy," said Brad, explaining that his son had been born.

"Sergeant Jordan, I've never seen him. A week or so later I was in the office when Kay came in with a package. I noticed Leah's name on the return address. It didn't take much to connect the overnight from Leah and the next day courier to the Benedicts' home to know what it was. I wasn't surprised. It was the kind of thing she'd do."

"You connected the dots yourself?" asked Liz.

"Well, it had been done before. The overnights and the courier accounts are right there. I can access any of it," he answered. "I was sure Kay knew nothing, so I didn't ask her. Then a few weeks later, there was a dust-up in the office. Helene discovered from the courier that an overnight package from Leah had been picked up at an address here in Columbia City. Helene freaked. She said that Leah hadn't kept her end of the agreement. Helene notified the Benedicts and advised them to stop receiving the packages. I don't know why she even cared," he said.

"I didn't hear from Leah again, for weeks. Not until after she had hired an attorney and decided to sue CER. She called me. She wanted to apologize, told me that she didn't blame me. She was concerned about the baby's placement. She said she knew Helene had lied to her and that it wasn't okay."

Brad went on, "I asked if that's why she had been back in town. This caught her off guard. She was concerned that she had been found out, but admitted it. I told her she could have stayed with me. She laughed. She said, 'Geez Bee, stay with you while I'm preparing to sue CER. Now, that would be interesting.' I told her how sorry I was about everything. Leah insisted it wasn't my fault, that it was her decision."

"Leah called you Bee?" Liz asked Brad.

"Everyone does," he said with a half grin. "Friends do, at least. It's been a nickname since college."

"We let things chill for a few weeks, Leah and myself. I'd been doing a lot of thinking about things," he said. "…Dad, his integrity and the businesses he built. I thought about my sister and how much she had pissed on my Dad, me, our clients, most of all, on Leah and the baby. And I started to worry about my own future, Detective. Finally, I got in touch with Leah and asked if she wanted to visit for a few days. We talked a lot while she was here. We discussed her lawsuit."

"I assured her that neither I nor my father were responsible for the way the adoptions, hers and many others, were handled. She said she knew that. I don't know how she knew it, but Leah's problem was with Helene, at that point. It turns out that the way the adoption papers were worded, all legal responsibility was placed with my father. I'm still trying to figure out how Helene managed that. My father didn't deserve this. Neither did our clients."

"Leah came back here and stayed with you? Can you tell me exactly how long, how many days?" Liz asked Brad.

"She arrived Wednesday, last week, by train. I picked her up at the station. She stayed with me until Friday," he answered. "Leah told me she was headed back to her mom's in Richland. That was Friday morning. I found out later she didn't leave town that day. If only she had," he groaned, miserable.

Liz asked him, "Did you see Leah after that?"

"Yes, but only for a little while. Saturday afternoon." That aligned with Malachi's statement. "I was in the office catching up on paperwork. Leah called and asked if she could buy me coffee." He smiled at the memory, but the happiness was fleeting. "I was surprised she was still in town. I asked her where the hell she was staying and she said The Suite. Leah had told me that the women's room at Avalon is called The Suite. She thought that was great. She said she planned to be there only a few days. She didn't want me to pick her up there. We met near the park since it's kind of on my way home. We just went for a drive. I had coffee. Leah still wasn't doing caffeine. Mint tea," he explained. That would fit. He could drive from CER to his apartment taking that route. And the other details fit.

"What did you and Leah talk about?"

"Leah was determined to confront Helene. I asked her, please, to let it go. Let the lawsuit deal with Helene. Actually, I advised her not to have contact with Helene, and that her attorney would agree." Liz nodded, but remembered that Diana Harrison's distrust was directed, not at Helene, but at her father. Had Helene engineered it that way? Had someone else?

Liz had to ask, "Would you say it was a calm chat or a heated discussion?"

"I'd say we were both insistent about our points of view. Leah could have been a great litigator, I tell you," he said, thinking of her. "I had to get home to change for dinner with my Dad that evening. She agreed not to confront Helene until we talked again." More details fit. The argument Malachi heard on Saturday and the awards dinner. And with that, Brad Ridgeman became very sad, realizing that he and Leah Bishop didn't speak again before she died.

Chapter 38

Liz continued the discussion by asking a few more pointed questions. "Okay, Brad. I want to ask you about a couple of other people. Do you know of a woman named Candy Schinde?"

"Yes." He thought for a moment before he continued. "I knew her in Spokane. She was a friend of Leah's. I'm not sure how long they'd known each other. According to Leah, Candy found out she was pregnant well into her second trimester. She was terrified to care for a child and decided on adoption. Leah told her to contact CER to arrange it. Candy was a mess. The poor girl was so, so sick. After the baby was born, the heartless people my sister chose to place the baby with refused to take her. Candy was heartbroken."

Brad continued, "I told her we would find a good placement for her baby, if she could give us some time. Helene told her to get lost, that we couldn't place a sick infant. I couldn't believe it." That closely jibed with Diana Harrison's account of Candy's dealings with CER. Candy's note told a similar tale but she had been unsure who was to blame.

"When did you last see Candy?" Liz asked him, careful not to provide any details of Candy leaving town and leaving her baby at Avalon. "Do you know where she is staying?"

"The last time I saw her was the meeting at CER when Helene told her the adoption was off. I don't know where she's staying, somewhere safe, I hope," he said. Yeah, thought Liz. I hope so, too. At least we know her baby is safe.

Liz continued, "Brad, do you know a guy named Malachi Evanson?"

Brad seemed a little surprised but not evasive and replied, "l know a guy named Malachi. He's an okay guy. He's got his problems, but he's okay. I've not heard his last name before. He knew Leah, too," he said. "Here's a story. Once I warned Leah that Malachi liked her. She rolled her eyes at me and laughed, said 'No, no, I'm definitely not his type.' She was trying to clue me in to the fact that Malachi prefers guys."

"When did you last talk to Malachi?" she asked.

"Sunday morning. We had coffee." he answered. "Why? Is he okay?"

"Yes, he's okay." She didn't mention detox. "Does he call you Bee?"

"Yes, he does. I don't think he even knows my name," Brad told her.

"How did you meet up with Malachi on Sunday?"

"I went to find him. It's not hard to do. He's usually in one of a few places."

"Why did you want to find him?" Liz asked Brad.

Brad sighed. "I wanted to find Leah. I was worried. Saturday evening got kind of weird. I was hoping he might have seen her." That fits, thought Liz.

"How did things get weird on Saturday evening?"

"I attended a dinner for my father. He was honored by a community group. I like to attend those events for him. It means a lot to him. Helene attended, as well. Toward the end of the evening, my father became ill," he explained. "My sister drove him home, but she insisted on trading cars with me. She said Dad would be more comfortable in the larger vehicle. I have an SUV. Helene's car is nice but it is small and low to sit in."

"So, you agreed with her point about your Dad's comfort. Had she ever asked to trade vehicles before for a similar reason?" Liz asked.

"She had a point, yes. But no, Helene had never asked to drive my car before." He sounded amused at the idea. "Then she calls me about Dad's award. She said he was concerned about leaving the dinner without it. I told her I was leaving shortly and would stop by with it. She hesitated, as if it was up to her if I stop by Dad's. I was about to ask, 'What's the problem, Helene?' but she said, okay, she'd wait."

"I was here, at Dad's, within an hour. Helene met me at the door. I handed her Dad's award. Kay was asleep, she said. Helene was staying the night to be sure Dad was okay in the morning. She had already put my car in Dad's garage and locked up so we decided to switch back cars the next day."

"The next day, meaning Sunday," clarified Liz.

"Yes," Brad answered, "except that I couldn't reach Helene on Sunday."

"So, when did you switch cars? And tell me where and how," said Liz.

"It was Monday morning, at CER. I was at my desk. She stopped in on her way to her office downtown. We just exchanged keys."

"Did you talk to Helene?"

"I said thanks for not getting back to me yesterday after I left about four messages. The last message just said I'll be at work in the morning. If she wanted her car back, it'd be there." He said, "I wasn't happy she was dissing me, but it's not unusual."

"What did she say? When you saw Helene at CER?"

"She said something along the lines of, 'Here's your POS'. That means Piece of Shit, and 'I'm so glad to have my car again.' Helene was unpleasant, as usual."

"I know what a POS is, thanks. I've owned a few," Liz told him.

"Then I told her I'd drive her Mercedes anytime. She left."

Liz thought back to her conversation with Malachi. She hadn't taken notes because she had it recorded. She remembered, though, that he claimed to have seen Bee's car pull out from near the park on Sunday morning. But, he had not seen Bee driving it.

"Brad, listen carefully to my next question. From the time you left the award dinner until Monday morning at CER, you were not in possession of your vehicle, correct?"

"That's right," he answered.

"And you didn't see Helene from the time you went to your father's home on Saturday evening until Monday morning at CER?"

"Like I said, I left messages for her. She never returned my call. I gave up, figured she could deal with it. My sister can be a real bitch, Detective."

"And that's why Saturday evening was weird? Trading cars?"

"Well, yes...but I kept thinking about Leah. And how she encouraged me to study for the bar exam. It's coming up in a few months. I use a room at CER to study. There's a law library there. I have everything I need to focus on studying. And on the weekends the place is empty, so I'm not disturbed," he explained, and continued. "When I left Dad's, I wasn't tired. I didn't feel like sleep. Actually, I felt motivated. I decided to use the energy to study. I headed straight to CER and hit the books."

"How long did you study, Brad?"

He sighed, thought about it. "I got there about ten p.m. Made coffee. I worked until about four, maybe four-thirty. I slept on the couch there. When I woke up about nine, I was kind of a mess, Detective. Hadn't changed or showered. I wanted coffee. Thought of Malachi, wondered if he'd seen Leah. I wanted to find her. I just felt like I wanted to know she was okay. Shit..."

He teared up again, rubbed his face with his hands.

"That's when you went to find Malachi?" He nodded.

"And you were driving Helene's car until Monday morning after you had started your workday at CER?" He nodded. Brad appeared to be thinking about something, something he was working out in his head, something he didn't like.

"Is there anyone able to confirm this? That you went to your office at CER to study? That you were there until after nine the next morning? That you were driving Helene's car until Monday?" Brad was thinking about it. He appeared hesitant to answer. "Listen," Liz prodded, "it would help the case a lot if we can confirm your whereabouts and what vehicle you were driving during that time frame. If you can do so, I'd recommend it. So, what have you got?"

"Well, there's an entry pad into the building, of course. But it's a single code. We all use the same one." Brad paused again, hesitated.

"I'm waiting, Brad."

"Okay, okay...the office isn't in the best part of town... and there's a variety of clients and professionals coming and going... so, I had a surveillance camera installed near the parking lot a few weeks ago, for everyone's protection. Helene went ballistic about the cost when I got the estimate. She doesn't know I went ahead and had the system installed. I figured she'd see the invoice eventually. I'd deal with her then."

"And I can access the videos?" Liz asked. "Are they on discs?"

"No, Detective. Data is uploaded to an internet server. More secure that way," he said. Exactly, thought Liz. Damn near tamper-proof. And if the surveillance video didn't support what Brad was saying, he wouldn't have mentioned it.

Chapter 39

Liz conferred privately with Connors. "My money is on one of two people, either Brad or Helene, as Leah's killer. If we can play this right, based on the evidence, the guilty one will crack it for us," Liz explained. Connors agreed, but a detail was nagging at him so when they returned to where Brad was waiting, he directed the question to Brad himself.

"Mr. Ridgeman, I saw the award your father received on Saturday at his office this morning. It's a beautiful piece. He said he was touched to receive it. Do you know how it got to your father's office?"

"He took it to the office with him, I guess...that's why I dropped it by after the dinner," he said, sounding confused. "Why?" Connors and Liz exchanged glances. Liz wasn't sure where Connors was going but she deferred, trusting him.

"Your father is under the impression that you brought his award to his office just this morning, Tuesday morning. Do you have any idea why he would think that?" Connors asked.

"I don't, Officer. I haven't seen that award since I gave it to Helene at the door to Dad's house." he told them. "Actually, I haven't seen it since the committee chairman placed it back in the box."

"The award was in a box?" Connors asked.

"Yes. At least it was when I brought it here. It was still on display on the dais when I asked to take it to Dad. The chairman put it back in the box it came in from the engraver. To protect it, she said."

"And you didn't take it out of the box?" asked Connors.

He shook his head no and said, "I didn't even open the box."

Liz looked at Connors and said, "Let's keep that as our secret, shall we?"

Liz asked Brad Ridgeman and Kay Sutton if they would both be willing to give formal statements at the precinct regarding the information they had shared with her. She would appreciate it if Kay could manage this within a day or two.

When they were alone, Liz addressed Brad again. "Brad, I have to tell you something," said Liz. "Your SUV was seen near the park in the Beau on Sunday morning. But you say that you can prove with surveillance video that the SUV was in Helene's possession until Monday. Is your car here, right now?"

"Yes. It's in the garage. Why?" he asked. Brad sounded worried, so Liz explained what she was thinking.

"I'd like you to voluntarily submit your SUV to impound. I think we need to have it examined for trace evidence."

"You think Helene killed Leah." Brad said it as a statement, not a question.

"Possibly," Liz went on, "and I think she wants us to think you killed her. I want to rule out the possibility that you could have."

"Oh, my God...Leah," said Brad, stunned, reality sinking in.

"So, here's the deal. With your permission, techs will check out your car. They may find something if the evidence hasn't been destroyed or compromised. And, as a precaution, I'd like to take you into protective custody as a witness, until we have your statement for the record. And you'll be talking only to me or Officer Connors."

Brad looked at her. "You want to offer me protection as a

witness, but you aren't charging me with anything. And you want me to offer up my personal vehicle for an evidence search. Do I understand you, Detective?" asked Brad.

"Yes, that's right. You can agree or we can wait for a subpoena. But I'll get the subpoena. I think you know that. Your cooperation could go a long way," Liz said, sure of herself. *And*...thought Liz to herself, *I need to create an illusion. I want to see how Helene reacts if she thinks Brad's been suspected of Leah's murder. And, further, how cooperative will Brad be?*

Brad was thinking, looking from Liz to Connors, back to Liz. "Detective, I'll agree to all that. I'll do whatever I can. I owe Leah that much. And I know I didn't hurt her." He paused. "But there's something else you should know. I said earlier that I saw weird things happening at CER. I mentioned that I made notes and copies of questionable documents."

"Yes, you did," said Liz, wondering where he was going with this.

"Well, when I saw Leah on Friday, when she said she was heading back to her mom's. I gave her a copy of a document. It was a copy of a money order that was paid to CER. I knew it was from the Benedicts, but I told her I couldn't prove that. Any judge would call it circumstantial."

"Then why did you give it to her?" they asked him.

"Because according to records," he explained, "the Benedicts paid 10K to CER for legal services and 8K to Leah for her expenses. The money order brought that total up to much more. And Leah told me she was given a check for $18,000. That's outside an acceptable range, Detective. I wanted her to have another piece of the truth, I guess." So, Brad had given Leah the copy of the money order. Liz was hoping Miles Carey, the financial sleuth, would link it to the Benedicts.

"You're pretty calm. Weren't you, aren't you now, worried

about being accused of collusion in all this?" Liz really wanted to know. "You're on staff at CER, after all."

"Yes, that's true." He hesitated. "But I haven't done anything illegal. And there's a whistleblower law. Besides, I'm not a licensed attorney, Detective. I'm only on staff. It's my father I was hoping to protect."

"By helping Leah?" Liz was confused now.

"Well, Detective...I made copies of a lot of documents, pertaining to many, many adoptions."

Liz's phone rang. It was Diana Harrison. She would be at the morgue with Connie Bishop in one hour.

Chapter 40

Liz and Connors organized themselves while they had Cryer keep an eye on Kay Sutton and Brad. Connors checked in with the eyes watching Helene and Brad's father. Helene had been at the law firm office until lunch and then at the courthouse. Carl had been in the office all day.

Trace evidence techs came for Brad's SUV, giving him a receipt, which he signed. Liz wanted a professional to deliver the vehicle to the lab, hoping to avoid problems with potential evidence. Connors took Brad into custody as a witness. Connors and Cryer headed to the precinct with him, with strict instructions that Brad was to be placed in a room. He was to have no contact with anyone, except Liz or Connors. Connors would settle Brad into a room and check in with Gibson to see what he had been able to come up with on the granite award. Brad would contact his surveillance company and request surveillance from the time in question.

Connors would then have Brad repeat his conversation with Liz for the official record. At some point soon, it would become his signed statement. Liz agreed to let Brad check messages, as long as he responded only to those which were work related. If it appeared he was conducting business as usual it would add to the illusion. Liz asked him not to contact either of the legal offices, Helene, or his father.

Liz agreed that Kathryn, or Kay, could give her statement at a later time -- as long as she was on the record within the next day or two. The only detail Liz was interested in, anyway, was that it had been Helene who had asked Kay to use the post office box to receive items on the sly, and then drop them at CER. Clearly, Kay was more concerned about her domestic duties for the Ridgemans than in her civic duty to make a statement involving a murder investigation. The degree of loyalty was puzzling, but Liz had had limited experience with domestic servants.

Liz headed to the morgue. On the way, she revisited the conversation she and Diana had had by phone with Leah's mother, Connie. She wondered how she was doing. Even if she was doing fairly well, the visit to the morgue and seeing Leah's body would set her back. Liz felt for the woman, as she always did when heading to the morgue to assist a family.

She pulled into the parking structure, parked, and stepped out of her vehicle. Her thoughts were on Leah and with her mother, Connie Bishop. As Liz turned, she collided with none other than Myers, himself. Myers was as stunned as Liz. He dropped the file he carried. Papers scattered.

"What exactly is wrong with you, Detective?" Myers exclaimed, glaring. "Are you incapable of navigating your way in and out of buildings without creating an incident?" He was red-faced but didn't break a sweat. He was angry as he knelt to retrieve his files.

"What's wrong with me? Don't you watch where you're going?" Liz was shocked to have collided with someone and irritated that it had turned out to be Myers. She knelt instinctively to help pick up papers. "Do you expect everyone to just move out of your way, like you're special or something?"

"What I expect," Myers stated, as calmly as possible, as he snatched papers from Liz's hands, "is to make my way safely to my vehicle without being unexpectedly assaulted by a moron with no physical control over their being! Get out of my way, Detective!" Myers was trying to organize his papers as he stomped away from Liz.

"You're the moron, Myers!" Liz yelled after the pathologist. "And one day soon I'm going to kick your ass! Or should I say, I'm going to kick your ass *again!*" Liz turned and leaned against her car, hands splayed. Her heart was beating wildly, from surprise and from anger, maybe from embarrassment, too. A couple of deep breaths would help. *Calm, calm,* she thought. *You're heading into a meeting with a grieving mother.* Why did she have to run into Myers? Literally, run into Myers – and right now? As unfair as it was to Connie Bishop, all Liz could think of at that moment was how much she hated Myers.

After a minute or two, Liz walked to the entrance and into the building. When she turned the corner into the waiting area, she saw Diana Harrison. There were two women with her. They were huddled together, more for privacy it appeared to Liz, than support. The woman in the middle was a couple of inches shorter than Liz. She was slender but not rail thin. Liz thought they may have met. Then Liz realized why the woman looked familiar; it must be Leah's mother because Connie Bishop was an older version of Leah's ID photo. They wore their hair in a similar style. Connie's hair was a shade or two lighter in color than her daughter's had been. The eyes were the same. The other woman was shorter, blonde and slightly heavier.

"Diana," said Liz as a greeting to the attorney. The two women shook hands, and then Liz extended her hand to the woman whom she had determined was Connie. "Ms. Bishop, I'm Detective Jordan. We spoke last night. I'm sorry to meet you under these circumstances." Connie answered hello while she shook Liz's hand. Then she introduced Liz to her friend, Ginny. Liz said hello and shook hands with the blonde woman. "I hope you haven't been waiting for me long," said Liz.

It was Diana who spoke. "No, Detective, we just arrived a few minutes ago and told the staff we're here. We were just talking about how we wanted to wait for you." They turned as an automatic door opened and into the corridor stepped Dr. Stein.

As he approached Connie, he said, "Are you Ms. Bishop?" Connie said that she was. Stein introduced himself, and indicated the sofa to their left. "Let's sit for a minute." Liz noticed that Stein spoke only to Connie, focusing his attention on the grieving mother. He and Connie sat, the other three remained standing.

"I want you to understand, Ms. Bishop, this isn't going to be easy," Stein told her, "but you have friends with you." Connie nodded. "Are you ready to go in and see her?" Connie said that she was, and took a breath. "Okay," said the Chief Medical Examiner, "I'm going to let you stand next to her, not through the glass. I can't allow you to touch her. After you see her, we'll go to my office. There are a couple of documents I need to ask you to sign, okay?" Connie nodded again, said thank you.

Stein stood and then waited for Connie to stand. She was flanked by Diana and Ginny as they followed him through the same doorway through which he'd come. Liz followed. Stein led them to a small, plain, less laboratory-like room that Liz had not been in before. There were no other bodies in the room. On a table was Leah's body, covered with a sheet.

They approached, Diana supporting Connie, Liz now supporting Ginny. Stein pulled the sheet back from Leah's face, one shoulder showing, careful not to reveal the Y incision made at autopsy. From this angle, the head wound was not as noticeable as when Liz had been with her in the alley. Connie looked at Leah. Even in death, as Liz had noted on Sunday, one could tell that Leah had been a nice looking young woman. Tears formed and fell slowly from Connie's eyes. She cried silently. Diana handed her a tissue and she dabbed her eyes and cheeks.

Without a word, she nodded her head, looked at Stein, and

then turned away. Ginny, sensing the worst was over, found her strength and took her place by her friend. Diana led the two women away from Leah's body. Liz and Stein looked at each other, shared a moment, like they had many times before. He gently covered Leah and they followed him to his office.

In Stein's office, Liz assured Connie she was looking closely into Leah death. Connie told her, "Yes, I know you are. Diana says everyone is working very hard. Thank you."

"If you have questions, please call and I'll try to answer them for you." She handed Connie her card. "And I need to get back to work. It may be necessary to speak with you at some point. Will that be okay?"

"Yes. Diana will know where I am," she said.

Liz nodded and looked at Diana. "Can I speak to you for a moment?"

Diana followed Liz out of Stein's office. "Thank goodness that's over. I feel badly for Connie. How are things going, Liz? Will you find who did this?" asked Diana.

"Yes, I think we already have, but it's too soon to talk about it," Liz answered. "I appreciated the information about Helene Ridgeman this morning, from your secretary. But I wanted to ask you, have you ever met her brother, Brad?"

"On a few occasions," Diana answered. "He hasn't been around long and I don't believe he's practicing yet. I know he's working at CER, admin and paralegal-type work. Why?"

"Just wanting your general impression, if you had formed one," answered Liz, and asked another question. "In any of your conversations with Helene, has she ever mentioned her brother?"

Diana studied Liz as she thought about the question, her attorney's mind trying to figure out the reason it was asked. "Not that I remember. We don't have chats of that nature."

"You attended the awards dinner Saturday evening, didn't you?" asked Liz.

"That's right," replied Diana.

"Helene and her brother were both there, as well," said Liz. "Did you speak with them?"

"Yes, I saw them. Just hello and a handshake," she responded.

"Anything you noticed that comes to mind that might be significant?" Liz asked and then apologized. "Sorry, I know it's a strange question. I don't have another way to phrase it. This is a strange case."

"Well, honestly, I don't know them well enough to judge if anything was significant," the attorney answered. "Can I ask where you're going with this, Detective?"

Liz shook her head and answered, "Nothing I can tell you at this time. I'll let you get back to Connie Bishop. Let her know for me that I'll be in touch as soon as I have any information." Liz turned and left, headed to the precinct on the other side of the complex.

When she arrived, Liz found Connors with Brad in one of the interview rooms. The blinds were closed and they were reviewing surveillance video over cups of coffee. It reminded Liz of two nerdy teenagers hunched over an Xbox, playing games.

"Great set up, Sergeant," the young officer told her. "Brad called the company, identified himself as the account subscriber. After verifying password information, they emailed the video directly. It took them about a minute and a half. Brad had them send the same download to my work email. So we already have the video we need. As Brad said, it clearly shows him driving Helene's Mercedes and the time stamps sync with Brad's account of things. It also shows Helene returning Brad's SUV on Monday morning and retrieving her Mercedes."

Connors clearly was impressed with the surveillance system. "With this capability, there's no excuse for useless surveillance video that's been recorded over. That is, if people are willing to invest a little more in their own protection."

Liz nodded and said, "No doubt Brad has already figured that out." The video of him at CER on Sunday morning proves he didn't have his own vehicle, and proves Helene had the SUV until Monday. "Let's see what Trace comes up with. Have you checked with Gibson since you've been on site?" Connors had not, so Liz suggested they walk over together. She wanted a few moments alone with Connors.

"How did the viewing go for Leah's mother?" asked Connors, who realized it was a dumb question, but more than anything, it let Liz know that the officer's thoughts had been with the family of the deceased.

"As well as you could expect, I guess," replied Liz, trying not to think about the run-in with Myers. "Stein handled it well. Leah's mother had a friend with her who accompanied her from Richland, and Diana Harrison was there for support. I told Ms. Bishop we'd be in touch as soon as possible with any developments." Hopefully to inform her we've made an arrest, thought Liz.

"Let me ask you a question. How did Brad seem to you after you left his father's home?" asked Liz.

"He was cooperative. He's mourning Leah and he's worried about his father." Connors paused and then continued. "He's also really upset that his sister has been using the adoption services that CER provides as a way of making a lot of money for herself. He doesn't see any other explanation for the activity he's been seeing. That's why he started to make copies of documents."

"Smarter than we assumed," said Liz, and she thought for a moment. "I know he's been cooperative, but let's not assume too much. We listen to indisputable evidence, short of a flat out confession. The video narrows the time frame, certainly for Brad. But it doesn't clear either Brad or Helene from suspicion, nor does it condemn either of them. We don't know where Brad was after he left Malachi on Sunday morning. He needs an alibi that we can confirm. He told Malachi he was going home to crash. He says he tried to reach Helene several times. We don't know where Helene was on Sunday. We know that Brad's car was seen in the vicinity of Leah's murder at the time she died, and we think it was in Helene's possession."

"But we can't prove it yet. I follow you, Sergeant, but either she did it, or the sighting of the SUV was a coincidence." Connors clearly didn't believe the coincidence theory. "That's hard to swallow because Malachi found Leah dead in the alley right after."

"And that is why they call it circumstantial evidence, Connors. Just ask any defense attorney. Let's see what Gibson says," Liz said, as they walked into the crime lab, in search of Alan Gibson.

Chapter 41

"Detective, someone tried to clean this piece of granite, but they didn't do a thorough enough job," said Gibson. "I found minute traces of blood on the rough, unpolished edge, just sufficient to test, and they match your victim. In my opinion, this was the murder weapon, but that doesn't surprise any of us, given the dimensions and weight of the object. What you want to know is that I've lifted a few partial fingerprints. From three or four individuals, I'd say. There are two sets I haven't identified, however, I can tell you that both Carl Ridgeman and Helene Ridgeman handled this object. I'm finding no prints belonging to Brad Ridgeman."

Bingo, thought Liz. But don't rush yourself, she said silently. Stay focused.

"We have witnesses who saw Carl Ridgeman holding the award at the dinner after it was presented to him. And we were told that the chair of the committee handled it. We were told she placed it back in the box for Brad. It may have been the same person who handed it to Carl." Liz was thinking aloud. Both Connors and Gibson were following her thought process.

"Get me exemplars, I'll tell you if one of the contributors was this committee chair," said Gibson. "Shouldn't be too difficult, right, Detective? And I'll keep searching for the other contributor."

Those prints, and any trace evidence from the SUV, were the remaining pieces. Gibson would get a message to Liz as soon as the techs were finished. They were ready to move.

Liz had duty officers contact both Helene Ridgeman and her father with urgent requests for them to please come down to the precinct and ask for Detective Sergeant Liz Jordan. The detectives watching were told to stay on them until they were inside the station house. When told they had arrived, Liz had them placed together in an interview room. She waited about fifteen minutes before she and Connors entered the room.

"Detective, where's Brad?" asked Carl. "He was to contact you and I haven't heard from him. Did you meet with him?" Ridgeman was clearly worried. Helene was sitting near her father, with her hand on his shoulder.

"Detective Jordan, I realize you have a job to do, but this is causing my father some distress," she said. "Can you just tell us if you've talked with Brad?" Helene almost sounded bored.

Liz and Connors exchanged glances and sat down. "Yes. We've talked with Brad at some length. That's why I've asked you both here. I have a few additional questions and I'd like to record our conversation, if you'll agree to that." Carl mumbled something that sounded like an agreement.

Helene looked at Liz blankly, and asked, "Certainly, whatever we can do to assist you. But after the extended meeting earlier today, what could you possibly have missed?"

"Well, Brad was able to fill in some details, but to be honest, the situation isn't looking good for Brad," Liz told them. "Actually, he's been detained as a person of interest. I'm hoping the two of you can provide some clarification -- to avoid our taking the next step."

"What next step? What do you mean?" Carl asked, incredulously.

"His arrest," she said plainly, "for the murder of Leah Bishop."

Carl Ridgeman turned a shade paler, and said, "Oh, my God, Helene."

Helene looked at Liz and then at Connors. She turned to her father and patted his shoulder with the hand that hadn't left it, and said, "Detective, there has to be some mistake. I know my brother. He's not capable of this."

"Don't misunderstand. He hasn't been charged. Yet," Liz told her.

"But I'd like to talk to him. As his attorney, you understand," said Helene. Ever the supportive sister, thought Liz.

"Again, he hasn't been charged," Liz responded, pointedly. "And Brad hasn't asked to speak with his attorney. If he hasn't been charged and hasn't asked for counsel, we don't have to let him talk to anyone."

"Detective, how can we help you?" It was Carl who asked the question.

"We have other questions about how Leah Bishop's adoption was handled. And about Leah, herself," said Liz. "Were either of you aware that Brad was acquainted with Leah, long before she needed arrangements for a private adoption?"

"I find that hard to believe," said Carl. "How would Brad have known this young woman?" Liz waited for Helene's response. Would she go for the truth here? Or would she bluff? Helene looked at her father, patting his shoulder again.

"Yes," she answered with a sigh, going for truth. "I knew. I saw them together a few times, after the adoption of her child. I never confronted Brad about it. I can't honestly say that the impropriety would have occurred to him." Helene's father was shocked by her words.

"What? Helene, how can you say that? Brad knows better than that. What was the situation where they were seen? It must have been professional," he decided.

"Dad, I don't think it was professional. They were friends. Maybe good friends, it seemed," she said, as if embarrassed for her brother. "Actually, I saw them coming out of Brad's apartment. It was a work day. I needed to go by one morning, something for work. When I saw them I left quickly. I had hoped without being seen."

"You said you never confronted Brad, Ms. Ridgeman. Did you ask Leah Bishop if she knew your brother outside of being a client of CER?" asked Liz.

"No," Helene answered. "I knew she did. I'd seen them together." She's sticking with the truth, thought Liz, but defensive.

"Ms. Ridgeman, you had no conversations with Leah Bishop about knowing your brother?" Liz asked again, to clarify.

"No, Detective, I did not. But you said Brad may have known her long before we arranged for her adoption. Why do you think that?" Helene asked Liz.

"We'll come back to that," said Liz, cutting her off. "When we talked earlier you gave us numbers estimating what fees run for private adoptions. You gave me a ballpark of $12,000 to $20,000 per adoption. Is that still your estimate?"

Helen looked Liz in the eye and said, "Yes, on average."

Liz returned the look and asked her, "Then can you explain how the adoption of Leah's child resulted in payments to Leah and to CER totaling $50,000?"

"What? That's preposterous!" Carl Ridgeman was shocked. "I've seen the accounting reports. That's a ridiculous claim, Detective."

"Mr. Ridgeman, we have copies of the payments," Liz told him, "including a check for an exorbitant amount written directly to Leah Bishop for 'expenses' from the adoptive parents. We have a copy of a money order paid to CER that we're linking to them, and for much more than Helene has estimated fees to have been."

Helene did not look happy. "You're talking about one adoption, one family. It's probably some clerical error, Dad, an accounting glitch. We'll straighten it out."

"Good. That's good, Helene, and while you're at it, you can straighten out how the other $900,000 was collected in fees," Liz said, leaning forward on the table. "And also, tell your father where most of it is because we've discovered the payments to CER but not where you've hidden the funds."

"What has Brad told you?" Helene screamed at them as she stood and said to her father, "Dad, we're leaving!" Connors stood too, maintaining control of the room. Carl Ridgeman looked at his daughter as if she was a stranger to him.

Liz looked at Helene and said, "I suggest you sit back down, Ms. Ridgeman. We're far from finished here. Mr. Ridgeman," Liz explained, directing her attention to Helene's father, "we believe that Helene has been accepting huge fees from wealthy adopting families, many of whom have not been properly screened. In some cases, in direct opposition to what's been recommended."

Carl Ridgeman sat very still, no longer shocked, looking very sad. He held one hand over his mouth in a pose Liz had seen before. "How," he asked, "do you know this?"

"A fiscal investigator has been looking into things, Sir. And actually, Brad has had suspicions. He's been accumulating evidence, partly in his own defense, but mostly to protect you."

"The little shit! He won't have anything you can use! He's worthless. He's been worthless since the day he was born!" Helene said, laughing it away.

"Don't underestimate him, Helene. But let's move on to other issues," said Liz. "It's my belief that you confronted Leah Bishop about the lawsuit she filed against CER. When she refused to drop her claims, and knowing she had proof, you killed her."

"What? That's absurd!" she exclaimed.

"You switched cars with your brother Saturday evening. You had Brad bring the granite award to your father's home. You went down to the Beau Sunday morning in Brad's car, knowing that your Mercedes would attract attention. Brad's car was seen in the area at the time of Leah's death. You sought out Leah, you confronted her, and you killed her by blows to the head with your father's award. I'm not sure you planned on killing her. It may have been an impulse kill."

"Oh, no, no..." she muttered. No longer fueled by anger, Helene now was stunned. "The money's one thing, but murder? No, no, no...I did not..."

"We know you had Brad's car until Monday morning. We know you had the granite award with you at your father's house." Liz hammered her with the evidence. "Leah's blood was found on it as were your fingerprints, Helene."

"I had the award in my hands at the dinner, Detective. My father and I are both holding it in pictures." She was desperate to offer alternatives to what she was hearing from Liz. "And, yes, I used Brad's car. It was for Dad's comfort. He wasn't well. But I didn't go downtown on Sunday or confront Leah Bishop. And I certainly didn't kill her."

"Detective," said Carl, "did I hear you say that my son's SUV was seen downtown on Sunday, near where this young woman was killed?"

"Yes, Sir," Liz told him, "and I don't believe it was Brad driving it."

"Detective, I know Brad wasn't driving it, neither was Helene, although I'm not sure of much else regarding my daughter right now..." said Ridgeman. "Helene was at my home with me on Sunday until early afternoon, at least two p.m."

So, Helene has an alibi. She was with her father. "Dad, please listen to me..." begged Helene.

Carl Ridgeman put his hand up to silence his daughter and said, "Stop. I don't want to hear from you right now."

Liz's phone buzzed. She read the message on the display. It was from Gibson. "Matched set of prints to those on file from an assault case twenty years ago. They belong to a Kathryn Sutton."

Chapter 42

When Liz, Connors, and a uniformed officer named Curry returned to Carl Ridgeman's home, Kay Sutton answered the door. "I'm coming to your office tomorrow to answer your questions. I thought we agreed that that was sufficient. It will be quite convenient for me before I do the marketing."

"Plans have changed, Ms. Sutton," Liz told her. "Your fingerprints were found on what has been determined to be the weapon used to kill Leah Bishop."

Liz saw no reaction from Kay, except that she sounded inconvenienced. "I don't know what you're taking about, Detective," Kay said. "But if I must accompany you right this minute, fine."

Confronted with the evidence against her, Kathryn Sutton didn't request counsel. Her demeanor was calm and Liz wondered if the woman fully understood the situation she was in. She agreed to go with them, but asked that she be allowed to return to the kitchen for a moment. "I have Mr. Ridgeman's dinner in the oven, Detective. I'll need to take it off the heat before I leave the house," Kay explained.

Liz and Officer Curry followed Kay through the house to the kitchen. With her back to Liz, Kay reached the kitchen a step sooner. Before Liz could react, Kay had a knife in her hand. She grabbed Liz, pushed her against the counter, and placed the knife against Liz's throat.

Curry reached for her sidearm. "Please don't pull your weapon, young lady. I would be forced to harm your Sergeant," said Kay with eery calm. Curry made eye contact with Liz, who shook her head slightly to say, "Don't." Curry moved her hand away from her weapon. Liz thought of the weapon in the holster she wore under her left arm. Her right arm was pressed against the granite countertop. Her left arm was twisted behind her, against Kay's body. She couldn't draw the weapon from the position she was in. And, she hoped, neither could Kay.

"You don't think I would have accompanied you without a chance to explain, do you?" Kay sounded calm. Liz found it hard to believe the woman was holding a knife to the throat of a police officer. But as it happened to be Liz's throat, she believed it.

"All right, Kay. What do you want to explain? Can we just sit and talk at the table? We did that earlier, remember?" Liz was aware of the blade. She could feel it. She could feel Kay's hand holding it. Her hand was steady. Liz's mind raced. Her thoughts vacillated between panic and an attempt at a plan.

"Why is it so hard to understand how important it is to protect the family?" Kay asked them calmly.

Officer Curry was trying to engage Kay. She sounded empathetic, the way she had been trained to sound. "We do understand, Ma'am. We do. But if you hurt the Sergeant, you're only hurting yourself, too. And that won't help anyone else," Curry said.

Liz heard a dog barking. Was it the Ridgeman's dog, the one Liz had seen in the yard with the gardener? Under these circumstances, why did she care? And where the hell was Connors? Liz realized that Curry was talking to Kay but she was focused on a spot over Liz's right shoulder.

"Put down the knife, Kay. Put it down now. I have a gun

aimed at your head. I will shoot you unless you do as I ask." It was Connors.

Liz felt Kay move quickly. She shoved Liz forward, toward Officer Curry. The blade was away from Liz's throat and this was all Liz could focus on for a few moments. Liz turned around as Kay plunged the blade into the inside of her own left thigh.

The paramedics that arrived to stabilize and transport Kay insisted on checking Liz. She was unharmed except for a small scratch on her neck.

Liz learned later that when Connors realized what had occurred in the kitchen -- that their suspect was holding a knife to the neck of his Sergeant -- he darted back out the front entrance. After calling in for help, Connors made his way around the side of the house. He discovered French doors leading to Carl Ridgeman's master bedroom. The doors were unlocked, and one side was open. Mr. Ridgeman often left it that way for Coulee, the Lab.

Connors knew that Coulee's barking might alert Kay, but he decided to chance it. It turned out that Coulee was receptive to having a new friend. The barking was more of a greeting than a warning. Connors closed Coulee in the bedroom and silently crept up behind Kay. Unsure of how the situation would end, Connors had decided to do more than wait for help. As it turned out, he had probably saved Liz's life.

Within a couple of hours, they were notified that Kay was not badly injured. Her aim for her femoral artery had missed. She had lost blood and it was recommended she be observed overnight. Kay was treated and released to the authorities the next morning. She was charged with assault on a police officer.

Liz spent Tuesday evening with Mike. When he found out what happened, he insisted that she not be alone. They stopped by Liz's apartment to feed Eddie and Little Kurt. They ordered take-out and ate at the little breakfast bar in Mike's apartment. It helped Liz to talk over what had occurred over of the past few days. And it helped Mike, too. "I can't believe I sat across a kitchen table from a killer and didn't realize it, Mike. I'm having a hard time with that," Liz shared with her friend. "We might have avoided the whole incident."

Liz had trained on the basic behaviors of sociopaths, but she had not witnessed them, experienced them, until now. She remembered the cold manner, and steely nerve Kay displayed. Liz wondered what had occurred in Kay life to cause that level of emotional damage. Then she realized Mike was talking to her.

"You'll be required to talk to a department psychologist, right?" Mike asked. "I'm asking because you probably should, after what you've been through." Their eyes met. Liz nodded. "Ridgeman's son, Liz, he knew Leah for a long time. Sounds like he wanted to make a life with her but she resisted. He told you he fathered her baby?"

"Yes, although if he wants to pursue custody of the child, that will need to be proven with DNA," she answered. "The guy is so different from his sister. They both seem to have good relationships with their father, but different relationships. Helene seemed caring but more of an equal, certainly in the law firm, and had betrayed him. Brad needed more help from his Dad and is proving himself to be more loyal." Liz thought about it all for a moment, and then continued. "Helene has pissed it all away now. Her career, her family, she risked it all. She had all the advantages and support in the world. What happened to her, I wonder?"

Mike looked at his friend, and replied, "Maybe she had too many advantages, and too much support. Maybe she never had to work for anything. You know as well as I do, we don't really appreciate what we don't work for, no matter how much we want it. She never had to doubt that she'd have a position in a prestigious law firm, Liz. It was a given, just by the luck of the family she was born to." Mike paused, thoughtful. "I think about how unfair it is that girls like Leah, even Candy, may have the scope of their futures determined simply by where they're born and to whom, and how well off their families are."

Liz nodded, listening to Mike's words. She said, "It's late. I need to wrap this up tomorrow."

Mike reached for her hand. "Sleep will help."

"I didn't think to grab a few things while we were at my place. I've got basic necessities here, right?" Liz asked. "That is, unless you threw my things out."

"No, I did not throw out your things." Mike shook his head. "They're where you left them, Liz," he assured her.

"Cool. Thank you. May I borrow a t-shirt?" she asked, "after I borrow the shower?"

"Yes, of course," he said as he tidied up, placing the food containers in the garbage. "Help yourself. We can talk more after you shower." They shared a glance. Then Liz headed to see what articles of clothing she had left in Mike's closet for tomorrow's work day. A few minutes later, fresh from a hot shower, Liz came out to the living room. Mike was asleep on his sofa. Sweet guy, she thought, and a good friend. She didn't want to disturb him. She turned and went to bed.

WEDNESDAY

Chapter 43

On Wednesday morning, Liz, Curry, and Connors were greeted in the precinct with high-fives from the other officers and investigators. Nice, they all said. Good, solid police work. Everyone had done their job. A dangerous situation had ended with no one harmed.

But Liz was circumspect. Why had she not cuffed Kay? Why had she not thought to enter the kitchen herself and turn off the oven? These were questions she would need to think about. Soon -- when this was over. Maybe with the shrink Mike had suggested.

Liz had calls to make. She contacted Leah's mother, Connie, as she had promised. She was clear that an arrest had not yet been made but that the evidence was solid.

Then Liz talked with Diana Harrison. Diana was glad to hear of Liz's success in the search for Leah's killer, but she was more than surprised that it was Helene Ridgeman who was responsible for the fraud and deceitful practices at CER. She would look into things, would give the circumstances a lot of thought, speak with Connie, and decide how to pursue Leah's case.

Connors had been busy, too. He had placed Helene Ridgeman under arrest for fraud. Helene had retained counsel and was hoping to be released on bail. But at the moment, was cooling her heels in lock-up.

Also, Connors learned that Brad had had a short conversation with a neighbor at his apartment complex when he returned home Sunday, around noon. The neighbor confirmed that Brad was driving Helene's Mercedes, and was sure the "flashy wheels" were parked there until Monday morning. So, Brad also had an alibi.

Liz had a conversation with Carl and Brad Ridgeman. After Helene's arrest, she knew the father and son had much to discuss. Liz was hoping that one of the topics between them would be that Brad had a child with Leah Bishop, a child that was placed for adoption. From what she had learned of Brad, he would tell his father the whole story, and possibly petition for custody of his son, Carl's grandchild.

Then there was the evidence that implicated Kay Sutton, the Ridgeman's loyal housekeeper, for the murder of Leah Bishop. Leah, the girl Brad had loved and with whom he fathered a child. Liz knew that CER's financial records would be dissected, piece by piece, and thoroughly studied, and she hoped that both Carl and Brad would be cleared of any wrongdoing. Brad's information would help in that regard, and would possibly return some monies to families who had been bilked. Also, it would help serve to convict his sister. Liz was sure that Brad wouldn't care.

Late Wednesday morning, Connors sat in while Liz interviewed Kay. Liz began by explaining that they were interested in Leah Bishop and Kay's fingerprints on the granite award. Liz had hoped to finish this yesterday, she said, before Kay had pulled the stunt with the knife. Liz kept her eyes on Kay, but turned her head so the scratch on her neck was visible. Kay sat in a wheelchair. She glanced at Liz's neck, then at Connors. Then she focused on her hands folded in her lap.

They recorded the following:

Liz: Can you tell me how you came to be employed by the Ridgeman family?

Kay: I used to live in Blaine. There was some trouble with an acquaintance of mine. I was accused of simple assault, took the plea bargain and received a sentence of time served. When I was released I wanted to leave town. A friend of mine was working here, as a domestic. This was twenty years ago. I moved here, applied with an employment service for positions as a housekeeper. I held two other positions before I was hired by Mrs. Ridgeman, thirteen years ago. I believe we covered some of this yesterday, Detective.

Liz: Yes, we did. But the circumstances have changed now. Tell me about the Ridgemans, Carl and his late wife, Amelia.

Kay: Lovely people, wonderful employers; caring, fair. When Mrs. Ridgeman became ill, she relied on me as much as any sister. I was happy to help her in any way I could. When she died about five years ago, Mr. Ridgeman was devastated. Both children were grown and on their own. He needed me to continue to run his house. I would never have deserted him.

Liz: You stated yesterday that you didn't know Helene very well; didn't see her often until she returned to Columbia City to work for her father. What else can you tell me about Helene?

Kay: Helene was a terrible daughter. She and her mother couldn't get along at all, no matter how much Mrs. Ridgeman tried to appease her. Helene has been manipulating everyone in her life as long as I've known her. She was in law school when she discovered my past and used it to gain my cooperation in a variety of ways over the years.

Liz: Including the post office box arrangements?

Kay: Yes, you know that, Detective.

Liz: Tell me more about Brad, Kay.

Kay: Brad was such a sweet boy. Still in school, as I told you, when I started working for the family. His mother would light up when he was around. He was so sweet to her. He loved to make his mother happy. There were disagreements but never arguments, unless of course, Helene was around. He came home to visit his mother often at the end, much more than Helene, and Brad was still in Spokane. It was beyond sense.

Liz: When did you learn about Leah Bishop?

Kay: (Sighs) I knew Brad was seeing someone, but he hadn't mentioned it to me. We were close so I was concerned as to why. I made a point to check on things when I was out and about. I'd go by his office or his apartment.

Liz: And Brad was okay with you, essentially, spying on him?

Kay: (Eye roll) Brad knew I wasn't spying, Detective. He knew I was looking out for his best interests. I saw the two of them together on a few occasions. She was obviously just a low class girl looking for a foot up. Then, she disappeared. I found out later that she was pregnant and with Brad's child. A disaster for him and the family, if not handled appropriately. I realized she was placing the child for adoption and was glad to know that she'd made the right decision to leave Brad and the family out of her mess. I knew some of the packages received were from her. I knew I may need to reach her so I got her number from Brad's phone when he was visiting his father. My happiness for the family was short lived. I overheard Helene talking on a phone call about the lawsuit that girl had filed. How dare she?

Liz: Did you contact Leah?

Kay: Certainly, I did. I told her to stay away, leave Brad alone. That this family was never going to be her family. She was so rude to me! She said I was crazy, and to mind my own business! Brad would never have allowed her to speak to me that way. Then I saw her with Brad again, just last week. She was never going to leave him alone, not even after causing them so much trouble by suing them.

Liz: So what did you do?

Kay: I phoned her; asked to speak with her.

Liz: When was this?

Kay: It must have been Friday. She said she was staying downtown. She laughed and said, "The Suite," and did I even know where that was. I told her no, and she hung up. But, Detective, it wasn't difficult to learn of a place where women can stay called The Suite. I found it. I watched her for a couple of days, in the evening, when I had finished my duties. She was living like a vagrant, and presuming to be a friend of Brad's. It was unseemly."

Liz: Okay, go on.

Kay: The family was so happy to be going to the dinner together on Saturday. Mr. Ridgeman is so often honored. I was glad for him. Then he returned home early, with Helene. He was not well, but she told me she did not need any help from me, and that she was staying the night. I was insulted and went to my room. Later, I heard Brad stop by. I saw the box on the table in the foyer. I opened it and saw the beautiful award, so nicely done.

The next morning, Sunday, the phone rang. It was Brad checking on his father; so considerate of him. Helene insisted on caring for her father. I had errands to run anyway. When I went to the garage, Brad's car was parked behind the sedan I use for shopping. Helene couldn't be bothered to move it, so she told me to use Brad's SUV. So, I did. I took Mr. Ridgeman's award with me, to admire it, read the inscription again, you understand.

Liz: Not really, Kay, but go on.

Kay: I was driving near the park when I saw her. She was talking to some other vagrant, a young man. There weren't many people out and about at that time on a Sunday in that neighborhood. It's not like there are decent people around there attending church services. All you'd find down there is low-life vagrants recovering from their carousing of the night before. I went around the block and then I pulled over down the street. There's an alley to that place she was staying. You can reach it from the other direction. I decided to show her Mr. Ridgeman's award. They don't give these beautiful honors to just anyone, certainly not to someone like her. I took it from the box. It fit in my coat pocket nicely, you see. I walked down the alley from the other direction and I waited for her.

(Pause) When she came down the alley, I approached her. I only wanted to talk to her, to reason with her. She refused to hear me out. I took the award out of my pocket to show her. I started to read the inscription to her, to make her realize how special the family was. She said to get away. She had a cup in her hand. She turned to walk away but I grabbed her arm and she dropped her cup. It spilled. She told me I was crazy, that I wasn't part of their family anyway. How dare she? How would she know? She was nothing. (Pause) I hit her with Mr. Ridgeman's award. She fell. She was still, but breathing. I hit her once more. (Pause) She didn't breathe again. I picked up her cup. I don't know why. I left quickly, back the way I had come, opposite the park, back to Brad's car, and returned home.

Liz: Where on her body did you hit her?

Kay: Here, (motions) on the right side of her head, near the temple.

Liz: And you had the granite award in your left hand when you struck Leah?

Kay: I'm left handed, Detective.

Liz: That's not an answer, Ms. Sutton.

Kay: Yes, in my left hand.

Liz: Were you sorry for it, Kay? That you had killed a young woman?

Kay: Yes... it happened so fast... But I was relieved she wouldn't be a problem any longer; for the family.

Liz: It was a head wound. What about blood?

Kay: There was blood...but more after she was on the ground. There was blood on Mr. Ridgeman's award. It didn't take much effort to clean it. When I returned to the house, Helene was ready to leave. She said her father was resting. I placed the award in my room. No one asked about it. For two days. Finally, early yesterday, Tuesday morning, I took it in to Mr. Ridgeman's office and told Lorraine that Brad had asked me to leave it, that he had a busy day and wasn't able to deliver it himself.

End of interview.

Chapter 44

Liz was in a daze after conducting Kay's interview, which was followed immediately by Kathryn Sutton's arrest for Leah's murder. She sat in her office alone, thinking about the confession. She felt chilled by what she had heard. She would review the recording later, as would countless others -- attorneys, prosecutors, judges, possibly a jury. But only Liz had sat across the table from Kay while she delivered, with matter-of-fact calmness, her account of stalking and murdering a young woman. And all of it based on her obsession with the family she served and her twisted belief that they needed her to intervene and protect them.

The trace evidence from Brad's SUV was somewhat inconclusive. There were minute traces of blood that matched Leah Bishop. There were prints from a few persons including Brad, Helene and Kay. There were prints on the passenger side matching Carl Ridgeman and Leah herself. But when Liz stood back from the evidence, it only told her that Leah's killer had driven the car and that Leah had been a passenger at some point in recent time. So, it would come down to the recorded confession and other possible evidence they could obtain from the search of Kay's living quarters. And of course, the evidence from the murder weapon, a small slab of granite. And, there were the alibis of the other people involved.

Liz made a second call to Connie Bishop, finally able to report that there had been an arrest in the case of her daughter's murder. Liz prepared the arresting officer's portion of the press release for the department's public relations office and was told that the public would receive the announcement within minutes.

Later that afternoon, Carl Ridgeman contacted Liz and asked to meet with her at the law firm. When she arrived, Lorraine took her directly to the attorney's office, saying that he was waiting for her. Carl Ridgeman was standing at the window when she entered the office. He turned and greeted her, saying, "Detective Jordan, please come in. Let's sit, and I hope you'll have a cup of coffee with me."

"That would be nice, Sir. Thank you," she said. Ridgeman directed his attention to Lorraine, and before he said a word, she told him she would return shortly with coffee for them. As she closed the office door behind her, Liz and the attorney took seats at the table. "I'm guessing you know about Ms. Sutton's arrest?" Liz asked.

"Yes. There's no doubt in your mind?" he asked.

Liz measured her words. "The evidence clearly points to her. And she's confessed, Sir. There's no doubt."

"Now I must reconcile myself to the facts. My daughter committed a series of crimes. She betrayed my trust in her. And I had a killer living in my home, in my employ." Ridgeman took a breath, shook his head slowly.

"Detective, my wife was a talented woman. Her areas of interest were human development and psychology. When we met, Amelia was contemplating graduate programs and was trying to choose which of the two areas she felt more passionate about. Of course, this was years ago, but I've thought of it many times. She was particularly interested in a theory called Nature vs. Nurture. Are you familiar with it?"

Liz said that, yes, she was somewhat familiar with the concept but had not studied it at length. "Basically," Carl explained, "the theory deals with the forces of genetic predisposition and the effects of our environment on our development, and which of the two impacts the individual more strongly. My wife's position was that no matter how an individual, a child say, is predisposed because of their genetics, the advantages of a healthy, secure environment and loving caregivers can determine a better outcome, or future, for the child. Do you follow the logic, even if you don't agree?" he asked.

"Yes, Mr. Ridgeman, I do follow the logic," Liz answered. "And as a law enforcement officer, I find it an interesting theory. But I'm not sure why you wanted to discuss this with me today."

"Because, Detective Jordan, I'm trying to make sense of things," he replied. There was a knock at the door and Lorraine entered with coffee on a tray. She offered to serve. Liz asked that she please allow her. Lorraine stepped out and Liz poured coffee for Carl and for herself. Carl Ridgeman reached into a cabinet and extracted a bottle of whiskey. He offered the bottle to Liz. Liz declined, but he poured whiskey into his steaming cup. Liz remained silent, sipping coffee, hoping the attorney would fill the quiet and continue.

"When Amelia gave birth to Helene, we were overjoyed. My wife was a wonderful mother, as I knew she would be. She gave Helene just the right balance of security and freedom to explore and be her own person. Helene was a handful, as we used to say. She was demanding, stubborn to the point of obstinate. Helene was often restless and hard to comfort. Having said all of that, she was very bright. She began speaking earlier than most and had an intense desire to learn."

"Interesting," said Liz. "Tell me about Brad as a child, Sir."

"I will, Detective, I will. In due course," he said. "Anyway, Amelia struggled with Helene emotionally. She didn't receive a lot of what you would call emotional response from Helene. She even said once that she wasn't sure that her daughter liked her. It was difficult, painful for my wife. We sometimes witnessed the same in her interactions with other children. It was as if Helene was so focused on what she wanted that it left no room for kindness. The struggle was made worse in that Helene seemed to gravitate to me."

"Instead of making that an issue, my wife just said she was glad for it. What I describe is normal in children to some degree, Sergeant. But it was exaggerated in Helene." He paused. "By the time Helene was in preschool, we gave up on conceiving another child and decided to adopt," he continued. "Brad entered our lives the next year."

"Brad was adopted?" Liz asked, taken by surprise.

"Yes. We contacted a state agency that places children for adoption who have been removed from their parents' custody permanently. We were contacted about a baby boy who had been through a terrible first year of life. When Amelia read his background information, she was positive that she wanted to give this child a home and a place in our lives." He paused. "And I agreed, especially after we met him. He was the sweetest child, had been in foster care for several months. Amelia and the boy bonded instantly, as if they were joined at their souls."

"Does Brad know?" Liz asked the attorney.

"Oh, yes, he knows," Ridgeman replied. "We were very honest with him. We thought it best."

"Brad thrived in our care, especially with my wife's consistent, loving parenting of him. He was a bright child, but worked harder to learn compared to Helene. He could master his challenges but it took a bit longer for him. And he was simply a joy. He was never mean or unkind, even to other children, even those younger than himself. In competitive sports, for example, Brad would excel but never at the expense of another's feelings. We became conscious of the difference in our children and worked very hard to be sure that we treated them the same, loved them both, and offered them the same advantages and freedoms."

"I'm sure you did, Sir," Liz told him, believing it to be true.

"Detective, Helene was unhappy to be a sister from the first day. She was spiteful and unreasonably angry, with us and with her little brother. We had to intervene a few times when we found her being particularly mean to Brad. Until he was bigger and stronger than her, and we felt he could defend himself physically, we didn't trust her. The emotional meanness took a different toll, of course, and it all served to prevent a loving relationship between them."

"It sounds like your wife was a wonderful person, Mr. Ridgeman. Obviously, you've given this a lot of thought," she said.

"Yes, but I cannot make sense of it! Helene is our biological child. I've loved her since she was born. I've been proud of her accomplishments. She's had every advantage her mother and I could provide. After what I heard yesterday, I'm disgusted. I feel like I don't know her. My son began life in risky, dangerous conditions. We received limited information about his biological family, but what we were told was terrible. But he never let it define him, Sergeant. He wasn't tainted by it. My son could have been angry about his first year of life, but he has kindness and empathy to spare, while my daughter has led a gifted life, full of support and has placed money ahead of kindness, integrity and family. I respect you, Sergeant Jordan, and I am simply asking for your thoughts."

Liz took a few moments. She poured each of them more coffee. Reaching for the whiskey, she uncapped the bottle and poured whiskey into Ridgeman's coffee. Then she poured whiskey into her own. "Mr. Ridgeman, I'm not a parent. I can only imagine the pain you feel about Helene." She paused. "My parents are both teachers. I don't talk about my family when I'm working but I will share with you that they are special people. My father once told me that as a teacher, he could only do his best, but even then, there were no guarantees." Liz took a moment, sipped, then continued. "It must be the same with parenting. My best guess would be that Nature and Nurture complement each other and that both forces determine who we become. Do not blame yourself. Grieve for what you have seen Helene become. But please, appreciate the gift you have been given in Brad. My impressions are that he's been an honorable young man through this."

Carl Ridgeman was quiet. He thought for a moment then said, "Thank you, Sergeant. I do need to remember that. And, Brad tells me I have a grandson."

Liz sighed. "That's what I understand."

"Brad doesn't think that Helene realizes that she placed her own nephew for adoption to the highest bidder. We haven't explored that issue, and it doesn't matter now." Ridgeman paused for a beat. "We are, however, looking to regain custody of Brad's child. He wants to raise him. I want to help. And we hope Leah's mother will want to be a part of his life, as well."

"I wish you the best, Mr. Ridgeman. You and Brad both," Liz said. "But may I ask one question, before I go?"

He half smiled and said, "After all you just sat through? Certainly you can."

"Yesterday, why did you tell Brad he needed to speak with me?" asked Liz.

"My award, the one I received Saturday at the dinner. After you left our meeting, I asked Lorraine about it, about who had brought it to the office that morning. I assumed that Brad had done so because she had made the remark earlier that Brad was busy. But Lorraine said it was Kay who delivered it along with Brad's message. At that point, it seemed Kay knew something." Carl Ridgeman paused, sighed. "And I was sure my award was the murder weapon. I wanted it out of here, in your hands. It was looking bad for Brad...but it made no sense to me. From the information you had, it sounded as if Helene's hand was involved. I'm not sure... I suppose I wanted him to have an advocate, even if it was me. If Helene was innocent, she would be able to handle it on her own. I wasn't sure of my son. I guess I underestimate him, don't I?"

"Maybe you do, a little. But I think you underestimate yourself as a father."

Carl Ridgeman nodded and thanked Liz for her kindness. Liz finished her coffee and left. There was one remaining detail she wanted to investigate.

Chapter 45

Liz returned to her office and spent the next couple of hours in research. Then she managed to find Gibson before he left for the day, to confirm what she discovered. She was convinced of the information she had found and was ready to address it. Liz went to the jail and arranged to talk with Kay Sutton, one last time.

"What do you want, Detective? I'm very tired," said Kay.

"You told me you were living in Blaine, near the Canadian border before moving here," Liz said. "Where did you live prior to Blaine, Kay?"

Kay studied her. "Why?" she asked Liz.

"I'm curious. Filling in gaps," Liz answered.

"I'd rather not say, Detective Jordan," the woman told her.

"Why keep secrets now, Kay? You were full of information earlier," Liz told her, and asked, "What could be so important to keep quiet about, now that you've confessed to Leah Bishop's murder?" Kay Sutton looked away, silent.

"Let me tell you what I've discovered, Kay. Before Blaine, you were living in Vancouver, B.C. You see, your prints match those of a woman who left Canada almost thirty years ago." Liz went on, "Her name was Katherine Sutherland." At mention of the name, Kay looked at Liz, her face paled, and although the expression was defiant, the calm demeanor was cracking.

"I don't know what you're talking about," she said, but her statement wasn't convincing.

"Katherine Sutherland was a Canadian citizen living in B.C. As a young woman, she had lived on the streets, escaping abuse at home. She had a few arrests for drug possession, domestic disturbances, and finally, was charged with involvement in a robbery scheme." Liz continued, "Katherine agreed to testify against the others involved and the charges against her were reduced. She was sentenced to time served and released."

"None of this has anything to do with me," Kay told her firmly, "and you can't prove that it does."

"Yes, I think I can," Liz told her. "Katherine gave birth to a baby, a boy. She had traveled across the border and gave birth in the States, thinking it would be better for them. She stayed here, trying to manage for a few months with a child she couldn't care for. She took up with a variety of men, but it was one disaster after another. When the child was taken from her by authorities, Katherine disappeared. She turned up a few years later, according to employment records. She had changed her name to Kathryn Sutton."

Kay's jaw was clinched tight, she was furious, trembling with anger. The calm façade had crumbled.

"It took you years to find him and when you did, you insinuated yourself into his life as the housekeeper for his adoptive family." Liz had almost finished the tale. "No one could have been as devoted to an employer as you tried to appear unless there was a deeper connection. You killed Leah because you believed it was your duty to protect Brad. Not because you cared about the Ridgemans, but because he was the son you lost."

Kay grew quiet. Finally, she asked, "Are you going to tell them? After all this time, are you going to tell them?"

"No, I'm not going to tell them. It's not pertinent to my case. I have no reason with your confession to murder, as well as the other evidence," Liz replied. "If you care about Brad at all, you won't tell him either."

ONE WEEK LATER

Chapter 46

Kelly Blevins was preparing herself. It was the day before Thanksgiving. Today she would defend her work with the homeless to the City Council. The group of civic leaders would determine whether funding for her position as Outreach Manager for the Homeless would be renewed.

The past week had been filled with fun, surprises, and a lot of work caring for Candy's baby girl, whom they were calling Caroline. She and Peter had started the foster parent process and were encouraged enough to think they would be able to care for her until an adoptive family could be found. Pete's mother, Alice, had arrived a few days ago to help, having been cleared by Carlton, Caroline's caseworker. Alice, an experienced grandmother, was having the time of her life.

Kelly entered the council chamber at City Hall and took a seat beside her supervisor, Councilman Don Collier. During proceedings for any other item before the Council, Don would be at his usual spot at the front with the others. He had excused himself from the panel because of his connection to the homeless outreach project, and because he wanted to support Kelly. But he would cast a vote when the time came.

Kelly glanced around the room and saw many familiar faces. Mike from Avalon was there as were Liz Jordan and Kyle Connors, the cops who had found Leah's killer. Darlene was there. She would be moving from The Suite into her own place soon. Ty was sitting with Gary from the men's shelter, and Fran, the nurse from the community clinic, was sitting next to a man Kelly knew as one of the doctors who donated time but Kelly didn't recall his name.

Kelly would speak first, followed by Don. Next, they would answer any questions posed to them by the council members. After Kelly and Don, the format allowed for anyone with an interest in the proceedings to speak for up to five minutes.

Kelly had practiced her speech. She took Mike's advice and after a brief overview of her work, she addressed the fiscal advantage of having an advocate in her position as a preventive measure for the folks on the street. She answered a few questions. Then it was Don's turn. Kelly felt touched that he would express his faith in her and the work she did on behalf of her clients.

Mike Dwyer spoke next, identifying himself and his position as manager at the Avalon Street Shelter. Mike talked about the progress of clients who worked with Kelly versus the ones who did not. He related to the council that trust was a big factor in working with people who were homeless, and that someone in Kelly's position had a better chance of earning their trust.

One or two other providers spoke about the necessity of Kelly's position because as providers of services to the homeless community, their work didn't allow time to seek people out. They were dependent on clients finding their way to them, which meant that many homeless people, those most needing help, fell through the proverbial cracks.

The council chair announced time for one more speaker from the community before they adjourned for discussion. Kelly looked up when she heard a familiar voice.

"I am Detective Sergeant Elizabeth Jordan with the Metro Division. I appreciate the chance to address the council today." Liz paused. "A young, homeless woman was murdered in our city recently. Her name was Leah Bishop. She was eighteen years old. Is she dead because she was homeless? I don't know the answer to that. Was she a drug addict, a prostitute, or a thief? No, Leah was none of those things. She was just a kid. But even if she had been in trouble we would have worked to find her killer. She deserved that."

"One week ago today, we apprehended the person responsible for Leah's death. This person was not a member of the homeless community, as many suspected. What I'm here to emphasize is that I don't know if we could have solved this crime without Kelly Blevins. Kelly advocated for us with people she knew, her clients. She assured them that we could be trusted. They believed that we wouldn't look for a way to discount their knowledge or cause more problems for them."

Liz, knowing her time was almost up, raised a hand and said, "Please allow me a few more minutes. Thank you. Speaking for law enforcement, we're trying to keep our streets safe, for everyone, including homeless persons. So, we need Kelly to continue to work for the benefit of our community. Personally, I think we need more people like her who can do this work. That's all. Thank you for hearing me out."

As Liz finished speaking, applause erupted in the council chamber and most of the audience was standing.

The meeting adjourned and attendees were filing out of the council chamber. Kelly and Mike approached Liz. She had hoped to leave the building without running into anyone. But Mike was different. Liz would never avoid Mike. And Liz liked Kelly. That's why she showed up today.

"Liz, thank you for coming here," Kelly told her. "And thank you for the support. It means a lot to me."

"You're welcome," Liz said. "I hope our paths cross again."

"I'm sure they will. Anyway, I need to run. Thanks again."

Kelly turned to leave, then stopped and added, "And I'm glad you're okay after what happened last week."

"Thank you. So am I."

As Kelly left them, Mike said to Liz, "I've got to get to Avalon. The shelter is busy during holiday weeks. But I was hoping we'd have a minute. Your mom called me. She hadn't heard from you and was worried."

Liz was upset with herself for the oversight. "Oh man, I have to call her, like right now."

"She understood after I explained that you'd been busy with a case," Mike said. "Anyway, she invited me to Thanksgiving dinner. I told her I'd love to accept, but I can't get away. Liz, she wants to wait until Saturday to have the holiday dinner. I told her I'd talk to you. What do you think? We can drive over Friday evening and back on Sunday."

"That plan sounds great to me, Mike. We can split the drive time. I'll ask the lady downstairs to feed Eddie and Little Kurt. It will be nice to get away. And it will be nice to have you join us." Liz paused, then she said, "Hey, the Apple Cup is Saturday. We can all watch the game together."

"Liz, your mom still thinks we're a couple, doesn't she?" Mike asked his friend, shaking his head.

Liz laughed. She gave Mike a hug, kissed his cheek and said, "I'd better call her. I'll catch you later."

Liz walked away, looking forward to the Thanksgiving weekend.

Epilogue

Kathryn Sutton, aka Katherine Sutherland, was not tried for the murder of Leah Bishop. The court appointed an attorney for her. Because she had confessed, Kay was allowed to make her statement before a judge in an open courtroom. She should expect to be sentenced to the maximum allowed by law. To Liz's knowledge, Kay never revealed the truth of her identity to Brad Ridgeman. Charges are pending regarding her assault on Liz. The court has ordered a psychiatric evaluation.

Helene Ridgeman was tried and convicted of arranging adoptions for profit. She was disbarred. Her case is currently under appeal. Lenora and Cyril Benedict, upon hearing of the conditions surrounding their child's adoption, voluntarily gave up their rights as adoptive parents. They have yet to decide whether to pursue another adoption.

Brad Ridgeman sought and was given custody of his son, having proved he was the child's biological father. After a few days together, the child began to attach to Brad and to his grandfather, Carl. Brad and his son now live with Brad's father, Carl Ridgeman.

Connie Bishop returns to Columbia City often to visit with Leah's child, her grandson. Connie helped Brad decide on his son's name. She told Brad the story of the Old Testament matriarch, Leah, the sorrowful wife of Jacob. Leah had a son named Judah. Brad named his and Leah's son Judah Bradley Ridgeman. Brad received the small slip of paper that Leah had kept with Judah's date and time of birth surrounded by a heart. He will someday share it with his son.

Carl Ridgeman closed CER Legal Services. He and Brad spent months looking into the fraudulent adoptions, repairing damage, and returning fees. Brad Ridgeman is scheduled to sit for his bar exam soon. Diana Harrison continues to practice law and still drives her Saab 900 with the vanity plates. She remains a staunch advocate for women and children.

Nyla Garrity and Skip Thibodeux, aka Millard, moved back to the Seattle area. They remain in contact with Keith Akeuchi, who continues to run the Greyson Avenue Hotel. Ty Phillips remains in Columbia City. He remains a prominent fixture at the men's shelter and visits with Mike on Sunday evenings at Avalon. He struggles with his demons. Malachi Evanson completed inpatient treatment with the help of his friends and his family. He is attending school and playing baseball. Darlene, Maria, and her son, Javier, are thriving. Maria kept in touch with Kelly for a while. Darlene calls Kelly on a regular basis.

Kelly and Peter fostered Caroline for several months, until she was placed for permanent adoption with a family named Baker. The Bakers liked the name Caroline and invited "Aunt Kelly and Uncle Pete" to serve as Caroline's extended family. Funding for Kelly's position was renewed by the City Council for another eighteen months, when it will again be under review.

Dr. Stein, the Chief Medical Examiner, hopes to retire next year. Dr. Myers will likely assume his position.

Detective Sergeant Liz Jordan and Officer Kyle Connors still serve the people of Columbia City. Kyle plays basketball with Peter every Wednesday. Eddie and Little Kurt are doing well. Mike Dwyer continues to manage Avalon Street Center, where every day is a balancing act. As with all social services, his work is two steps forward and one step back. He remains an advocate for the homeless. Liz's mother still thinks Liz and Mike are a couple.

Marco and Genevieve, the seniors, disappeared. They may have headed south to California. No one has heard from Candy Schinde.

The End

Acknowledgements

There are many special people to whom I owe debts of gratitude for the help they provided as I wrote this novel. Several friends and family members read the manuscript at various stages and offered great feedback. Their encouragement was much appreciated and their comments always helpful. Thank you, thank you, to Denise Wiseman, Jennifer Weidner, Trisia and Russell Deojay, Margaret Wilder, Abby Wiseman, Frankie Mulloy, and of course, David Conine. Thanks, too, go to Jordan, Taylor, and Shae Wiseman for tech support and for cheering me on. Thanks to Kate Wilder and Edde Rolstad, for proofreading; an onerous task, in my opinion. And finally, a very special Thank you to Jac Versteeg, for serving as Editor. His advice and suggestions were invaluable.

To all professionals working so diligently in the fields of law, law enforcement, and chemical dependency counseling: please excuse errors or inaccuracies made regarding the work you do for the sake of telling a story.

Resources

For information on how to contribute to the fight against homelessness, contact the United States Interagency Council on Homelessness at www.usich.gov for links to services in your area, your local Department of Social and Health Services (HHS), and community food banks in your area. Information also may be provided by the house of worship of your choice.

Printed in the United States
By Bookmasters